Paradise Pawn

OZ
CUPS

"Reading *Paradise Pawn* was an absolute delight, there's treasure to be found on every page. Richardson is the genuine article, and the charming, wise, and hilarious debut novel in your hand worth any number of hocked wedding rings."

—**Elissa Schappell**,
author of *Blueprints for Building Better Girls*

"Brilliant and bighearted, *Paradise Pawn* transported me back to the electrifying intensity of young friendship. It beautifully captures the feeling of slowly waking up from childhood and emerging into the adult world only to realize it's often not what we thought it would be. A total gem of a debut!"

—**Charlee Dyroff**,
author of *Loneliness & Company*

"*Paradise Pawn* cleverly captures the absurdity of adulthood through the eyes of a child. As an employee in a pawnshop—where love and desperation, poverty and wealth are on display just as much as the wares—our young narrator bravely clings onto how the world should be, even as she is reminded daily of how it really is. Hopeful, heartbreaking, and oftentimes hilarious, Richardson artfully paints a vibrant, colorful world with only black ink on a white page."

—**Kat Tang**,
author of *Five-Star Stranger*

"From the first page to the last of *Paradise Pawn*, Meg Richardson establishes herself as a writer with a singular voice and vision. With fearless and exacting prose, she captures the beauty and hurt of youth, friendship, and class. I loved it, and you will too."

—**Tillie Walden**,
author of *On a Sunbeam*

"*Paradise Pawn* introduces us to a world that feels deeply lived in, and Meg Richardson gets every detail just right. In the pawn shop, we are privy to the pendulum of human desperation: what people need and what they're willing to sacrifice. The friendship between Jackie and Kayla perfectly captures the feeling of being caught between: between new friends and old friends that feel like family, between childhood and adulthood, between wanting to be close and wanting to be your own person. *Paradise Pawn* is a touching ode to the gleeful delusion and quiet heartbreak of growing up."

—**Katie Yee**,
author of *Maggie; or, A Man and a Woman Walk Into a Bar*

"You've never read a coming-of-age novel like this before. Meg Richardson manages to capture the exact moment when childhood tips into puberty. Funny and sweet without shying away from the darker moments of adulthood, Richardson transforms our ideas of what it means to be a girl in this laugh-out-loud novel about best friendship, growing up, and working class life."

—**Molly McGhee**,
author of *Jonathan Abernathy You Are Kind*

"Meg Richardson's *Paradise Pawn* joins the ranks of novels helmed by heartbreaking child narrators (think Kaye Gibbons's Ellen *Foster*, Lisa Shea's *Hula*, Karen Russell's *Swamplandia!*) who are up against themselves and the world trying to figure out who they are and who they might be. In a voice filled with authority and authenticity, Jackie tries to navigate an unfair world while caring for and about her single father and her best, best friend, sometimes succeeding brilliantly and sometimes failing spectacularly. With deft compassion, Richardson paints a clear-eyed portrait of the world of pawn shops and beach towns, allows Jackie to get into all sorts of messes, and sticks with her while she figures her way out, reminding both her characters and her readers of something we all could use a reminder about: You can't control what the world throws at you, and everyone makes mistakes, so being a grown-up might mean nothing more and nothing less than owning what is yours to take responsibility for."

—**Karen Shepard**,
author of *Kiss Me Someone*

"*Paradise Pawn* makes me ache for younger versions of myself, to hear the voices of childhood friends I haven't spoken to in years. Richardson brilliantly and compassionately explores the contradictions of adulthood against the zany backdrop of a pawn shop in a beach town. Charming, funny, and sweet, but also clear-eyed and painfully honest in its views of the cost of growing up. A fresh debut from a writer of great talent and heart."

—**Jean Kyoung Frazier**,
author of *Pizza Girl*

"A lovely book that captures the rhythms and travails of working-class life. Meg Richardson is a rising new talent."

—**Gary Shteyngart**,
author of *Vera, or Faith*

Paradise Pawn

a novel

Meg Richardson

Tin House
A zando IMPRINT
NEW YORK

Tin House

Tin House is an imprint of Zando.
zandoprojects.com

First US Edition 2026
Cover and text design by Beth Steidle

Library of Congress Cataloging-in-Publication Data is available.

978-1-963108-73-6 (paperback)
978-1-963108-81-1 (ebook)

10 9 8 7 6 5 4 3 2 1

Manufactured in the United States of America

LSCC

To my family and to my friends
who feel like family.

Paradise Pawn

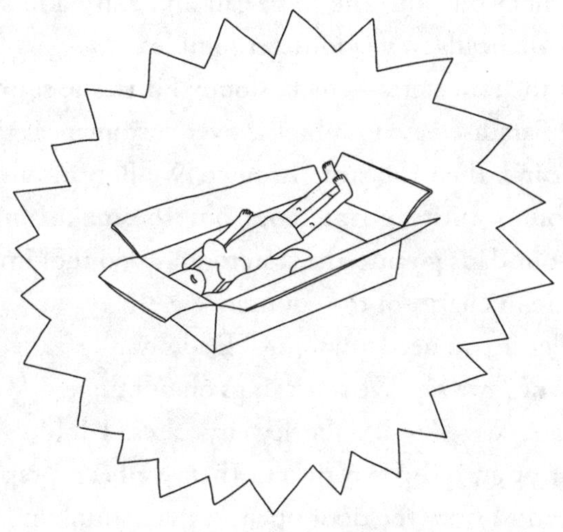

CHAPTER 1

WE MAKE TONS OF MONEY OFF OF CHRISTMAS IN July because everyone in Cherry Beach is lonely. We wrap tinsel and lights around the bars on our windows and play Christmas music through big car speakers out front and lonely people come crashing through our doors like waves.

They aren't really Christmas shopping. They are paying for us to listen to them talk about their sister in Georgia, their wife in Cuba, or their boyfriend in Texas. We help them pick out presents for the people they miss, they give us $10, and we put the presents on layaway for a month. They are paying for a funny kind of hope that in thirty days, when their next payment is due, they will be rich.

By noon, me and Kayla have deposits on a set of hubcaps, a surfboard, a baby bracelet, a big eighteen-karat Gucci link chain and two iPads. Our Santa hats are heavy with sweat. We squeeze them out into the trash can and rub hand sanitizer into our foreheads so we don't get pimples.

Then the rain starts—thick, sloppy hurricane season rain. We hold Paradise Pawn umbrellas over customers as they run to their cars. Then the store is quiet. We flop in our chairs. Carter, our security guard, goes out to smoke under the awning, our dads go into the storeroom to do tool inventory, and we are in charge of the counter.

"Holler if you need anything," Dad says.

"Will do," we say. We stack rings on our fingers. We strum the guitars. We Windex the jewelry cases. I fold a fortune teller out of an old pawn ticket. Then we hear a tap on the window and I buzz the door open. A man stumbles in carrying a wet cardboard box. He drops it on the floor and grunts.

He is soaked. White, wet hair sprouts out the sides of his pink neck. He's wearing a tank top and pink swim trunks that are almost the same pink as his skin. His eyes dart around the store. Kayla swings open the counter and puts on her customer smile. Our customer smiles are tight and fake, but the customers don't know that. They think we're smiling for real.

"Good afternoon, sir. Welcome to Paradise Pawn. How can I help?" Kayla says.

"You? No, no thanks," he says. He looks from his sandals to his box. He's breathing fast. "Is the manager here?"

"The manager had to step in the back for a moment, but we would be glad to assist you," Kayla says.

"There's nobody else here? Nobody older?"

"We're in charge, sir. Here, let me help you with that," Kayla says. I open the counter and run to help her lift the box. It's heavy. There's something rolling around in it.

"Look, there's no need," the man says, wiping his face with his shirt. We keep walking and set the box on the counter.

Customers often get nervous and sad while they walk from the door of Paradise Pawn to the counter. You can see it in their bodies. They slouch. They hold necklaces from ex-husbands or trumpets they never learned how to play close to their chests, the way kids hold their blankets. Then me and Kayla talk to them in deep voices. We look them right in the eyes and make them do what we want them to do.

"I really don't think you girls should be helping me with this," the man says. I pretend not to hear him.

"Would you like some water, sir?" I say sweetly. It's a trick I learned from Dad. If you give people something, even something as small as a Styrofoam cup of water, they will feel like they owe you. That's right where you want to be, Dad says.

"Sure, I'll take some water," the man says. I smile at him, keeping eye contact as I hold the cup under the gurgling jug. I hand him the water and he downs it in one swallow. Then he starts stamping patterns into the Styrofoam with his fingernails.

"Rainy out there, isn't it?" I say, just like Dad does. The man nods. Kayla peels a piece of tape off the cardboard box and I lift the flaps. Inside is a giant Barbie doll. She's beautiful. She has wavy blonde hair down to her waist. She's wearing a shiny red dress. One of her arms has fallen off her body. I touch her fingers. Her skin is squishy like real skin.

"We love dolls!" Kayla says to the man, even though we are fourteen. Three years ago, Kayla decided we were too old to play with dolls and I never played with a doll again.

The man's face relaxes. He smiles.

"Yep. She's just a very fancy doll. I paid a shitload of money for her. Sorry, I mean, a crap load. Pardon my French. Fifteen hundred when she was new and she's hardly been used."

"Wonderful. We'll do an evaluation and come up with an arrangement in just a few moments," Kayla says. "Have you heard about our Christmas in July layaway promotion?"

"Just ten dollars to put any item in the store on layaway," I say.

"Not today, but thank you," the man says. We lift the doll out of her box and set her down on the floor behind the counter. She's as heavy as a real girl. We crouch beside her so the man can't see us. I slip my hand under her head. It feels wrong to make her lie on the cold tiles. She looks so real. Her long eyelashes fall closed. Her breasts bounce up and down. I've never seen a real person with breasts that big. I touch one of them. It feels like a water balloon. Kayla reaches into the doll's box again and pulls out an instruction manual. I watch Kayla's eyes move across the words. She chews on her sleeve.

"Apparently her name is Cheri," Kayla says. Kayla turns to the next page in the manual and makes a face like she's bitten into a lemon.

"What?" I say.

"Look," she says, pointing to a chart with pictures of guys wrapping themselves around Cheri in eleven different ways.

"Are they having sex with her?" I whisper.

"I think so," Kayla says.

"Ew," I say. I reach for Cheri's hand. It's cold and rubbery. Her fingernails are pink and smooth. I wish my fingernails looked like that.

"We should do a loan on her," Kayla says.

"Would someone buy her secondhand?" I say.

"For the right price," Kayla says, combing her fingers through Cheri's hair. I nod. "Plus, it would be good for us to read this manual. We need to know the stuff in here."

"We do?" I say. Kayla looks at me like I'm stupid.

"Yeah, we majorly do," she says. "Especially when we start high school." I shrug.

"I already know a lot of it," I say.

"Sure, you do," she says, rolling her eyes at me.

"I do!" I whine. I find Cheri's model number stamped into her neck and I read it out loud to Kayla. She types it into eBay to see how much Cheri is worth. We click through pictures of other Cheris, then of dolls named Angel and Lolo and Rosie—pictures of their plastic faces and vaginas and breasts. The guy wasn't lying. They're expensive. I watch numbers swirl in Kayla's notebook. She's in Gifted and Talented math, and Gifted and Talented everything else. I'm in regular everything.

"Maybe we shouldn't tell the dads about this," I say.

"Why?" Kayla says.

"Because it's embarrassing! Look at this thing," I say, waving the manual in her face.

"Well, we can't lie," Kayla says. "If we do the loan, they'll see the money is missing at the end of the day."

"Maybe we can count the cash when we close and we can make it look like nothing happened," I say.

"That would be lying. Plus, it won't work," Kayla says. She loves to tell me my ideas won't work. "I'll think of something else." She chews on the side of her thumb and squints at her notebook. Then she says, "Okay, let's give him five hundred dollars and put in the system that she's a really nice chainsaw. We can leave her in the box. We'll just make sure the dads are distracted when he comes to redeem her."

"Fine," I say. Sometimes I get annoyed by how smart Kayla is without even trying.

"How do you know he'll come back?" I say.

"It's just N.E.H.A.," she says. N.E.H.A. is how you decide how much money to loan somebody. It stands for "Need for cash, Emotional attachment to the item, History of paying loans back, and Ability to pay."

"Right?" Kayla says. "He's rich, clearly, so he has the ability to pay the loan back. I'm sure he has an emotional attachment to Cheri, because he, you know, has sex with her. That's like maximum emotional attachment."

"True," I say. "Okay." We stand up and peer over the counter. The guy is looking at phones. Kayla swings open the counter and he jumps. I count the phones to make sure he hasn't stuck one in his swim trunks. He hasn't.

"We'd be pleased to offer you a loan of five hundred dollars on this item," Kayla says, smiling a perfect customer smile. The man wipes his mouth on his shirt.

"That's all?" he says.

"You won't find a better deal anywhere in Cherry Beach," Kayla says sweetly. The man leans his elbows on the counter and looks at Cheri lying on the floor. He wipes his nose with his wrist.

"Could I hold her for a moment?" he says softly. I look at Kayla. She almost starts to laugh, but then she looks at the man's drooping face.

"Certainly," Kayla says, as if the man is asking to do something totally normal, like try on earrings or test a tile cutter. We pick Cheri up and her eyelids glide open. Her eyes are friendly. Kayla passes Cheri to the man, being careful not to scrape her jiggling skin on the counter. I pass him Cheri's fallen-off arm.

"I just need to make sure, you know, that her batteries are charged and everything," he says. He pops her arm back into her shoulder.

"Of course," we say. We step away from the counter and bow our heads like we're at a funeral. He's not checking her batteries. He's saying goodbye. He presses her against his chest and takes a few deep breaths. Then he cups his hand around her cheek like she is a real person. We pretend to be busy loading paper into the printer to give them privacy. He runs his fingers through her hair and then he says, "Alright. I'm done. Sorry," and passes Cheri back over the counter to us.

"No problem," Kayla says gently. She bends over the computer, signs into MasterPawn, and types up a loan for a chainsaw. I scan the guy's driver's license. His name is Ian Burger. His face is thinner in the driver's license picture and his hair is brown instead of white. I wonder if kids used to make fun of him for having the last name Burger.

We press each of Ian Burger's fingers into the fingerprint reader. He's wearing a wedding ring, which means we're supposed to ask when his anniversary is so we can send him reminders to buy jewelry for his wife every year, but we don't ask.

Kayla prints a contract and a statement of ownership form for him to sign. His writing is messy. Then Kayla counts out five smirking Ben Franklins and hands them to him.

"It'll be six hundred fifty dollars to pick her up next month, sir," Kayla says. We stick out our hands for him to shake, but he doesn't shake them. He just mutters, "I'm sorry you had to see that."

"Nothing to be sorry for, Mr. Burger," Kayla says. "Thanks for coming in." We buzz the door and he runs through the rain to his car. We grab two pairs of whale-watching binoculars and zoom in on him. He's shivering and hunched against the steering wheel. He's looking at pictures of Cheri on his phone and he's crying as if she were a real person and he's just said goodbye to her.

"Poor guy," I say.

"Poor Cheri too," Kayla says.

"Yeah," I say. Sheets of rain crash against the window. Ian Burger puts his phone in the cup holder of his car and drives away. We walk back behind the counter in silence. Kayla prints out a barcode sticker for Cheri's box. I feel bad putting her away on the floor of the storeroom, where she'll get cold.

"I'm going to put my sweater on her," Kayla says. It's like she can read my mind.

"Good idea," I say. "I'll make her a little pillow." I fold a rag from the jewelry cleaning room into a rectangle and slide it under Cheri's head. Only one button on Kayla's sweater will close around Cheri's chest, but it's better than just leaving her in the cold with only a sleeveless dress on. We slide her box into the storeroom as quietly as we can.

"Everything good?" Dad says, and we jump.

"Yes sir," we say. Then we close the storeroom door and sit under the counter and study Cheri's manual. Kayla highlights the important parts.

"Would you want to look like Cheri if you could?" I ask Kayla.

"Yeah, probably. I could make guys buy me stuff."

"Because they would love you?" I say.

"No, because they would all want to do it with me," Kayla says.

"Oh."

"What do you think it feels like?" Kayla says.

"What, doing it? I don't know," I say.

"You know we're going to someday."

"Ew, Kayla," I say.

"What? It's a part of life! How do you think you got to be born?" she says. I slap her arm with the instruction manual. I hate thinking about my parents doing it. It's basically all they ever did together.

They met at a bar that is now a nail salon. Mom came to Cherry Beach for spring break when she was in college. Dad had just started working at Paradise Pawn. He was wearing a new gold chain the night they met. There was popcorn at the bar. There was a fishpond by the parking lot and they went outside and fed popcorn to the fish in the dark. They talked about the Iraq War.

Then they did it at the Best Western where Mom was staying, and they made me. After they did it, Dad made coffee for them with the hotel coffee maker. He let Mom have all the little creams and sugars in hers. They were going to meet at a bar the next day, but Mom went on a tour of the turtle farm instead.

A few months later, Mom called Dad from her college in Texas to tell him I was inside her. She was planning to give me to a family who needed a baby because they couldn't have one, but Dad said he wanted to take care of me.

Dad drove sixteen hours to Texas the day before I was born. Mom didn't want Dad in the hospital room while I was being born. Nobody was there with her, except doctors and me, and I couldn't talk to her or hold her hand. Kayla's mom, Giselle, says that having a baby hurts more than anything else in the world.

While Mom was pushing me out of her, Dad got a huge tattoo on his chest. It says *Jackie* and the date of my birthday in swirly blue letters. They gave him 20 percent off when he told them his daughter was being born at that very moment. Dad says getting a tattoo that big hurts just as much as having a baby. The thing is, he'll never know for sure, because he'll never have to push a baby out of his body.

Mom wanted to name me Grace, but Dad wanted to name me Jaqueline and call me Jackie, and since Dad was going to be saying my name more than Mom, he got to pick. Also, he already had the tattoo that said "Jackie," so it would have been awkward if Mom had said my name couldn't be Jackie. Sometimes when I go to the tourist smoothie place and they ask what my name is, I tell them it's Grace and they believe me.

When I was two weeks old, Dad brought me back to Cherry Beach. When I was two and a half weeks old, I met Kayla. She was seven months old. The dads used to put us in baby backpacks and take us jet skiing. When we were three, the dads bought us eighteen-karat gold necklaces with their employee discounts that are two halves of a heart. We've worn them ever since. Kayla's says *Best* and mine says *Friends* and we're going to wear them for the rest of our lives.

Mom died when I was eight. The last time I saw her was when she came to Cherry Beach for my seventh birthday. She stayed at the Margaritaville Hotel on Five Mile Beach, which is pretty expensive. She said I could sleep in her hotel room for the week if I wanted to, but I used to get scared of sleeping anywhere besides my house or Kayla's apartment. Mom gave me the tiny bottles of shampoo and lotion from her room, because she washed her hair with special shampoo from her hairstylist. I still have the tiny shampoos and lotions. I've never used them. I just smell them sometimes. I keep them in my underwear drawer with my baby teeth and a folder with pictures of Mom in it.

Kayla reaches for my hand.

"Hey," she says. "Sorry. I wasn't trying to be mean."

"You weren't being mean," I say. "It's okay."

Kayla and I read Cheri's manual twice and then quiz each other. It's like studying for a test, tucking information into our brains like rings into a ring pad. The test will come when we have boyfriends. Kayla will probably have a boyfriend way before I do. She's prettier and better at talking to people than I am. But now, whenever I do have a boyfriend, I'll be ready. It never hurts to be ready for things early. Dad always says if you're early, you're on time. If you're on time, you're late. If you're late, you're fired.

At 5:30, the rain stops and waves of colored polo shirts and name tags come crashing through our door—Ritz-Carlton blue, Häagen-Dazs red, Margaritaville pink, 7-Eleven green.

Me and Kayla run back and forth between the door buzzer and the people in colored shirts. They have just finished a day of fake smiling at people and they are hungry for someone to fake smile at them.

I place white-gold rings on a pad for two women in Westin shirts. Westin just got new name tags, to make it easier for tourists to talk to the people refilling their waters and folding their towels. *My passion: family. My passion: reading*, the women's name tags say. I slide a CZ stone ring onto the woman whose passion is family.

"My ring size changed since coming here. Too much scrubbing," she says. She whispers to her friend in Tagalog and they laugh. "Too small for me. Maybe for my daughter," she says. She opens her phone and shows me a picture of a girl who looks about fourteen, like me. She's holding up two fingers and grinning. "She's in the Philippines," the woman says. I nod.

"All grown up and beautiful. The last time I saw her, she was much littler."

"This ring would be perfect for her," I say.

"Show me earrings," the woman orders, and I do. "Put them on me," she says. Her earlobe is fat with delicate hairs on it. I lean over the counter and push a white-gold hoop onto it.

"Tell me if it hurts," I say. Her hair smells like ironing and tea. I fasten the earring but I don't lean back. For a few seconds I stay there, with my thumb and fingers on her ear and my face against hers, smelling her. I wonder if her daughter remembers how she smells. I want to ask her, "What does sex feel like? Can you move while a guy does it to you, or are you supposed to stay still like a doll?" but instead I lean back and say, "You can put these on layaway for just ten dollars. It's Christmas in July." She clicks her tongue and says, "Not today. Maybe when I get paid." I shake her hand. It is hard and warm and I want to keep holding on to it, but I know she's not going to buy anything. Dad is snapping his fingers at me because he needs my help.

"Have a nice day," I say to the women. Then I run over to the main counter.

"Hi, baby," Dad says. He sets down the chainsaw he's testing and kisses my hair. "Test this ring for me. I need to get this customer out of my hair pronto." He hands me a pavé ring with all the stones missing. A woman with a purple tooth is watching me. She must be the customer.

I scrub the ring on the touchstone and dab acid on the line it leaves behind. The ten-karat acid holds, but the fourteen-karat acid eats away the line in a second. I weigh it and look up the spot price for gold.

"Hi, ma'am," I say. She doesn't seem to speak English. I write *$15* on a Post-it note. She shakes her finger at me. I shrug and hand the ring back to her. She puts her hands together like she's praying to me. I shake my head no. She looks sad. Then she mimes rocking a baby. I don't know if she's trying to tell me that she had a baby or she's going to have a baby or what, but it doesn't really matter. I write *$17*. She sighs like a pool floaty being stepped on. I give her a thumbs-up and she gives me a sad thumbs-up back. I put the ring in the scrap gold pile and count out $17 for her. She blows me a silent kiss. I try to mime "Come back soon" by making my fingers walk through a door made out of my hand, but she looks confused and I shrug and we laugh and she leaves.

At 7:00, we pull the grates down over the windows. We pile the jewelry and phones and laptops in the safe in case we get robbed. We wheel the bikes inside. The broken ones make a soft ticking noise, like the sound the moms at Kayla's church make when their babies cry. Dad counts the cash and whistles "All I Want for Christmas Is You." Then he clicks through the computer and sends our numbers to Corporate in Miami. I crawl on the floor unplugging the TVs.

"Y'all did a pawn on a chainsaw?" Dad says. My stomach feels cold. I try to meet Kayla's eyes but her head is inside the ring case. I crouch behind a TV and pretend to unplug it, even though it's already unplugged.

"Yep," I say, the word like Styrofoam in my mouth. A part of my brain wants me to stand up, run to him, and tell him that we lied, but my knees stay stuck to the dusty ground. I've lied to him about brushing my teeth and putting sunscreen on my feet, but never about something like this.

"Good stuff," Dad says. I feel myself exhale. I turn off the *Cash for Gold* sign and watch the tiny bulbs fade from red and blue to clear. Then Dad sets the alarm and we all walk out to the parking lot together. Dad's truck and Kayla's dad's car are parked side by side. They were pawned by the same guy a few years ago and they have the same weird smell—like horses and rice.

I hug Kayla and say, "I'll miss you!" I really will miss her, even though I'll see her tomorrow.

"I'll miss you too," she says. I climb into Dad's truck and wave to Kayla until I can't see her anymore. Dad turns on the radio and drums his fingers on the steering wheel. I roll down my window and make my hand dive in and out of the wind like a dolphin.

The puddles on the road glow like watch faces. The sun is starfruit orange. Kayla says we should remember how lucky we are to get to look at orange skies and blue ocean every day. Some people only get to see places as pretty as Cherry Beach on their phone backgrounds. I try to make myself feel lucky, but I feel shaky.

I can't believe what a gigantic lie Kayla and I just told. We aren't liars. Or at least we weren't before today. Part of me wants to just tell Dad everything so the feeling will go away. But another part of me knows that I can't tell him. I just have to wait for the feeling to go away on its own.

We drive past the golf course. The cruise ship families are out, dressed in all blue or all white, grinning at photographers. Dad turns down the music and says, "Are you good, baby? Anything on your mind?" He knows something is wrong. Usually, I love that he can tell what I'm feeling, but I don't love it right now.

"No," I say. I sound rude even though I don't mean to. "Is anything on your mind, Dad?" I say, trying to sound less rude. Dad laughs a little. It's a nice laugh. He's not laughing at me the way some grown-ups laugh at kids.

"I'd say you're the main thing on my mind," he says. I lean my head on his shoulder. He takes one hand off the steering wheel and combs his fingers through my hair the way he does when I can't fall asleep. I watch the truck swallow the yellow lines on the road until we are home.

CHAPTER 2

ME AND KAYLA GET THE MORNING OFF ON FRIDAYS in the summer, but we have to help with the lunch rush. The bike ride from my house to Kayla's house is ten minutes and the bike ride from her house to Paradise Pawn is fifteen minutes, if we don't stop to feed the baby chicks who live under the helicopter pad or to pick the clover that grows through the cracks in the sidewalk by Save A Lot, or to spy on the girls at St. Bridget's.

St. Bridget's is the best private school in Cherry Beach. We're going there in the fall for high school. We'll wear mint-green pleated skirts and tiny silk scarves. We'll learn to play the violins hanging on the walls of Paradise Pawn and how to draw apples with shadows that look real. Our friends will have yachts and skin cream and dads who work at banks. My dad is taking out a loan on his truck to pay my tuition and Kayla is going to get the full-ride scholarship.

At 12:30, we slide into the Paradise Pawn parking lot and I lock my bike to a palm tree. Carter is outside taking his smoke break. He's wearing his Santa hat. Carter is our favorite guard. We think he's cute. He has big, brown eyes and a tattoo of a pirate flag on his neck. He has a bullet stuck in his arm, but it doesn't hurt anymore, and it's useful because when we need to test metal detectors, we don't have to bury stuff in the sand, we just use Carter's arm. Carter's girlfriend, April, works at a bakery in a hotel and sometimes she brings us cupcakes that are too old to sell to tourists.

"Afternoon!" Carter says. He gives us each a fist bump. "Ready to get in there and do some layaways?" he says.

"Yes sir," we say. We hear the door buzz and we go inside. The store is swarming. Dad is fingerprinting a lady with a glass eye. Kayla's dad, Aubrey, is showing a power drill to a man jiggling a baby.

Aubrey and my dad are best friends, just like Kayla and me. Aubrey is tall and squishy, and my dad is short and muscley. They look like Pooh and Piglet when they walk around together. Aubrey wears a ten-karat Gucci link chain. My dad wears a fourteen-karat Cuban link. Aubrey is the store manager for Cherry Beach. My dad is the regional manager for all the Paradise Pawns in central Florida. Me and Kayla are sales associates. We officially started working at the shop this year, but we have been hanging out here since we were in diapers. I wait until Dad is done with the customer, then I give him a hug.

"Hi, baby. Hi, Kayla. How we doing?" Dad says. Before we can answer, a man dumps a bag of PlayStation controllers on the counter. Dad turns to him and fake smiles. "I'll be with you in just one moment," he says. Then to us he says, "Hurry and get dressed. We need you out here." We run to the storeroom and lock the door. We clip our panic buttons and jewelry loupes to our belts. We button up our Paradise Pawn shirts. Our shirts are size extra small, but mine is still too big for me. I hate the way it sticks to my chest.

Kayla has been wearing a bra since sixth grade. She has a bright blue one and two skin-colored ones. She says I'm lucky I don't wear a bra yet. She says they're uncomfortable, but I think she's lying to make me feel better. Even if bras were uncomfortable, even if they were made of broken glass, I would wear one to make my shirt fall over my chest like Kayla's does.

Kayla's body looks like God carved her out of one beautiful piece of marble. All the parts of her fit together the way they're supposed to—the curves of her tan shoulders with little blonde hairs on them, her boobs, perfectly smooth in the cups of her bras, her strong legs, her squinty brown eyes.

I look like I'm made of a bunch of leftover parts that weren't supposed to go together, but God said, "What the heck? I might as well make a girl out of these." I have the proportions of a pelican. My stomach is too round, my legs are too skinny, and my face is too long and pointy.

My shirt has two little bumps poking out of it like I'm a tree with a disease. Dad tells me not to cross my arms when I'm talking to customers, but it's hard to calculate layaway payments or make someone buy a dishwasher when I can tell they're looking at the bumps under my shirt and not at my eyes. Kayla sprays us with her body mist that smells like cucumbers.

"You want a bun or a ponytail?" she asks me. Kayla always does my hair before work. Kayla and I have the exact same haircut—long layers and side bangs. She got it first, and I copied her, but it looks way better with her hair. Her hair is dark blonde and thick and shiny. My hair used to be blonde too, when we were little, but it's turned a gross light brown, like the color of a hearing aid.

"Bun," I say. Kayla's warm hands comb over my scalp, and then I feel my hair twisting together on top of my head. Kayla is amazing at doing hair, but her mom is even better. Giselle cleans rooms at the Marriott, but she's going to go to beauty school someday to be a real hairdresser. She already knows everything she needs to know, she just has to get her license. Giselle has given me every single haircut of my life. Sometimes when I sit on the edge of Kayla's bathtub while Giselle combs and clips and blow-dries my hair, I pretend that she is my mom.

Dad knocks on the storeroom door.

"Let's move it!" he yells. We tuck in our shirts, yank on our Santa hats, and move it. "Took you long enough," Dad says.

"Sorry," we say.

"Don't say sorry. Just don't be slow next time. Now go get some stuff on layaway. Hustle," Dad says, and we hustle. When the rain comes and the store empties out, Dad gives us a box of watches that people defaulted on.

"Get these polished up and priced and set to 10:10," he says.

"Roger that," we say.

Watches are like people. When they're smiling, it's easier for them to make money. That's why whenever a new watch goes out for sale, we set it to 10:10, so the hands make a smiling face. The Cartier store and the Rolex store downtown do it too.

There are a lot of bankers in Cherry Beach. They make so much money that at the grocery store where the rich tourists and the banker families go, they sell blocks of cheese that cost as much as a moped.

A lot of the bankers are obsessed with watches. They come into Paradise Pawn and go insane over watches the way weird kids go insane over Pokémon cards. I think it's because they want to stop time. The ones who like watches all have that I-wish-I-was-younger-than-I-am look. They have big, glowing veneers, like cartoon rabbits. They have orange skin, sunglasses with neck straps, and girlfriends who could be their daughters.

I can't blame the bankers. I understand how they feel. I don't want time to pass either. I wish I could be ten forever. Being ten was so much better than being fourteen and I'm worried that fifteen and sixteen and being a grown-up will be even worse. At least I'm not fooling myself the way the bankers are. I'm not dumb enough to think that spending thousands of dollars on watches will stop the hands on them from turning and my boobs from growing and the hair under my arms from getting thick and gross. Buying watches isn't going to keep the bankers' faces and bellies from sagging either.

But the watches aren't completely useless to them. The watches show off how much money they have. Showing off how much money they have can help them find new, perfect-looking girlfriends when their old girlfriends wear out and start to remind them that time is passing.

I think when the bankers look at their girlfriends, it's like wearing virtual reality goggles. Looking at their young girlfriends makes the bankers feel like they are young too.

If I could find a way to make Kayla look like she was ten sometimes, so I could feel like I was ten, I might do it, but I would never replace Kayla with an actual ten-year-old. I love Kayla a lot more than any of the bankers love their girlfriends, and she loves me more than any of the girlfriends love the bankers.

"If you were a watch, what kind would you want to be?" Kayla asks me, winding an Omega's hands into a smile.

"Something twenty-four karat, so I could sell myself if I ran out of money," I say. "No wait, actually a G-Shock, so I'd be indestructible."

"I'd be something automatic," Kayla says.

"Why?" I say.

"'Cause then, no matter whose wrist was swinging me around—no matter what they did to me, it would give me power. I wouldn't need anyone to change my battery or plug me in, ever. Anything automatic is actually more indestructible than a G-Shock, if you think about it."

"Actually, I'd be something automatic too," I say. Kayla gives me a mean little laugh.

"Copier," she says. I try to spray Windex at her but she ducks.

"Geez, watch it," she says. "It could have gotten in my eyes."

"Sorry," I say. A girl with rhinestones on her shirt walks up to the door and we buzz her in. She folds her umbrella nervously.

"Good afternoon," she whispers.

"Hi there," we say. She shuffles to the counter and hands Kayla her driver's license. She doesn't meet our eyes. She is here to do a pawn.

"How can we help?" Kayla says. The woman unfastens the watch on her wrist. It's a Ballon Bleu de Cartier. We used to have one in the store just like it.

"I need a loan," she murmurs. She's wearing fake eyelashes and acrylic nails but she looks only a few years older than us. She's shorter than me. When she leans on the counter, the corner of it stabs into her boobs.

Dad comes out of the storeroom. He looks at the girl. Then he eats a breath freshener strip. He thinks she's pretty.

"What have we got there?" he asks.

"Ballon Bleu de Cartier," I say.

"Seriously?" he says. He takes the watch from Kayla and looks at it through his loupe. The girl drums her nails on the counter. Dad leans over the computer and looks up the Ballon Bleu de Cartier that we used to have in the store. We sold it to a wrinkled old banker named Mr. Barnes with a wrinkled old wife named Mrs. Barnes. Mr. Barnes buys tons of watches for Mrs. Barnes. When he bought the Ballon Bleu de Cartier for her, he told us a whole story about how it was their anniversary and he was going to take her out on a yacht and then give it to her. We told him she was going to love it.

I always thought it was sweet that Mr. Barnes bought watches for his wife even though she isn't pretty anymore. In the pictures of Mrs. Barnes that Mr. Barnes has showed us, she has the look of an old woman who used to be gorgeous and is panicked about not being gorgeous anymore. Her eyes and eyelashes are still pretty, but the rest of her prettiness is all blurred.

Sometimes when I get mad that I'm not prettier, I think about how at least I'll be used to being ugly when I'm an old woman. The people who are pretty now, like Kayla, will be scrambling to figure out how to make it as ugly people, but I will have had a lifetime of practice.

Dad squints at the serial number on the Ballon Bleu. Then he nods. It's the same one that we sold to Mr. Barnes. He nudges me and Kayla, then rips off a Post-it note and writes: *stolen*.

"Are you sure?" I whisper.

"Shh," he says, and presses his panic button to call the police. Then he writes: *distract her* and underlines it.

"So, how's your day going?" I ask the girl. It's never a good question to ask when someone is doing a pawn. The answer is always that their day is going bad, but I can't think of anything else to say. The girl shrugs.

"My son wouldn't sleep last night, so mama didn't sleep. He was screaming his head off. Usually, I put him in front of the dishwasher and the noise of it knocks him out, but my electricity got shut off." She doesn't look old enough to have a son—even a baby one.

"Well, if you're looking to replace your dishwasher, we have some great models I could show you," I say.

"I'm not," she says. "It wasn't a problem with the dishwasher. It was the power getting shut off. I'm just looking for two things—money and my son's dad. I haven't heard from him in weeks. He was supposed to be paying the electricity bill." I nod. I hope the police get here soon. I feel awkward. The woman shows me a video of her son saying "Mama."

"He's a cutie," I say. "We just got some beautiful fourteen-karat baby chains in, actually. Let me show you." She follows me to the jewelry cases. She smiles as she holds up the little chains. Usually, we're only supposed to let customers handle one chain at a time, but I let her touch as many baby chains as she wants. She deserves a nice moment before she gets arrested.

Then I see red and blue lights flashing outside. I take the baby chains she's holding and put them back in the case. Two police officers stomp in the door. They look like Transformers in their bulletproof vests. They shake hands with Carter and Aubrey and Dad.

"Excuse me, ma'am?" Dad says to the girl. The girl turns and stares at the police officers.

"I didn't do anything wrong, I swear," she says quietly.

"Come with us," one of the officers says. Dad, the girl, and the police walk into Dad's office. Me and Kayla watch them on the security cameras and bite our nails. The girl is crying and flailing her hands. Dad and the officers cross their arms and shake their heads. Dad picks up the phone. In a few minutes, a Mercedes-Benz squeals into the parking lot and Mr. Barnes, the banker who bought the Ballon Bleu de Cartier, gets out of it, slams the door, and jogs through the rain into the store.

"Good afternoon," we say. He yanks off his Oakley sunglasses and nods at us.

"Could you direct me to the manager's office please?" I point to Dad's door.

"That way," I say.

"Thank you so much," he says. His voice sounds deep and friendly, like a politician's. On the security cameras, we watch him enter Dad's office. He tugs on his pants, sits down, and leans back like he's sitting in a cabana chair at the beach. He puts his huge hand on the girl's small shoulder and clamps it there. She looks like she wants to scratch him with her nails, but she makes her mouth into a smile. Mr. Barnes chops his hands through the air like he is a conductor and everyone else is in his orchestra. Dad and the officers smile. Mr. Barnes claps everyone on the back and shakes everyone's hand. When they walk out of the office, everyone is chuckling except for the girl. Mr. Barnes's hand is still fastened on her shoulder.

Dad hands the Ballon Bleu de Cartier back to Mr. Barnes and shakes his hand—the hand that's not squeezing the girl.

"Sorry for the misunderstanding," Dad says.

"No problem at all," Mr. Barnes says, flashing front teeth the size of coins.

"Have a nice day," Dad says to the girl. I can tell Dad feels bad for her. Mr. Barnes jerks her out the door and into the parking lot. I look at Kayla.

"Let's follow them," she says.

"We're taking the trash out!" I yell at Dad. We pull the trash bags out of the bins and run after the girl and Mr. Barnes. We shoo the chickens away from the dumpster and crouch behind it. Mr. Barnes is screaming at the girl.

"Are you slow or something? Seriously, what is wrong with you? Why would you bring that here?" He's shaking her like she's a rug with crumbs on it.

"I needed money," she says calmly.

"Why didn't you tell me?"

"I did," she says. "And if you do this again—if you leave us with no lights, I swear I'll show up with the baby and I'll introduce him to Mrs. Barnes and his half brothers."

Mr. Barnes grabs her again. His whole face is quivering and red. He raises his hand like he's going to hit her. Kayla stands up with a jolt. I grab her arm and whisper, "Stop!" and try to pull her back down, but she shoves me away. She reaches for the lid of the dumpster and bangs it hard. Mr. Barnes jumps, then lets go of the girl. Their eyes snap toward us.

"Hello, girls," Mr. Barnes says, back in his politician voice. His face is still red and scary, but he twists it into a smile. He looks like the Joker in *Batman*.

"We were just taking out the trash," I say. My throat is cold and dry. Mr. Barnes walks closer to us and I wonder if he's going to try to hit us, too.

"Tell your dad thanks for the help today," he says to me. I feel like I'm going to throw up. I hate the idea that Dad helped Mr. Barnes. It wasn't Dad's fault. Dad was just doing his job. He thought the watch was stolen.

Mr. Barnes must be able to tell that I feel weird. He winks at me. I force myself to smile. He holds out his hand—the same one he was about to slap into the girl. He wants me to shake it.

"Always a pleasure doing business at Paradise Pawn," he says. I feel my arm lifting and my hand fitting into his and being pumped up and down. Then I watch his hand move toward Kayla like a claw. She doesn't shake his hand. I nudge her, but she doesn't move.

Finally, Mr. Barnes puts his hand in his pocket, laughs, and says, "I tell you, pretty soon the boys will be lining up for you girls." He says it to both of us, but he's looking at Kayla. Usually, this kind of thing makes me jealous of her, but I'm glad Mr. Barnes isn't looking at me. Kayla and I stand there, stiff. I look to the girl, but she's looking at the ground.

"Yeah, totally," I say. I don't know what else to say. Kayla puts her hand on my wrist and guides me away from Mr. Barnes.

"So long!" he says cheerfully, like he doesn't realize how creepy he is.

We stand behind the dumpster and watch Mr. Barnes press the girl's face into his. His hands rub her butt and her glittery nails comb through his gray hair. Then we watch him drive away, and we watch her walk to the bus stop. Kayla holds my hand as we walk back to the store.

"That was messed up," I say. Kayla nods. There are tears in her eyes.

"God, I want to be rich," she says. "I don't want to date somebody rich, or have a baby with somebody rich, or marry somebody rich, I want to *be* rich."

"Me too," I say. I can tell she's deciding whether or not to get mad at me, whether to say that I *am* rich—richer than her, because my dad is richer than her dad—but she doesn't get mad. She squeezes my hand and says, "We will be rich. Don't worry."

"Someday, Mr. Barnes's kids will work for us," I say. I mean it like a joke, but Kayla nods slowly, like it isn't a joke.

"Exactly," she says. She looks out toward the pier as if she can see it—us wearing high heels in a glass room at the top of a skyscraper, Mr. Barnes's kids following us around with files of important papers and cups of coffee, worrying that we'll yell at them if they make a mistake. I squeeze her hand and she squeezes back.

There's a line at the counter when we get inside. A tourist is yelling and waving a DVD in Dad's face, a kid is having a tantrum by the small appliances, and someone has spilled a box of drill bits on the floor.

"Girls, what's the holdup? Let's move it!" Dad yells, and we move it even though we still feel a little sick.

CHAPTER 3

SOMEBODY JACKHAMMERED THROUGH THE CEILing of the Daytona Beach Paradise Pawn and stole a bunch of phones and laptops, so Dad has to go meet with the police there. Rob at Corporate is really mad. Dad is mad too, about the phones and laptops, but I think he's happy he gets to go to Daytona Beach. He has a friend there named Alexis, who works at a hotel. She's really good at folding towels into swans. She has pink hair and too many freckles. I've never met her, but I read her texts to Dad when he's in the shower. She sends him pictures of the towel swans she makes, and selfies where she's making kissy-faces at him. Dad is staying the whole weekend in Daytona Beach so he can hang out with Alexis. I get to stay with Kayla's family while Dad is gone.

Kayla's apartment is as loud as my house is quiet. There are eighteen kids on her street, counting Kayla and her brothers—

nineteen, counting me. There are zero other kids on my street, just a bunch of old people who walk around like tortoises.

Me and Kayla sleep in the living room at her apartment because Kayla shares a room with her brothers, Mason and Bobby. They're nine and five—not old enough to have a conversation about anything interesting, but old enough to be annoying. When I sleep at Kayla's, we make a little nest out of the couch cushions and my camping mattress and my sleeping bag. Kayla doesn't have a sleeping bag but she folds her blankets into one.

Once we've eaten dinner and made our nest, I want to start whispering to Kayla about if God exists and what bras feel like, but we can't because Kayla's brothers have to take their baths and run around and scream for a while. Then Kayla's grandpa and grandma come over and they have to mess up our nest and put the couch cushions back so they can watch the end of a NASCAR race with Aubrey. Then Kayla's cousin Courtney comes over for Giselle to dye her hair. Courtney has a boyfriend named Anthony, who she talks about like he's Jesus. We have to sit in the kitchen and listen to her go on and on about how Anthony's going to get promoted to meat department manager at Publix and he's going to save up to buy a boat and she's going to have to buy a bunch of swimsuits.

Kayla wants to know everything about Anthony, but I get bored before Giselle is even done rinsing Courtney's hair. When it's finally quiet, Kayla says she's too tired to stay up late and talk to me. I poke her and try to talk to her anyway, but she pretends to be asleep, and then she actually falls asleep. I make an obstacle course for an ant on the floor with my fingers. Then I watch Kayla's stomach glide up and down as she breathes until I am asleep.

In the morning, chalky light streams through the grate on the window and wakes me up. Kayla is in the kitchen. No one else is awake. I wiggle out of my sleeping bag and walk toward her.

"What are you doing?" I say.

"Look," Kayla says quietly. She's holding out an envelope the way the priests at her church hold the Bible. It's an envelope from St. Bridget's—the same kind that our acceptance letters came in. The loopy gold letters say *Aubrey and Giselle McCabe*.

"It's your scholarship! Right? It totally is!" I yell.

"Shush!" Kayla says. "You'll wake everyone up."

"Sorry. Okay, but it's got to be!" I run to hug her. "I'm so fricking happy!" I say, as quietly as I can. Then I kiss her cheeks.

"Stop," she says, and pushes me off her. "Don't jinx it."

"They wouldn't waste their expensive paper to be like, 'Oh, sorry. No scholarship for the smartest, coolest girl in Cherry Beach.' Here. I'll open it if you're too scared. Give it to me," I say. I reach for the letter.

"Don't, Jackie. Stop," Kayla whisper-yells. She grabs the letter out of my hands.

"Okay, geez. Sorry," I say.

"We have to open it on Lucky Island," Kayla says.

"Seriously?" I say. She nods. I'm sleepy and I don't feel like getting wet, but I look at her face and say, "Fine."

Lucky Island isn't really an island. It's a concrete slab in the ocean, but it really is lucky. We go there to pray sometimes. I don't know how to pray, but Kayla does. When Hurricane Ike was about to hit Kayla's aunt's house, we prayed that her roof would stay on, and it did.

Two summers ago, me and Kayla both had one last baby tooth to lose. We swam out to Lucky Island and clipped our *Best Friends* necklaces together and pulled our teeth out at the exact same time. The tooth fairy used to pay each of us one dollar every time we lost a tooth, but that time the tooth fairy paid me $20 and gave me a little bracelet with fake diamonds in it from Paradise Pawn. She only paid Kayla one dollar, like normal. That's how we knew for sure that the tooth fairy was just our parents.

We opened our acceptance letters from St. Bridget's on Lucky Island too. I didn't think I would get in, because my grades aren't very good, but Lucky Island made it happen. Kayla obviously got in with her grades and now she's obviously going to get the scholarship. Kayla runs to her room. Bobby and Mason are fast asleep. It's earlier than I realized. The sky is still pink.

"Here," Kayla whispers. She hands me her rosary, which is from Paradise Pawn, and the envelope of four-leaf clovers that her pen pal, Chelsea in Ireland, sent her when we were in fourth grade. My pen pal was a boy and he never sent me any clovers. I told him I lived in a skyscraper with my mom and dad and five sisters and he believed it.

"Go put these in a plastic bag," Kayla says. She takes off her nightgown and shimmies into her red-and-white swimsuit. She looks beautiful in her swimsuit. I wrap the St. Bridget's letter and Kayla's lucky stuff in two layers of cling wrap, a Ziploc bag, and a grocery bag. Then I put on the swimsuit that I keep at Kayla's house.

"Ready?" Kayla says.

"Ready," I say. We slip out the door. Kayla sits on the handlebars of my bike and I pedal past Save A Lot, past Pleasant Palms, to Five Mile Beach. The ocean is pink and shimmery. Lucky Island belongs to the Radisson and there's a fence around their part of the beach, so we have to pretend to be tourists to get to it.

"Hey!" I yell to a guy jogging on the beach. He has no shirt on. "I left my key in my room. Can you let us in?" He doesn't seem to speak English, but he opens the gate and jogs away. Kayla wheels my bike onto the sand and we lock it to a cabana. Then we run down the beach and into the water. We push ourselves up onto Lucky Island, panting. Everything is silent, like the ocean is holding its breath, waiting for Kayla to open her letter.

Kayla slides the rosary out of the two layers of plastic bags and the cling wrap. She starts to pray. Her rosary beads clap against each other. I pick at some barnacles on the side of Lucky Island. Then I close my eyes and imagine me and Kayla twirling in green-and-white St. Bridget's uniforms.

"Okay," Kayla says finally. She unwraps the letter and holds it against her chest with her eyes closed.

"Just read it," I say. I squeeze her hand. She unfolds the letter and holds it in front of her face. I curl my toes into the sharpness of Lucky Island, ready to lunge at her and hug her and jump into the ocean with her and scream with joy. I watch her eyes move across the page. Then she shuts her eyes again and a tear wobbles down her cheek. She tries to crumple up the paper but it's so fancy that it doesn't crumple like normal paper.

"Frick!" I yell. I reach for Kayla's arm, but she yanks it away and dives into the water and swims away so fast and so far that I would be scared to save her if she started drowning.

"Hey!" I scream to her tiny head, bobbing in the waves.

"What?" she yells.

"Come back! I have an idea." I don't actually have an idea, but I don't want her to drown and then me to drown trying to save her. She paddles back to me, pushes herself onto Lucky Island and says, "What?" Water drips off her face. I can't tell which drops are tears and which drops are ocean.

"It's just twelve thousand dollars. It's just money. We can get that much money," I say.

"You're joking, right?" Kayla says, looking at me like I'm the stupidest person who ever lived. "School starts in a month. And we make fifteen dollars an hour. And pretty much all my money from work goes in a bank account for my future. Not my in-two-weeks future, my grown-up, pay-my-own bills future. We definitely can't get that much money."

"Okay, geez, sorry. I'm just trying to think of ideas," I say, feeling like I might cry too, which would make Kayla even madder at me. She would say this is her sadness to cry about, not mine. "We could buy lottery tickets, we could start a YouTube channel, we could send those emails to old people saying we're princesses in a foreign country who need to get out of jail." Kayla shakes her head.

"Those are stupid ideas," she says. "I'm sorry, but they are."

"What, so you're just going to give up? We're going to go to different schools? You're going to throw away all our plans about going to St. Bridget's?"

"I don't know. I need to think," she says. She lies down on her back and I lie beside her on my side. I watch a barge inch across the horizon. It makes me mad that the people on the barge have no idea that this horrible, unfair thing has just happened to me and Kayla. It feels like everyone in the world should know about it and feel sad at the same time, like when a guy shoots people at a mall.

But nobody knows what has happened except for me and Kayla and some stupid person at St. Bridget's who decided not to give her the scholarship. I take deep breaths and try not to cry. I dig through my brain for a not-stupid way to get $12,000.

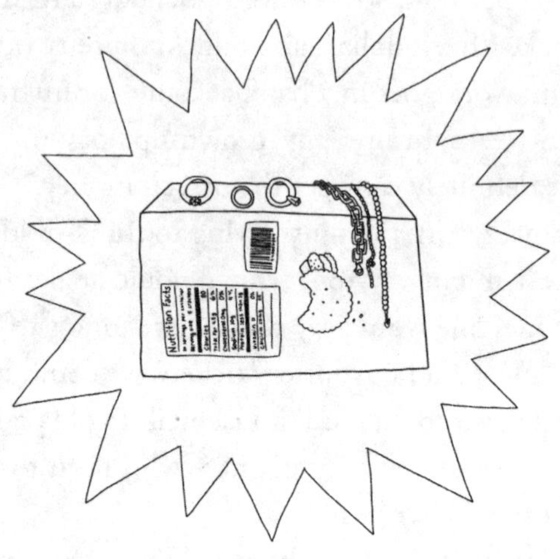

CHAPTER 4

WHEN DAD AND I WENT TO DALLAS FOR MOM'S funeral, Dad gave me my own disposable camera with twenty-four pictures on it. I used up two taking pictures out the window of the plane. I remember thinking it looked like there were animals made of diamonds swimming around in the water and crashing into each other and breaking.

I used the rest of the camera to take pictures of Mom in her casket. She was wearing a tight white dress and pink-orange lipstick. There was a wreath of lilies on her stomach. In the envelope under my bed with pictures of Mom in it, I have five pictures of her when she was alive and twenty-two pictures from that disposable camera of her when she was dead.

I don't remember the church part of the funeral very well, but I remember the part where everyone looked at Mom's body. There was a big air-conditioned room with green-and-purple carpet and a long line of people in black, picking at their fingernails as they walked past Mom lying there, dead, while they got to be alive.

One of the women said she was my aunt. She gave me a box of cheap crayons that broke if you pressed too hard. She took me into a corner of the room where there were sandwiches and mini bottles of water and she made me a word search on the back of the program for the funeral. They were all words I didn't know, like "solace" and "angel." The only one I knew was "paradise" because of the pawnshop.

The aunt held my hand and showed me a display with pictures of Mom when she was a little girl, biting into a big chocolate rabbit, doing a cartwheel, holding a parrot on her shoulder and laughing. I kept waiting for the aunt to say that Mom looked like me, but she never did, even though Mom did look exactly like me in some of the photos.

Then the aunt had to help put out more trays of sandwiches for everybody, and then she had to stand in a line by Mom's casket while people hugged her and cried. I wanted to be hugged by all the people there too, but when I went to stand by the aunt, she made me another word search and told me to go sit in a folding chair far away from the people giving hugs.

Then someone said it was time to take a picture of the family. Dad went in the other room with the sandwiches. He knew nobody wanted him in the picture. The women went to the bathroom to mop the bottoms of their eyes, where their makeup was smeared from crying. I went with them, even though I wasn't wearing any makeup. A photographer set up a big light and arranged everyone against the wall—tall people in the back, short people in the front. I went to stand in the front. The aunt put her hands on my shoulders for a few flashes of the camera. Then she whispered to me, "Could you go over there for a second, sweetheart?"

I sat on the floor by the photographer watching everyone else grin like they weren't in the same room as a dead person and like they hadn't just kicked me, their literal family, out of their family photo.

Up until then, I hadn't cried once that whole day. When people made speeches about Mom and it seemed like everyone was supposed to cry, I poked myself in the eyes with my finger to try to make them water, but it didn't work. As I sat on the carpet all alone under the photographer's flashing light, I finally felt tears in my throat. It was a bad time to cry. Everyone was lined up, looking right at me. I breathed in through my nose and out through my mouth, just like Kayla taught me to do when I needed to stop myself from crying at school. I kept breathing like that and I went to find Dad.

"Can we leave?" I said.

"You didn't want to be in the family picture?" he said.

"No, they didn't want me to be," I said, and then I cried, finally. Dad didn't say a word. He picked me up. It was back when I was small enough that he picked me up a lot. He carried me to the car and we drove to a Denny's with no other people in it.

While we waited for our food, Dad built me a card house out of the sugar packets. When I tried to help, I kept knocking it down, but he never got mad. He just kept rebuilding it and he kept letting me help. Eventually it was so big that it took up half the table. We got more sugar packets from the table next to us and built little houses around the main house. Dad made up a story about how he and I lived in the big house, which was a castle, and we were the bosses of everybody in the little houses. There was a pink wing of the castle for me and Kayla, a blue wing for Dad, and a brown wing for Aubrey and Giselle. When the waitress came with our food, she got mad at us. She said it was unhygienic for us to put our fingers all over the sugar packets.

"We'll buy them then," Dad said. I remember thinking he sounded like a really rich person. We looked like rich people too, because Dad was still wearing his black suit and I was wearing a black dress and tights and a ribbon in my hair and a new bracelet from Paradise Pawn. I didn't understand money back then. I knew we had spent a lot of money on the plane tickets and I got a little worried about how we would afford all the sugar packets, but it made me happy looking at the waitress's face. She was so shocked. I thought she must have thought two millionaires were at her Denny's.

After Dad ate shiny eggs and sausage and I ate French toast sticks, the waitress gave us a little to-go box for all our sugar packets. We took apart the castle and the houses carefully, putting pink sugar packets in one corner of the box, blue ones in another, yellow ones in another, and brown ones in another. Then we got in the car and we drove to a hotel parking lot.

"Get out," Dad said, "and bring your sugar packets." He looked at his watch and counted down from ten. A spray of pink fireworks shot into the sky, then gold, twinkling, dripping ones, then ones in the shape of smiley faces. It was the most fireworks I had ever seen in my life. They were the Six Flags fireworks, but I thought they were just for me. Dad ripped open a pink sugar packet and handed it to me. I poured it into my mouth and it felt like my teeth were full of sweet sand. When I'd crunched it all down, Dad opened another packet for me, and another one.

"Are you happy?" Dad yelled to me over the booms.

"Yeah!" I screamed. Then, when the sound died down and the sugar melted in my throat, I remembered that my mom was dead and I wasn't supposed to be happy. I was still wearing my black clothes. I was sweating through my tights and I'd spilled sugar into the velvet of my dress.

"Why did you do that to me?" I asked Dad when we were back in the car.

"Do what?" he said.

"Trick me into being happy. I'm supposed to be sad."

"Babe, no you're not. You're eight," he said. "No one who's eight is supposed to be sad."

A FEW DAYS after we got back from Mom's funeral, I was playing Barbies with Kayla in the back of Paradise Pawn. We used to lay out a mini pawnshop for them. We made a counter out of a Ritz crackers box and we pretended that rings were bracelets and bracelets were necklaces for them. Necklaces were leashes for their pets. Kayla made her Barbie say something funny, I don't remember what, and I was laughing so hard that I fully forgot, again, that Mom was dead. Then I started to cry. Kayla didn't ask what was wrong. She knew. She crossed her legs and I put my head in her lap and I cried into her shorts.

"I have an idea," she said. She went to the safe and took out the two $20 bills she got from her grandparents for Christmas. Then we put away our Barbies and walked out into the sun.

"Where are we going?" I said.

"You'll see," she said. We walked through the Burger King parking lot, then we crossed the big road and walked into the tourist grocery store. It was so air-conditioned inside that our teeth chattered. Kayla gave me her sweater. She walked to the fish counter and I followed her.

"Kayla, I hate it over here. You know that. Because of the lobsters," I said.

"I know," she said, squeezing my hand. "Hang on." We stood by the fish counter, breathing in the stink of fish guts and bleach.

The dead fish with their eyes and teeth still in didn't bother me, but the live lobsters in the tank made me feel like crying. Their feelers were so gentle. Their cartoony black-and-white eyes were so hopeful looking as they scrambled on top of each other and tried to crawl through the glass walls of their tank. They were working so hard, trying to take some control over their lives. But no matter what they did, they would end up boiled alive by tourists.

"Hey," Kayla said to the man behind the counter. She had to say it three times before he noticed us. "We'll take one lobster, please," she said.

"Kayla, to cook? What is wrong with you?" I said.

"No, dummy, to set free."

"But they're like fifty dollars," I whispered.

"Yeah, but it's worth it. I want to help you feel better," she said. I hugged her and she hugged me back. We picked the smallest lobster in the tank because it was the cheapest and because we thought it was a baby.

"Is it a boy or a girl?" I asked the man behind the counter.

"No idea," he said. "Look, I'm not going to package this thing up if you kids can't pay for it."

"We can," Kayla said, flashing the two $20 bills at him. "Look."

"Are your parents going to help you cook it?" he said.

"We're not going to cook it. We're going to set it free," Kayla said. The man heaved a sigh, like he thought we were stupid.

"Please," I said. "It's really important." I squeezed Kayla's hand and she squeezed mine. The man looked over his shoulder at his boss chopping up a salmon.

"You're going to let it go in the ocean? You know it'll just die out there, don't you?" he said. I looked at Kayla.

"No, it won't," she said.

"No, it won't," I repeated.

"Give it to us," Kayla said. Her voice sounded so powerful that he stopped arguing. He put the lobster in a Styrofoam box filled with ice and handed it to us.

"Have fun," he said, which was an annoying thing to say to us, given that we were saving a life, not having fun, but we ignored him.

We unwrapped the lobster as soon as we got outside. We wanted to let her walk beside us through the parking lot, but we couldn't get her to walk in a straight line and we worried she might get run over, so I held her in my arms like a baby and we walked to Five Mile Beach.

We found a quiet place where there were no jet skis or boats. Then we slid the rubber bands off her claws and let her crawl into the water.

"Thank you," I whispered to Kayla.

"Of course," she said. She squeezed me as we watched all her Christmas money scuttle away into the waves. "Do you feel better?" she said. I nodded into her shoulder.

We were so sure the lobster would live a long, happy life. We used to imagine she could see us when we went swimming at Five Mile Beach—that she was looking up at us from the ocean floor and feeling thankful that we saved her.

About a year ago, Dad was buying tilapia to grill for some cruise ship woman he had a crush on. Our grocery store was out of tilapia, so we went to the tourist store. While Dad got the fish, I stared at the lobsters stacked on top of each other, flailing their antennas around. It dawned on me that the lobster me and Kayla thought we saved from that tank probably died a few hours after we set her free.

We didn't give her any food. If she even found other lobsters to be with, she probably smelled weird to them and they probably ganged up on her. Her claws had been rubber banded together for so long that she had probably forgotten how to defend herself with them.

We thought we were doing this amazing thing for the world, but we weren't. It was probably more painful for our lobster to see the ocean and then die than it would have been to just get boiled alive in some rich family's Airbnb.

CHAPTER 5

KAYLA HAS BEEN ACTING LIKE SHE'S MAD AT ME ever since the letter about her scholarship came. She says she's not mad, but I can tell she is. When we hug, I hold her way more tightly than she holds me. When she has a fruit roll-up, instead of giving me half of it, like she used to, she just gives me a tiny piece.

We're in the parking lot of Paradise, detailing a car that someone didn't pay their loan on. The car has been in the sun all morning and it's hot. We roll the windows down. Sometimes a nice-smelling breeze comes in off the ocean, but mostly it smells like sweat—my sweat, Kayla's sweat, and the sweat of whoever used to own the car.

Usually, detailing cars with Kayla is fun. When we were younger, she made up all these special games when we cleaned cars. There was this game where we were spies driving across lava catching bad guys, and all the dust in the car was poison that the bad guys put there.

Then there was a game where we were spies driving to go on dates with bad guys. We had to get our car really clean so the bad guys would fall in love with us and tell us secrets, like the codes to set off their nuclear bombs. Then, as we got older, we started just talking about stuff and planning what we will do when we can actually drive.

But detailing a car isn't fun when Kayla won't talk to me. The only game we're playing is counting how many used Crest Whitestrips we find under the seats. It's not even fun. It's just gross.

As we're wiping dust out of the air vents in silence—Kayla in the front seat and me in the back, Kayla finally says, "Hey, I'm sorry I've been kind of weird lately."

"You haven't been weird," I say, even though she has.

"Well, I feel like I have been and I'm sorry," she says.

"It's okay," I say. I lean into the front seat and wrap my arms around her shoulders.

"I've been thinking about what you said, about how we could earn money for the St. Bridget's tuition, and you're right," she says.

"Really?" I say. I can feel my heart beating in my whole body, but I try to stay calm. I can't make Kayla annoyed at me again, just as she's getting un-annoyed.

"Here's what I'm thinking," Kayla says.

"Uh-huh," I say breathlessly.

"You know how we got that nice new camera in the store? I was practicing taking pictures with it and I'm pretty good. I think I could be a photographer. Tourists will pay like fifty dollars for a nice picture of themselves on the beach. I could just go to a hotel and set up the tripod and take a bunch of pictures of people and then, cha-ching—St. Bridget's tuition."

"You're a genius," I say. She really is.

"I did the math already. Twelve thousand dollars divided by fifty is two hundred and forty. I would just have to take two hundred and forty pictures, which really isn't that many. I wouldn't be able to earn all of it by the time school starts, but I probably could by the middle of the semester, so I could transfer then."

"Yes!" I can't contain myself anymore. "Yes yes yes! I'll just catch you up on everything you miss for the first few weeks. This is perfect!" I stand up in the back seat and launch myself across the car's console and press Kayla into my chest. "When should we start taking pictures? Like after work today?"

"Oh, you don't need to come. I can just do it myself," Kayla says. Some of the happiness drips out of me.

"Don't photographers need assistants?" I say.

"Well, for it to work, people will need to think we're old, like twenty. I can look old if I put on my mom's clothes and makeup, but—I just don't know if people would believe you're old. No offense." I stop hugging her and I droop into the back seat again.

"You're being mean," I say.

"No, Jackie. I didn't mean it like that," she says. She climbs from the front seat into the back and nestles into me. I scoot away from her.

"Just because you have boobs, you don't have to act like you're better than everyone," I say.

"I don't think I'm better than everyone," she says. "I really don't. I think I'm worse than most people." At first, I think she's joking. It's such a ridiculous thing for her to say. I am the one who is worse than most people. She is so much better than anyone else we have ever met. Maybe the pope or Rihanna or someone like that would have the same kind of glow that Kayla has, but as far as people in our normal world, she is the absolute best. I thought she knew that.

I usually give her a pass on acting like she's better than me and everyone around us, because it's the truth. She just is better. I want to say this to her, but we're in the middle of a fight. We are quiet for a while. I rub a Clorox wipe around and around the cup holder in the back seat of the car, even though it's already clean. Kayla is on her knees, fishing Skittles wrappers out from under the driver's seat.

"Seems like this guy was having some kind of identity crisis about his teeth," she says.

"What?" I say.

"Like, he was using way more Crest Whitestrips than you're supposed to, but also he was going to town on Skittles, which are really bad for your teeth." She holds up two handfuls of crumpled red wrappers.

"Kayla, I don't really care about this guy's teeth. Why are you changing the subject? Did you just forget what we were fighting about?" I say. I climb down onto the floor of the car to make better eye contact with her. Kayla stuffs the Skittles wrappers in a garbage bag.

Then she says, "Fine. You can come to take pictures, but you have to promise to do exactly what I say and to be really, really mature and professional."

"I promise," I say, snapping my chest upright to show her how mature and professional I can be. "I really do think it'll seem more legit if you have an assistant. I can bring a comb and comb people's hair before the pictures, like they do for picture day at school."

"I guess," Kayla says.

"When should we start?"

"Let's go tomorrow morning. Come over to my house. My mom works early, so we can take her clothes without her knowing."

"Okay," I say.

"And I'll put the camera and tripod in my backpack tonight as we're closing up," she says. "If we bring it back tomorrow morning, the dads won't notice."

"Okay," I say again. As we vacuum the car, the picture in my head of me and Kayla at St. Bridget's gets brighter and brighter.

*

THE NEXT MORNING, as the sky turns pink, I bike to Kayla's apartment. I climb up the fire escape and knock on the window of her room. She puts a finger to her lips. Her brothers and Aubrey are still sleeping. Then she opens the window and I climb in.

"Hi," she whispers. I give her a hug. She's wearing a black dress and blazer that make her look like a grown-up. She's also wearing makeup. Not just lip gloss, but makeup on her eyes.

"You look amazing," I say.

"I know," she whispers. "I watched a bunch of videos about how to do this makeup and it took like four tries, but I got it."

"Nice," I say. We tiptoe into Kayla's parents' room, where Aubrey is sleeping. Silently, Kayla slips a blue-and-white dress off a hanger. Then we creep into the bathroom.

"You have to be so careful with my mom's clothes, okay? She needs them for when she goes to beauty school, so we can't mess them up. Okay? Promise?" Kayla says. I nod. I wiggle out of my clothes and step into Giselle's dress. The fabric is swishy.

Kayla studies me. "I think you should wear a bra with some toilet paper in it," she says.

"Seriously? Okay," I say, trying to seem casual about it, even though I'm so excited my stomach hurts. Kayla hands me one of her bras, the bright blue one, which is her favorite. She helps me slip my arms through the straps and she fastens it around my chest. She pulls two long ribbons of toilet paper off the roll, crumples them into boob shapes, and tucks them into the cups of the bra against my skin. Then she pulls the dress up around my shoulders, zips it, and stands back to examine her work.

"Good," she says, nodding. "Can I put some eyeliner on you?"

"Of course," I murmur. She pulls the eyeliner out of Giselle's makeup bag.

"Stay still," she says. She sits on the bathroom counter and wraps her legs around my waist, holding me in place. I feel her breath on my cheeks. Her heels press into my back. "Close your eyes," she says, and I do. I feel her tracing my eyelid with the sharp, cold pencil. It hurts a little and I want to scrunch my eyes up, but I make them stay still. "Now pout your lips like a fish," she says. I do, and she dabs sweet-smelling lip gloss onto them. "Good," she says, nodding. "I'm going to write a note to my parents saying we went to the beach, which actually isn't totally a lie, and then we can go."

"Okay," I say. I'm hardly listening to her. I can't stop looking at myself in the mirror. I am wearing a bra and eyeliner and lip gloss. Kayla goes into the kitchen. I stay in the bathroom and stare at myself. I'm looking at a grown-up woman. I unzip the dress and pull it down around my waist. You can't see the toilet paper inside the bra I'm wearing. It just looks like I have boobs. I shiver. I wonder if Dad would be mad if he saw me. I wonder if I look like my mom. I pose with my arms above my head like a girl on a Victoria's Secret billboard. I shiver again. Kayla knocks on the door.

"Ready?" she says. I pull the dress back up around my shoulders.

"Ready," I say. We climb down the fire escape. Then I get on my bike and Kayla gets on the handlebars, holding her backpack with the camera and tripod in it.

“Whatever you do, don’t get sweaty,” she says. “If you feel yourself getting sweaty, we have to stop and switch places because these are clothes you have to dry-clean and dry-cleaning is super expensive.”

“Got it,” I say. I bike up the coast as the sky turns blue. We bike past the cheap spring break hotels and the big construction site, toward the nicest part of Five Mile Beach. I try not to let myself get sweaty, but eventually I do and I stop to fan my armpits. Then Kayla pedals and I sit on the handlebars with the backpack until we get to the Ritz-Carlton.

There’s a tall, white gate around the grounds. Quietly, we get off my bike and lock it to a lamppost. There’s a guardhouse by the door to the gate. The guard in the guardhouse is eating a sandwich. Mayonnaise drips out of it and onto his collar. As he looks down to wipe it off, we scramble over the gate and run. A golf course stretches out on either side of us like a soft, green ocean. There are giant black cars racing around in front of the hotel. Rich people in bright clothes get out of them and employees in tan uniforms get in them and drive them away.

The lobby is thick with air-conditioning and piano music. There’s a table the size of an oil tanker piled with breakfast food. Two kids, a boy and a girl about our age, are draped over gold chairs that look like thrones. The girl is peeling open a croissant and rolling its insides into little balls. She’s not even eating them. She’s just treating the croissant like modeling clay. The boy is playing a game on his phone and picking sunburned skin off his forehead.

We duck into the bathroom. Everything is white and gold and it smells like a spa. There’s a basket of hairspray and tampons and mouthwash.

“Is that stuff free?” I say.

"Yeah, if you're staying here, which we're not, so don't even think about touching it," Kayla says. Her bossiness is starting to annoy me a little.

"I wasn't," I say. "Geez." Kayla runs her fingers under the gold tap. Then she slicks back the bits of her hair that got curly and loose while we were biking. She does the same thing to my hair.

"Ready?" Kayla says. I nod. "Just act like you know what you're doing," Kayla says. I nod again.

We walk past a pool the color of blue Gatorade and then out to the beach. We set up the tripod and the camera like we know what we're doing. Then we scan the beach chairs for customers. Most people are sleeping or on their phones. Nobody is looking at the ocean.

"Should we just go up to people and ask if they want a picture?" I whisper.

"No, let them come to us," Kayla says. We wait for twenty minutes and no one comes to us. I can feel myself sweating and I try to stop.

A little girl toddles out into the waves and a woman with fake boobs runs after her.

"Wait for Mommy! Arlo, wait for Mommy!" the woman yells. The girl stops and wobbles on her chubby legs. The mom crouches down and takes pictures of the girl with her phone. "Are you so pretty, Arlo?" the mom coos. I catch Kayla's eye. This is perfect. Kayla tucks her hair behind her ears and walks toward the mom.

"Your daughter is precious!" she says in a deep voice. The woman turns around.

"Thanks," she says. "She's a handful sometimes, but a cute handful."

"I'm a photographer, actually, and I couldn't help but notice how perfect you two look together. Could I interest you in a professional portrait?" She sounds so convincing, I can't even believe it. The woman looks over at the tripod and me. I push out my toilet paper boobs and smile.

"Oh, what a sweet idea! Let's do it. I'll just go grab my husband," the woman says. "Babe! Kevin!" she yells to a balding man in a Hawaiian-print swimsuit. He puts his finger to his lips and points at his phone. "We're going to take a family portrait, babe!" the lady yells.

"I'm on a call, babe," Kevin says. The woman rolls her eyes. She sits down in the sand and starts building little sandcastles, which Arlo squashes. When Kevin hangs up the phone, he says, "Emma, I don't want to be in a portrait."

"He's a little camera shy," she says to us, smiling, like it's some sort of inside joke.

"I'm not camera shy, I'm just not in the mood to be in a photo right now, babe," Kevin says through his teeth. The little girl runs toward the water and Emma runs after her. Kevin types on his phone.

"Arlo! No going in the ocean without Mommy!" Emma yells. The little girl starts to cry. Emma wraps her in a hug. "Mommy just wants you to be safe. Mommy doesn't want you to get eaten by a shark!" Emma says. I think about telling her that actually the number of sharks killed by people is way higher than the number of people killed by sharks, but I decide not to. It seems like she's just trying to scare Arlo into listening to her. It doesn't seem to be working. Arlo wiggles out of her grip.

"Kevin!" Emma says, snapping her fingers at him. Kevin doesn't move. Under her breath she says to us, "He's losing his hair, so he doesn't like to be in photos. I'm trying to build his confidence up." Kayla nods sympathetically, as if she too has a husband who is losing his hair, so she understands. Emma keeps talking, the way very lonely people will just talk and talk to you if you look like you're listening. "He keeps saying he's going to go to Turkey and I keep saying, 'For who? I don't care if you're bald! Who are you trying to impress?' You know? Like, I don't think he would cheat on me, but I feel like I'm safer if he's bald," she whispers.

"Totally," I say, even though I'm completely confused by what she's saying.

"Daddy's handsome just as he is, right, Arlo?" Emma says. Arlo has taken off one of her sandals and is chewing on it. Emma hoists Arlo onto her hip and marches over to Kevin. I can't hear what they're saying, but I can tell they're arguing. Emma keeps glancing over at us and fake smiling.

Finally, Emma pulls Kevin up out of his chair and they walk toward us. Kevin drags his feet in the sand and doesn't look up from his phone.

"Here we are!" Emma says in a high, fake-cheerful voice. Kevin winces, like he's embarrassed by her. It makes me kind of nervous to be around them, but Kayla takes charge.

"What a gorgeous family," she coos. "Let's have you stand right about here, where the lighting is nice." She puts her hands on Emma's shoulders and guides her. "Now, sir, you stand here and put your arm around your gorgeous wife," she says to Kevin. "And you hold your parents' hands like this, sweetheart," she says to the little girl. Kayla reaches out to me and holds my hands to show the little girl what to do.

"That looks perfect," I say, trying to make my voice sound as grown-up as Kayla's.

"Now," Kayla says, "on the count of three, I want you each to think of something that makes you really, really happy. One, two, three." The camera flashes and the anger that was on their faces melts. I wonder what they're thinking about. I want to ask them, but it wouldn't be professional. "Lovely," Kayla says. "Now look into each other's eyes and keep smiling those beautiful smiles." They do as they're told and Kayla snaps pictures. I look at them in the little screen on the camera. They look like an ad for an airline credit card. They will hang this picture on their wall as proof to all their friends and to themselves that they love each other. "These are amazing. You're so photogenic," Kayla says.

"Thank you," Emma says.

"Can I get your email address and I'll email these to you?" Kayla says, holding out a little notebook that she brought.

"You don't print them?" Kevin says.

"No, we'll email them," Kayla says calmly. I think about telling him we could Photoshop more hair onto him if he pays us extra, but I don't. I think that would make him mad. Plus, we don't know how to use Photoshop.

"Email is perfect," Emma says, and writes down her email in Kayla's notebook.

"How much do I owe you?" Kevin says.

"Two hundred dollars," I blurt. Kayla blinks at me. We were only planning to charge fifty, but Kevin is wearing a Van Cleef watch on the beach, which tells me that two hundred dollars would be like a piece of Kleenex to him. I feel Kayla breathing nervously. I keep smiling at Kevin.

"Here," he says. He pulls out his wallet and hands us $200 in cash. Kayla zips it into her backpack. I push my feet into the sand to stop myself from jumping up and down.

"Thank you so much," Kayla says. "I'll email you the pictures shortly."

"Enjoy your vacation!" I say. When they walk away, I squeeze Kayla's waist. "It's working!" I yell in her ear.

"I can't believe they paid two hundred dollars," she says. "Good move."

"Thank you," I say. "St. Bridget's, here we come!"

"Don't count your chickens before they're hatched," Kayla says.

"But they're hatching!" I say. "Their little pink faces are pecking to get out." I pretend my nose is a beak and I peck Kayla's shoulder. "Bawk bawk bawk," I say.

"Okay, chicken," she says. "Back to work."

"Bawk to work," I say, still pecking her. She laughs and I hug her. I want to make the moment last forever—Kayla laughing at my jokes, me hugging her, and a plan that is working. We scan the beach chairs for more customers. A man in a Ritz-Carlton uniform with a curly wire in his ear is bringing people fresh towels. He glances over at us and looks suspicious.

"Let's go inside until he leaves," I whisper.

"Good idea," Kayla says. She zips the camera and the tripod into her backpack. We walk into the lobby, casually, gracefully, like we belong there. There are two stores in the lobby. One sells sunscreen and condoms and mugs with turtles on them. The other store sells jewelry. The jewelry cases have no scratches on them. They glow in a way that no amount of Windex could make our Paradise Pawn jewelry cases glow. I smile at the guy behind the counter. His name tag says *Bryan*.

Just like us, Bryan spends his days fake smiling while people tell him about anniversaries and birthdays and weddings. He only hears the happy stories though. He never hears about what happens to the rings he sells when people fall out of love or die. He never has to test his jewelry either—all of his gold is gold. All of his diamonds are diamonds.

"Look," says Kayla. The same style of Na Hoku palm tree necklace that somebody pawned last week is hanging around a white plastic neck in a line of other necks locked in the case. We ask Bryan to let us hold the necklace. I keep my eyes glued to his eyes so he can't say no.

"Be careful with it," Bryan says, which is something you should never say to a customer. You have to make them think you trust them, even if you don't. Kayla looks at me and rolls her eyes.

"This hotel should hire us to train Bryan," I whisper, and she laughs. I run my hand along the smooth gold trunk of the palm tree. Kayla rubs the chain between her fingers. Bryan watches us closely.

"It's sort of creepy how no one has ever worn this necklace before," I say.

"Yeah," Kayla says. "Maybe it'll end up at Paradise Pawn." She fastens the necklace around her neck, then leans toward the scratchless mirror on the counter.

"Get that one out," I say to Bryan, pointing to a white-gold engagement ring, and he does. I squint at the inside of the ring. It has a fourteen-karat stamp on it. I bounce the ring in my palm. It can't be much more than five pennyweights. I squint at the diamond, wishing I had my loupe. I'm sure it has inclusions that I can't see.

"How much is this ring?" I ask.

"Five thousand dollars," Bryan says. Me and Kayla bite our lips and try not to laugh. The gold is worth only about four hundred. The diamond is tiny, and probably lab grown. Kevin probably gave Emma a ring like this—a rip-off ring. She will wear it until they get divorced, having no idea how little it's really worth.

We make Bryan take out watches and bracelets and chains. I know we're being over the top. I can tell it's making Kayla nervous. It's making me a little nervous too, but it's so fun to be a customer for once—to have someone running around behind a counter and doing what we say instead of the other way around.

It's also fun to laugh at Bryan with our eyes. He wouldn't last an hour at Paradise Pawn.

He shows us a wheat-link chain and calls it a Byzantine link. He leaves a whole pile of watches unlocked on the counter, where they could get stolen.

As I'm stacking diamond rings on my fingers and breathing on them to make sure they're real, Bryan picks up the phone at his desk and whispers into it. I take the rings off my fingers and put them back on the counter. I catch Kayla's eye and point at Bryan on the phone. She starts trying to unhook the palm tree necklace. I help her get it off, finally. We are about to leave, but it is too late. I feel two hands on my shoulders. A man in a suit with a curly cord in his ear is standing behind me.

"Hi, miss. Are your parents guests at the resort?" he says to me. I feel my heart beating in my throat.

"Yes," I whisper. I try to wiggle out of his hands. I arch my back and I feel one of my fake boobs slipping out of the cup of Kayla's bra. Before I can stop it, the wad of toilet paper slides down my stomach, then down my leg, and falls noiselessly onto the floor. Bryan and the guard look at the toilet paper and then look at my one deflated breast.

"What's your room number? Where are your parents?" the guard says. I feel like I've swallowed sandpaper. I don't think I have it in me to lie again.

"Sorry, I forgot. I'm not actually staying here," I say. Kayla kicks my foot and glares at me. The guy talks into a radio. Then he tells us he's going to have to ask us to vacate Ritz-Carlton property. He says if we're caught here again there will be serious consequences. He still hasn't let go of my shoulders. He pushes me toward the door of the jewelry store and Kayla follows. My toilet paper boob is still on the floor. Everyone in the lobby stares at us.

When we make it across the lobby and through the hotel door, the guard lets go of me. Kayla and I take off running.

My chest burns. Palm trees rush past the sides of my eyes. We throw ourselves over the gate. Kayla yanks open my bike lock, shoves me onto the handlebars, and pedals away so fast that I can hear the wind whistling in my ears. We lurch to a stop at a gas station by the highway. I topple off the handlebars and reach for Kayla to give her a hug. Sweat pours out of our skin.

"Stop!" she yells. She lets my bike fall onto the pavement and twists out of my hug.

"Geez, calm down," I say.

"I knew I shouldn't have brought you," she says.

"You were the one who took so long to get that necklace off!" I say.

"You were the one who said we should go in that store!" Kayla says.

"Okay, but attitude of gratitude!" I yell. "We made two hundred dollars! That was because of me! You were only going to charge fifty!"

"I can't have an attitude of gratitude right now. I'm sweating on my mom's clothes so much," Kayla groans. She takes off the blazer. Then she opens the ice machine by the door to the gas station and sticks her face and torso in it.

"I don't think I even want to go to St. Bridget's anymore," she says, her voice echoing off the walls of the ice machine.

"What?" I say.

"Rich people are awful. I don't think I want to be rich anymore, so I don't need to go to St. Bridget's."

"Of course you want to be rich," I say. I stick my face in the ice machine too.

"I don't know," she says. I unbutton the front of the dress I'm wearing and I fan cold air from the ice machine onto my sweating chest. I pull my face out of the machine as a yellow Jeep careens toward the gas station. The pavement shrieks. The Jeep is full of boys. Their music is so loud that I cover my ears. Their chests are pink like raw hamburger meat. One of them stands up on his seat.

"Hey!" he yells at us.

"Hi!" I yell back. Kayla elbows me in the ribs.

"Hey, sexy!" another one of them yells, and then they all laugh. Nobody has ever called me sexy before. Maybe they're just talking to Kayla, but some of them are looking at me. I want to take their picture and get money out of them. I want to show Kayla that it was worth letting me come with her—that I am grown-up and sexy and useful. I tug on the empty bra to make it stick out.

"Jackie, stop. Let's go," Kayla says, pulling on my wrist.

"Hang on," I whisper. "Maybe we can take their picture."

"They're drunk!" she hisses.

"Yeah, and? Maybe that means they'll give us a lot of money."

"You are so stupid. We're leaving!" Kayla says, dragging me and my bike away from the Jeep.

"What's your number?" one of the boys yells. As they get closer, I realize they aren't really boys. They're more like men. They look almost as old as Dad.

"Come over here," one of them says. He's holding two beer cans. The back door of the Jeep opens and three of them get out and lumber toward us. I look around. There is no one else at the gas station to help us. The sexy feeling slides out of me and I panic. I turn around. Kayla is already on my bike.

"Get on!" she screams, lifting me onto the handlebars. She shifts into the highest gear and pedals. I watch her strong legs shove the air underneath the pedals. We bounce over the curb and speed away on the side of the highway.

"Come back!" one of the guys yells.

"Don't be shy!" yells another one. We bike in silence until we get to Kayla's street. Kayla is panting hard and sweating. We get off my bike and sit down on the curb outside her building. I'm worried she's going to be mad at me. I would deserve it. I should have realized the guys in the Jeep were creepy. If they had come into Paradise, I would have known they were creepy right away, but my radar for creepiness was off. I don't know why.

"That was weird," I say.

"Yeah," Kayla says. She puts her hand between my shoulder blades and rubs little circles into my muscles. I'm sweating into Giselle's clothes. She can probably feel my sweat on her hand, but she doesn't get mad at me about it.

"Sexiness is so weird," Kayla says. "It's like, one minute it's fun and people are extra nice to you if you're sexy, but then if a guy decides he actually wants to do it with you it's like the scariest thing ever."

"Yeah," I say. "Exactly." She just put into words what I was trying to figure out. My radar for creepiness didn't work, because at first when the men yelled that we were sexy, I felt great. Of course I did. I worry all the time that I'm not sexy and I never will be—and then all of a sudden in the middle of a gas station parking lot, someone screamed at me that I am sexy. People have been telling Kayla that she is sexy for at least two years, so it probably doesn't mess with her creepiness radar anymore. After today, I won't let it mess with my creepiness radar either.

I lean my head on Kayla's shoulder. She twirls some of my hair into a curl around her finger.

"Boing, boing," she says quietly, bouncing the curl up and down.

"Am I sexy?" I say, without looking at her.

"Do you want to be?" she says.

"I don't know."

"Yeah, me neither," she says.

"Well, you just are. You don't have a choice."

"Yeah, but if I did have a choice, I don't know what I would want," she says.

We flop down on our backs in the scratchy grass by the curb, my head still touching Kayla's shoulder. Kayla picks some little pieces of grass and sprinkles them on my forehead.

"What are you doing?" I say.

"I'm seasoning you," she says.

"For what?" I say.

"Thanksgiving dinner," she says, and we burst out laughing. Then we stand up, brush ourselves off, and lock my bike to the fence outside Kayla's building. We climb up the fire escape into Kayla's bedroom. Mason and Bobby are standing on Bobby's bed, pushing their Hot Wheels cars down a wrapping paper tube.

"Where were you?" Mason says.

"The store," I say. Kayla elbows me. She doesn't like lying to her brothers, but I think it's fine. Everyone lies to kids. Grown-ups lied to me all the time when I was a kid.

"Why are you wearing makeup?" Bobby says.

"We had to do some important stuff," Kayla says. We fold our $200 and push it deep into Kayla's underwear drawer. We hang Giselle's clothes up in her closet and spray them with body mist. They don't smell too much like sweat. Then we put on muddy clothes from the hamper so Aubrey and Giselle will think we were playing at the beach.

Then we help Bobby and Mason tape toilet paper tubes to the ends of the wrapping paper tube so their cars have a longer ramp. They think we're magic. We let them climb on the dresser to hold the ramp high in the air.

"Be careful," we say. We stand on chairs and hold on to their waists so they don't fall. I wonder if the guys in the yellow Jeep ever had older sisters who held on to them to keep them safe. I wonder if Kevin did. I wonder if Bobby and Mason will yell at their wives or yell at random girls at gas stations someday.

CHAPTER 6

IT'S THE END OF THE MONTH, SO NO ONE HAS ANY money, but they come into Paradise anyway. They run their fingers along the big speakers and tell us how someday they will be famous DJs, or they try on big chains and peer into the jewelry mirrors like they are crystal balls showing a future when they're rich.

Usually, I don't waste time talking to customers who clearly don't have money, even for a layaway, but today I do, because Kayla is being weird and not talking to me.

I came to work with a pile of brochures for hotels that I got from the tourist bureau, thinking we could go through them and pick some places to go to and take pictures, but Kayla put them in the paper shredder. She said she's not going to St. Bridget's and I should mind my own business. Then the dads came in, just as I was about to yell at her, and we had to pretend like everything was okay. We've been pretending all morning. We fake smile at customers with no money and our real feelings get shoved deep down into us, like a foot sinking into sand.

When the rain starts, we have to make phone calls. Phone calls at the end of the month can be sad, so the dads let us do them on the La-Z-Boy chair on pawn as a special treat. We lie on the chair with our heads on the footrest and our feet on the headrest. We have to put paper towels under our heels so we don't sell somebody a chair with a headrest that smells like our feet.

When we make phone calls, I hold the clipboard and dial the numbers and cross off the names and Kayla talks in her grown-up voice.

Trying to get people to pay loans back is worse over the phone than in person. On the phone it's harder to remind yourself that people are probably lying. If somebody tells you to your face that their dog got run over by a tour bus and their kids are all broken up about it and they'll be even sadder if we take their Xbox, you can tell that they're lying. You can stick your eyes to their eyes. Then you can make a joke and they will laugh and you will know they were lying, because they wouldn't be able to laugh if their dog had just died. When you're on the phone, though, you start to believe every dying grandfather and burst pipe and kid-in-the-hospital story you hear, because you can't see people's eyes.

When we check off all the calls on our list, we let our heads droop off the footrest. Our mouths hang open and drool pools on the roofs of them. The sadness you get after making phone calls isn't a sadness to cry about—just a sadness to breathe beside your best friend about for a few seconds. Kayla starts to flop her legs over like she's going to stand up and I kick her.

"Wait," I say. "I'm still a little sad."

"If you thought that was sad, you're a baby," she says.

"No, I'm not sad about the phone calls. I'm still sad about St. Bridget's and the plan not working and you shredding my brochures," I say, twisting my legs around hers so she can't leave me.

"*You're* sad about St. Bridget's? You realize that's an insane thing to say, right?" she says.

"It's not insane. I'm sad!" I say. Kayla shoots air through her teeth at me.

"Not everything is about you," she says.

"I know," I say.

"So you don't get to be sad about this. I'm the one who doesn't get to go to St. Bridget's. I'm the one who gets to be sad if I want to be, but I'm not going to lie here like a dead fish. I'm going to get back to work." She yanks her legs away from mine and the places where her skin touched mine are suddenly cold.

"That's not fair. I get to be sad too," I say. "Who am I supposed to be friends with if we go to different schools?" She rolls off the chair and stands in front of me. I'm still upside down.

"What do you want me to say? You'll make new friends. You'll figure it out," she says.

"But I don't want new friends. I want everything to stay the same," I say. I sound whiny and annoying, but I can't help it.

"Well, you can't control that," Kayla says. "If you want things to stay the same, you'll spend your whole life being disappointed, because nothing ever stays the same. I have to go meet a customer about a dirt bike he's trying to sell. I'll see you out there," she says.

I punch the La-Z-Boy chair and then I kick it and it wobbles and I get scared I'll break it and we'll be stuck trying to sell a broken chair, so I scramble to stand up. I feel blood sloshing around in my head like I'm a gas station slushy machine. I tighten my face into a customer smile and follow Kayla out into the store.

CHAPTER 7

THE GUY WHO OWNS ALL THE PARADISE PAWNS IN the world is named Rob. He has seventeen of them all over Florida. Rob shows up every couple of months to walk around the stores and yell at us about the Paradise Pawn core values and the Paradise Pawn vision statement and about how the storeroom is a mess. He has a tattoo of Snoopy on his ankle. He covers it up with a Band-Aid, but I saw it once when the Band-Aid fell off at the beach. His face is always red and he takes a long time to walk anywhere. He likes to call people "pal."

Rob has a son named Blake who is exactly me and Kayla's age. We've met Blake twice—once when we were all in swim diapers and once when we were ten. Rob divorced Blake's mom, Gretchen. Rob says she let herself go, which means she's ugly and Rob thinks it's her fault. Rob is way uglier than her, but he didn't seem to be thinking about that when he decided to divorce her.

I've never met Gretchen, but she owns part of Paradise Pawn too. Rob didn't make her sign a prenup because he didn't think she would get ugly. Every year we get two Christmas cards—one from Rob and one from Gretchen, both covered in little pictures of Blake doing things—snowboarding, petting dogs, holding up trophies in big grassy fields. Sometimes when I'm planning my wedding in my head and I need a face to put on the boy, I use Blake's face. Blake is so handsome that it's almost hard to believe he came from parents who are so ugly. I would like to think that Blake knows it's not really someone's fault if they're ugly. It's at least 75 percent just luck.

Waiting for Rob to come look at the store is like waiting for a hurricane. Dad wakes me up before sunrise and we drive to the store to check the model numbers and serial numbers on the TVs, even though we checked them yesterday and the day before. A regional manager in the panhandle just got fired for switching barcodes on TVs and selling expensive ones to his friends for the price of cheap ones. If Rob finds any model number and serial number mistakes, he could think Dad is doing that too and Dad could get fired.

Dad unlocks the door and turns off the alarm. Then he logs into the computer and I crawl on the floor yelling out numbers.

"Panasonic TV. Item number 8847, model number TH50-PX50U, serial number YP5350019!" I yell.

"Good, next," Dad says.

"Philips TV. Item number 8771, model number 32PFS5-82312, serial number FZ1A1801000001!"

"Fine, next," Dad says. I crawl and yell and crawl and yell until I get to the giant Sony TV that Kayla always says she will put in her house when she's rich. I look at my hands on the floor. Slivers of black dust have wedged themselves under my fingernails. I look up at the row of TVs—slabs of black and gray money. I look at the bikes—money. The guitars—money. I look at the safe, stuffed with little envelopes of sparkling, delicate money. Some of those envelopes could pay for a year of St. Bridget's. Some of them could pay for ten years of St. Bridget's.

"Dad," I say.

"What?" he says. "Hurry up. We gotta get this done." I stand and brush off my knees. Then I lock my eyes with Dad's, like he's a customer.

"Dad, you need to pay for Kayla to go to St. Bridget's," I say. He cracks his neck and looks at the floor. "You have to. She didn't get the scholarship."

"I heard, baby. Her dad told me. That really sucks."

"But it doesn't have to suck! Dad, we have twelve thousand dollars, don't we? You can feed me rice and beans for a while. Okay? I really wouldn't care. I like rice and beans."

"You're a good friend, baby," Dad says.

"I'm more than a good friend. I'm basically Kayla's sister. And it's completely unfair that I get to go to St. Bridget's and Kayla doesn't because you happen to have more money than Aubrey."

"You'll still get to hang out here, sweetheart. It's not like one of you is moving to another country," Dad says. He twists his chain around his thumb.

"Dad, stop changing the subject. You need to pay her tuition," I say in a low, grown-up voice.

"I can't do that, baby," Dad says. He looks down at the computer keyboard. "I'm really sorry." I feel like ants are crawling around inside my chest. I want to knock over the row of TVs and smash them, smash the jewelry cases, smash the phones. Dad keeps talking. "For one thing, I don't have that kind of money lying around. I already put a loan on the truck to pay the first installment of your tuition and now I gotta pay 33 percent interest on that, and even if I did have the money, I'm Aubrey's boss. That's not professional. It would hurt his pride."

"What does that even mean? Doesn't it hurt his pride more to not be able to send his daughter to the school she wants to go to? And to know that his friend, aka you, Dad, could help him, but you're deciding not to?" I ask.

"Jackie, I'm saying no, okay? I know you'll miss Kayla at school, but you'll be okay. She'll be okay." The point of our lives is not to be okay. Normal people are fine with just being okay, but me and Kayla aren't. We need to be rich and important and powerful, together, and we can't do that if we don't go to St. Bridget's together.

"Well, can Rob pay? Doesn't Rob have actual millions of dollars? Can I ask him?" I say. Dad rubs the skin between his eyebrows with his thumbs. Then he twists and untwists his chain.

"That's not a good idea, baby," he says. He reaches out to touch my hair and I slap his hand away.

"Stop it!" I scream. Dad jumps like he's just heard a gunshot. I run to the storeroom and lock the door. I sit next to a pile of chainsaws, crushing my knees into my chest. I touch my throat. The scream that came out of it didn't feel like mine. It was an older, meaner girl's scream. Dad knocks on the door.

"Baby," he says softly. I hear him crack his neck. I don't answer. I want him to keep knocking on the door and saying "baby," but he walks away. I hear him typing on the computer. He's checking the TVs by himself. It's hard to crawl on the floor and then go back and look at the computer, but I don't care. I want things to be hard for him. Things are too easy for him most of the time. I carve patterns into the dust on the chainsaws until the door buzzes. Kayla and Aubrey and Carter are here.

"Hey-hey!" Dad says in a cheerful voice. "Jackie's in back." He doesn't say anything about me yelling at him. I unlock the storeroom door.

"Morning," Kayla says to me. She has been like this since the Ritz-Carlton, acting like she's always in too much of a hurry to talk to me. She puts her lunch and Aubrey's lunch in the fridge, slips on her Paradise Pawn shirt, sprays her body mist, and starts carrying the jewelry from the safe out to the cases. She doesn't ask me if I want body mist, or if I want her to do my hair.

I want to tell her that I yelled at Dad for her—that I really tried to fix what is wrong, because I know it's wrong, but there's no time. It's 8:57. A lady with gold teeth is banging on the door. She wants to pawn her teeth to help pay for her sister's wedding. We tell her we can't take her teeth, so we take her phone and her rings and her earrings. While Kayla is testing the rings, I try to catch her eye to say, with my eyes, "I would pawn my stuff to help you pay for your wedding, because you're basically my sister," but she doesn't look up. I want to say sorry to Dad too, but a tourist from Russia is yelling at him about the price of a GoPro and a construction worker is yelling at me about a band saw.

ROB WILL BE HERE AT 3:00. Every model number and serial number in the computer is perfect. The store is gleaming. We are dusty and sweaty and we smell like Clorox wipes. Dad puts the *Beach Scenes* DVD into the DVD player and all the TVs light up with the same palm tree, which fades to the same little bird, then the same crashing wave. Normally we just play movies on the TVs, because there's a real beach right outside the door and people like movies better, but Rob likes the *Beach Scenes* DVD, so we play it whenever he comes to the store.

Rob is late—more than an hour late. Dad bites his nails. The *Beach Scenes* DVD starts over twice. Then, finally, a big black Escalade pulls into the parking lot. Rob gets out and walks toward the door. Dad and Aubrey and Carter run out to greet him, then they walk behind him into the store like his backup dancers.

"Hey, pal!" Rob says to me.

"Hi, sir," I say. He gives me a one-armed hug and breathes on me. He smells like he's just eaten something fried. I give him my best fake smile. Then I twist myself out from under his arm and stand behind the counter beside Kayla. Rob waddles toward the plastic Christmas in July mistletoe.

"Hey, Kayla," he says. He makes kissing noises and laughs.

"Good afternoon, sir," she says. Aubrey cracks his knuckles and looks at the floor.

"Y'all have grown since I was last down here, huh?" Rob says.

"Yes sir," we say, our fake smiles sparkling.

"Good stuff," Rob says. He's looking at Kayla's chest. I watch her shoulders hunch and her smile get tight.

"Girls, why are you just standing around? Let's get back to work," Dad says.

"Yes sir," we say, and we crouch beneath the counter, pretending to organize the ring boxes. Kayla's hands are shaking.

"Are you okay?" I whisper to her.

"What do you think? No, obviously not. I hate Rob," she says.

"Well, he is the boss, so what he says goes," I say. That's what Dad always says when Rob is being hard on us. Kayla blinks at me like I've said something mean. "What?" I ask. She shoves the ring box cabinet closed and runs to the bathroom. I try to follow her but she locks the door. "Kayla, I'm sorry," I say through the door. "Don't be mad."

"Don't tell me not to be mad when I'm mad," she says.

"Shush, Rob's coming," I say. Rob lumbers out of the storeroom, followed by the dads. Their smiles are fake and their hands are nervous.

"Hey, pal," Rob says to me.

"Hi, sir," I say, pressing my cheeks into a big smile.

"Where's Kayla?" he says.

"In the bathroom," I say. I expect the dads to make her come out and help with impressing Rob, but they don't. They just let her stay there while Rob checks model numbers and serial numbers and the rest of us have to follow him around and laugh at his jokes and let him breathe on us. When we close, Kayla comes out of the bathroom. Aubrey puts his hands on her shoulders and keeps them there. Rob sits on the La-Z-Boy chair in the storeroom like it's a throne.

"Pop a squat," he says to us, and we squat. "Y'all did good today."

"Thank you, sir," Dad says.

"It's good to know at least I can trust some of you people," Rob says, and smiles at us.

"Thank you," Dad says, even though what Rob said wasn't exactly a compliment. Rob keeps talking.

"They got me good in Pensacola," he says.

"What did they do?" I say.

"This little twerp of a sales associate was finding pawns that he knew wouldn't be picked up, then giving people, say, fifty dollars, but putting the loan into the system as seventy dollars and pocketing the extra twenty."

"Geez, terrible," Dad says, shaking his head.

"Wow," I say.

“He kept it up for months. He quit the job just as we started realizing something was weird about the numbers coming out of that store, but it took a sec for us to catch him. He was living large for a little bit, up in Tennessee with his sons. He bought them every video game in existence, I think. He got about ten thousand dollars all together,” Rob says.

“Ten thousand dollars?” I repeat. I feel my heart drop into my stomach and start beating fast. I’m scared to look at Kayla, but I can’t help it. She meets my eyes and then looks at the ground.

“What a story,” Dad says.

“The guy’s in jail now, obviously, but yeah, it was some scheme,” Rob says.

“Well, you know you never need to worry about integrity issues with us here,” Dad says.

“And I do appreciate that,” Rob says. He stands up and we do too. Then he shakes hands with Dad and Aubrey. Then he reaches to hug me and Kayla, but the dads stand in front of us. Aubrey coughs and Dad says, “How’s business elsewhere? I heard we got some good conch pearls in Miami?”

“Sure did,” Rob says. He keeps talking. Long vowels ooze out of his fish mouth. The dads and Carter stand like soldiers, nodding and yessir-ing to everything he says while my brain and my stomach churn, thinking about the sales associate in Pensacola and Kayla’s St. Bridget’s tuition.

Then Rob says he has to take off. He wants to try out the waterslide in his hotel. It’s over one hundred feet long. I smile, because I am imagining Rob getting stuck in a waterslide, and because I have a plan.

CHAPTER 8

DAD HAS TO GO GOLFING WITH ROB TODAY, SO I get to go to church and then to the beach with Kayla's family.

I like going to church with the McCabes. I wear the shiny church shoes that Kayla grew out of last year and I sit in the pew pretending I am Aubrey and Giselle's daughter and Kayla's sister. The best part of church is the singing. The songs start out quiet and mysterious. The moms open their hands like they're catching rain coming down from the ceiling. Then the music swells, and Felix, who me and Kayla have crushes on, straps on his electric guitar, and everyone's voices swirl together like dust in a beam of light.

Even if God isn't real, it feels like he is when we're singing, and it feels like he can hear us. I sometimes think that, even if he isn't real, it wouldn't matter. The idea of him still helps people, just like wearing a plated gold chain still makes people happy if they think it's solid gold, or a fake smile to a customer still makes them feel important and special if they think it's real.

Usually, when everyone else prays, I just look at my reflection in Kayla's shiny shoes. I've never had anything real to pray about—no cancer, no broken bones, plenty of food. I used to ask for millions of dollars when I was little, but then I got worried God would think I was greedy. I can't ask him for big things like making Mom alive again because I know he can't do that. People say bad things like that are God's plan—wars and dogs getting left in hot cars and moms dying. It was a bad plan to have my mom die, but I don't want God to know I think that. He could get offended and do something that would wreck my life.

I also don't feel like I can ask God for little things like making a pimple dry up, because then he'll think I'm spoiled and he won't help me when I really need him. I'd be like the customers at Paradise Pawn who tell us their husbands have just gotten run over by cars every month when their interest is due.

Everything is different today. I need God more than I have ever needed him in my life. I smash my eyelids together so tightly that I see pink light squirming around in the dark. It's hard for me to think words without saying them out loud, but God listens to prayers in Spanish and Tagalog and Creole and every other language, so I hope he will understand what I'm trying to say even though it's not coming out in words in my brain. I need him to tell me if my plan is sinful. I really don't think it is, but I want to make sure, so me and Kayla can go to heaven together.

"Amen," the reverend says, and we all say, "Amen" and sit down. "Turn to Luke 19:1–10," the reverend says, and the grown-ups crinkle their Bibles. Aubrey leans toward me and Kayla and points to the tiny words.

The reverend says the usual stuff about what a good person Jesus was and I watch a gecko scuttle up the wall. Then he talks about Zacchaeus. He says Zacchaeus was a tax collector, but he collected more money than he was supposed to and kept it for himself and his friends. I feel my heart pounding. I lean so far forward in the pew that I almost fall off it.

"Are you okay?" Kayla whispers. I nod, my eyes glued to the reverend's face. He says Zacchaeus lived in Jericho and everyone there hated him. But then, Jesus came to visit. Zacchaeus climbed up in a sycamore tree, and Jesus noticed him and said, "In the eyes and the heart of God you are a true son of Abraham." That was Jesus telling Zacchaeus that he was still a good person. Then Jesus went and hung out at the house that Zacchaeus had built with the money he stole from everybody. Zacchaeus and Jesus became friends. Zacchaeus stopped stealing and decided to give half of everything he owned to the poor.

The reverend says, "If you have a Zacchaeus in your life, remember to see him or her the way the Father does. Release the heart of God over him or her in prayer." I want to raise my hand and ask, "What if you *are* the Zacchaeus in your life?" but you're not allowed to raise your hand and ask questions like that in church. I decide that if you are the Zacchaeus, God doesn't care, as long as you have a good heart, which I do and Kayla does too. When me and Kayla are rich, we will give half of what we own to the poor, just like Zacchaeus, and then we'll get into heaven. We'll be so rich that we'll hardly even notice if half of our money disappears. That's how it is when you're rich. You have so much money that money stops being important.

After church, we all change out of our church clothes and into our swimsuits in Aubrey's car—first girls, then boys. Then we drive to Five Mile Beach—me and Kayla and Bobby and Mason all squashed in the back seat. The plan is crashing around in my head like shoes in a dryer.

As we drive, Giselle reaches into the back seat and dabs sunscreen on us. When Giselle isn't looking, me and Kayla scrape our sunscreen off because it will give us pimples. Bobby and Mason won't stop talking about the sand garage they're going to make for their cars. They paw through their backpacks full of cars and plastic tracks and yogurt containers to dig with.

"Will you help us?" they ask me and Kayla.

"Of course," Kayla says. I roll my eyes.

"What's your problem?" she says.

"I need to talk to you," I whisper. "Alone."

"Not everything is about you," Kayla hisses. I glare at her and push my cheek into the cold window.

As soon as Aubrey parks, Bobby and Mason leap out of their seats like kids going to the beach in a happy car commercial.

"Kayla! Jackie! Hurry!" they shriek. We follow them to the sand. Five Mile Beach isn't actually five miles long. It's two and a half miles long, and the public part of it that you can sit on if you're not staying at a fancy hotel is tiny and crowded. On a Sunday, you can hardly stretch your legs out without kicking someone. We sit with Bobby and Mason, patiently digging and patting, the way Jesus would build a sand garage. I look up at the sun and hope God is watching through his eyes and his heart—seeing what good people we are. We see some kids we know because their parents come into Paradise Pawn at the end of each month to pawn their PlayStation. They help us dig a moat around the garage. We add a parking lot lined with shells and a carwash and a seaweed highway. Then the tide comes in and ruins all of it. Bobby throws himself in front of the waves and gets salt water in his eyes and starts to cry. He runs to Giselle, and Mason follows. Kayla looks worried.

"They'll be fine. Can I please talk to you now?" I say.

"Okay," she says. I look at Giselle and Aubrey and they wave to us.

"It's something secret," I say. "Follow me." We walk through barbecue smoke and music and screaming little kids, trying not to step on people.

"Kayla!" some boys yell from the water. They're playing catch with a football. One of them throws it extra far, because he knows Kayla is watching.

"Hey!" she yells back. None of them yell to me. I take her hand so she doesn't go and talk to them. We step over a rope onto the Seagull Suites part of the beach. There is no music and no barbecue smoke. There are rows and rows of the same chair with the same fancy umbrella on top. Each chair has a number and a sunburned tourist in it. They're like chickens being roasted in a factory. Hotel people step between the rows of chairs adjusting their umbrellas and bringing them drinks.

"Mom!" a boy about Mason's age yells from the water. "My AirPod fell in the water!" One of the chairs creaks. A lady pulls a towel off her face and yells, "Not my problem!" The boy drives his heel into the sand and yells, "Frick!" Then he yanks a snorkel over his face and goes underwater.

"Excuse me," I say to the woman. "We sell AirPods at Paradise Pawn on the waterfront by KFC."

"What?" she says.

"She said we know a place to get new AirPods for your son," Kayla says.

"At a bargain price," I add.

"No, that's okay," the woman says, pulling the towel back over her face. "We're going back to Columbus tomorrow." I wait for her to say thank you, but she doesn't.

"It was worth a try. Never stop selling, right?" Kayla says. I nod. That's something in the Paradise Pawn employee handbook—never stop selling. We walk into the waves until the water is up to our waists.

"So, speaking of worth a try," I say. I wipe the sweat out of my eyebrows and hold on to both of Kayla's hands like we're getting married. I take a deep breath and I let the plan spill out of my throat—we'll find pawns that aren't going to be picked up, we'll tell people that they're getting loaned less money than what we put in the computer, we'll take the difference out of the cash drawer and save it for ourselves. Then we'll type up a letter to Aubrey and Giselle saying that St. Bridget's made a mistake with the scholarship applications. If we can do about $3,000 each month, and a little more at Christmas, then we'll have $12,000 and Kayla will be able to start at St. Bridget's in January. The letter said you have to pay the $12,000 up front, even if you're starting in the middle of the year, unless you talk to them and do some kind of payment plan. They'd probably be suspicious if two fourteen-year-olds walked in there and tried to do the payment plan, but if we just give them a stack of cash, they wouldn't need to know we're fourteen.

"How could they say no to that? It's money. They love money, clearly, or they would have given you the scholarship," I say to Kayla.

"Jackie," Kayla interrupts.

"Wait," I say. "Don't shoot it down yet. I know what you're going to say. You're going to say it's a sin. But it's not! It's pretty much the exact same thing Zacchaeus did, and Jesus knew he was a good person, and we're good people, so it'll be fine." Kayla blows a big breath out her nose.

"Jackie," she says. "You don't understand how anything works." She pulls her hands away from mine and strides through the water back to the sand. By the time I make it out of the water she's already halfway across the Seagull Suites beach.

"Wait!" I yell, running to catch up with her.

"I thought of that plan too, as soon as Rob said it, but it's not going to happen," Kayla says.

"But you heard the sermon today. We'd still get to go to heaven."

"It's not about heaven. Did you hear what happened to the guy in Pensacola? He went to jail. He had sons who love video games. And now he won't get to play video games with them for years and years."

"But we're kids, Kayla. We wouldn't go to jail."

"I'm not a kid," Kayla says.

"What, because you have boobs and I don't?" I say.

"Yeah, actually, that's part of it. A judge would be like, 'You look mature. You should have known better.' And don't say that's unfair because it's just the way it is," she says.

"But they would still know you're fourteen. They would have documents that would say that," I say. She starts walking away faster and I jog to catch up with her.

"We're done talking about this," she says.

"So I should just be fine going to a different school than my best friend?"

"Yes. You should," Kayla says. "I'm handling this. I'm applying for other scholarships, but if I don't get them, so what? Public school will be fine. I have way more friends there anyway. I don't know anyone going to St. Bridget's besides you."

Kayla saying she has other friends makes my heart sting and she knows it. She keeps power walking away from me, weaving through the sandcastles and towels on the public beach until we get back to her family. Giselle is lying on her stomach with her eyes closed. Kayla taps her leg.

"Can we go?" Kayla says. Giselle blinks and sits up sleepily.

"This is a first—you asking to leave the beach early, especially with Jackie." She smiles at me and I smile back, trying to act like nothing is wrong. "We can go in half an hour. I want your brothers to get some more of their energy out," Giselle says. She lies down again. I look at Kayla pleadingly.

"We're done talking about this," she says again. She stands up and walks toward the water where the boys from school are playing football. She says something to them that I can't hear and they all laugh. Soon she is sitting on the shoulders of one of the boys, Hunter. Hunter has a ton of pimples on his cheeks, but he's the tallest guy in our grade, and he has a little bit of a mustache, so he always has a girlfriend. I don't know who his girlfriend is now. I hope he doesn't want Kayla to be his girlfriend. Another boy who has a long rattail, Paxton, gets up on the third boy's, Alex's, shoulders. Paxton is trying to knock Kayla into the water. I hear her shriek in a flirty way as she swats at Paxton and holds on to Hunter's bleached hair. It feels like she's doing this just to be mean to me. She knows I don't know how to shriek and swat at boys like that, and I don't like to be reminded that she does. I watch as Paxton yanks on her arm, hard, but she stays upright. Then she shoves Paxton in the stomach and he lurches into the water.

"Oh, shit! Kayla for the win!" yells Hunter. Alex high-fives her. She gets off Hunter's shoulders and takes a bow. Paxton pretends to punch her in the face, but then gives her a hug. She waves to them and then prances out of the water back to me. As we fold up the beach chairs, I feel like yelling at her, telling her that she can't just ignore me and flirt with boys, but I can't do that in front of Giselle and Aubrey.

Giselle brushes sand off all of us and makes us sit on towels in the car. Bobby and Mason talk so much about their garage that I hope the grown-ups don't realize me and Kayla aren't speaking to each other.

"See you in the morning, Jackie," Aubrey says when they drop me off. Everyone waits for me and Kayla to say, "I'll miss you," but we don't. I get out of the car in silence, type in the code to get through my gate, and trudge toward my house without looking back.

I walk through the back door into a wall of Dad's cologne. His cologne is called Eternity by Calvin Klein. A guy named Pedro from New York pawned it a few years ago and never came back. The smell of it automatically makes me lonely, because it means Dad is going on a date.

The door to Dad's bathroom is open. He's playing a Pitbull song on his phone and combing gel into his hair. He's wearing a white shirt unbuttoned halfway, so the "ie" of his Jackie tattoo is showing. He leans close to the mirror and cracks his neck. His eyes are shining. I will probably have to eat breakfast with a Leslie or an Amy or a Cheryl tomorrow.

Dad isn't amazingly handsome or anything, but he's really good at making people think he's listening to them. He does it at Paradise to customers, and he does it at bars to women from cruise ships. Most people are dying to be listened to, so Dad gets a lot of people to do what he wants from acting like he's listening to them.

"Hi," I say. Dad jumps and turns off the music.

"Hi, baby," he says. "How was the beach?"

"Terrible," I say, and walk away dramatically, to make him feel bad about going on a date and leaving me alone. I walk down the hall and slam the door to my room. I count to fifteen and he knocks.

"Why was it terrible?" he says.

"Kayla," I say.

"You want to talk about it?" he says.

"No," I say. I want him to open the door and talk to me about it anyway, but I hear him walk away and then I hear the Pitbull song playing again. The next time he knocks on my door, I open it.

"Baby, are you going to be okay if I go out for a little while tonight?" he says, like I wouldn't have realized that he's going out from the stench of Eternity by Calvin Klein and the Pitbull music.

"Sure," I say. I watch his shoulders relax. He sits down on my bed. "Who is she?" I ask.

"Her name is Becca. We met at the golf course," he says, and shows me a Facebook picture of red-faced lady with sunglasses on her head.

"Okay," I say. He kisses my hair, then tucks some of it behind my ear. "I won't be home too late."

"Whatever," I say.

"Fish sticks sound okay for dinner?" he says, rubbing at the lines between his eyebrows. I decide I have been too mean to him, so I say, "Sure," even though we had fish sticks every night last week. He kisses me again. After he shaves, we sit on the couch sharing a plate of fish sticks and apple slices and Ritz crackers. I can't really taste any of it, because my nose is too full of Dad's cologne. When he leaves, I lie on the floor feeling mad at Dad and mad at Kayla and mad at everything.

There are a bunch of ants on the floor. I block their paths with my hands and make them run really fast. Then I get worried they'll get too tired and die of exhaustion, so I stop. Then I squirt some honey on the floor for them to eat, partially to help them and partially because Dad doesn't like it when I feed ants inside and I'm mad at him.

Kayla once told me, when we were both mad at Chloe Yoder in second grade, that when you're mad, it's like there's a tangle of a bunch of tiny necklace chains inside you. You're never mad about just one thing at a time. If you want to stop being mad, you have to pick through all the different chains and get them smooth one by one.

Me and Kayla are supposed to have the same tangles inside us. We're supposed to be mad at the same people at the same time. We're not supposed to be chains in each other's tangles, but now we can't go more than a few days without me being mad at her or her being mad at me.

I pick at the tangle in my heart and try to slide out one chain—I'm mad at Kayla because she's acting like it doesn't matter if we go to different schools. Then I slide out another one. I'm mad at her because if she goes to school without me, she won't be lonely. Friends just appear around her, like tarpon at the wharf when tourists feed them. Nobody appears around me. Girls only pretend to like me because they have to, because I'm Kayla's best friend. Boys don't like me because I don't look the way you have to look for boys to like you.

Then I get to the tangle I've been trying not to think about—maybe deep in her heart, Kayla wants to go to a different school than me. Maybe she wants to be free from me. Even if she would never say it to me, or even to herself, maybe she wants to get a boyfriend and go to boat parties and be sexy, and she can't do that if a greasy girl with tiny boobs is following her around everywhere she goes.

I roll onto my stomach. I feel the tile pressing into the start of my boobs and it hurts. I shove myself into the floor, hard, and imagine the two gooey patches of tenderness sinking into me and melting like ice cubes. I imagine Kayla's boobs melting too, so we can be ten again—boosting each other into trees, flailing around in our swimsuits—no hair or lumps on either of us—our legs climbing and running, splashing and scraping, not being looked at by boys—nothing to be mad or sad about except for having to go inside for dinner.

I feel like I have a fever. I bang my forehead on the tile a few times. Then I roll over onto my back. My pimple-boobs throb and I push on them with my thumbs, which makes them hurt even more. Then I hear Dad's truck pulling into the driveway and I run to my room and turn out the light so I don't have to be nice to Becca from the golf course.

CHAPTER 9

THE LADY WHO PAWNED THE LA-Z-BOY CHAIR DIED over the weekend. It was in pawn for two years—long enough for us to feel like it belonged to us. Now it has to go out on the floor and we aren't allowed to sit on it anymore. The only place to sit now is the wicker porch furniture on layaway that makes our legs itch. Me and Kayla are mad at each other and mad about the La-Z-Boy chair and mad at so many other things that we can't even name. All the little necklace chains of anger twist into hard lumps inside us. We slouch on the porch furniture, scratching our legs and glaring at each other while the dads move our La-Z-Boy chair out to the floor.

"Look alive," Dad says, and hands us a jewelry inventory list. We kneel by the safe and count envelopes of rings. I keep messing up because I'm watching Kayla's eyes, hoping they'll soften and say she forgives me, but they don't. Each time I mess up, Kayla sighs like she's blowing up a balloon.

At 8:45, a customer bangs on the window and I slide across the floor to tell them they have to come back at 9:00, but it's not a customer, it's Giselle. She's wearing red eye shadow to match her Marriott uniform. I buzz open the door for her.

"Hi, baby," she says, and pushes past me without giving me a hug. My stomach sinks. Kayla told her about my plan and now Giselle will hate me too. She'll tell Aubrey and Aubrey will tell Dad and then everyone will hate me. Giselle jogs behind the counter and into the storeroom.

"Did you tell her about the plan?" I whisper-yell to Kayla.

"No, of course not," she whispers.

"You swear?" I say. She holds out her pinky and I curl mine around it.

"Swear," she says. We press our ears against the storeroom door. We hear Aubrey and Dad talking in soft voices, but we can't make out their words. We hear the toilet flush twice.

"Frick," I say. "I bet they found Cheri. They're probably flushing her manual down the toilet." Kayla pushes her fist into her forehead. I wrap my arms around her waist and she doesn't pull away.

"It'll be okay," I say. She squeezes my hands. I feel her ribs moving as she breathes. Then the door bangs open. Giselle looks startled when she sees us.

"Oh! Girls!" she says. Her lipstick is smeared and she's sucking on a lemon wedge left over from when we gave out sweet tea on Customer Appreciation Day.

"Back to work," Dad says.

"Mommy, what's wrong?" Kayla says. Giselle looks at Aubrey and smiles.

"Nothing's wrong," Giselle says. Aubrey puts his hands on her shoulders and she says, looking at Kayla more than at me,

"Actually, something really good is happening. I'm going to have a baby—a little girl. You're finally going to have a sister." I wish she hadn't said "finally," because Kayla basically already has a sister, who is me, but I'm still happy. The baby will be like my sister too.

"Seriously? That's awesome!" I say. Giselle and Aubrey nod. I hug Giselle and kiss her stomach, then I hug Aubrey, then I hug Kayla.

Kayla's body is stiff and she doesn't hug me back. She's mad, which seems like the most selfish, weird reaction to this news. She's going to have a sister—a baby best friend who lives in her house and will never leave her. Even though me and Kayla are like sisters, I know there is a difference between being like sisters and being actual sisters. I would give anything to have a baby sister.

"When?" Kayla says quietly.

"End of February," Giselle and Aubrey say together, smiling dreamily.

"Maybe she'll have the same birthday as you!" I say to Kayla.

"Yeah," Kayla says, looking at the ground and scuffing her shoes. Giselle kisses Kayla's cheek. I want her to kiss my cheek too, but she doesn't.

"It'll be good. I promise," Giselle says. Kayla nods and gives Giselle an unconvincing fake smile. "I promise, baby. I really do," Giselle says, rubbing Kayla's back. "The money will be okay too. I'm going to work extra hours in the mornings until the baby comes and Daddy is going to work at the car rental place on Sundays and at night."

"Why?" I say.

"Because diapers don't buy themselves," Giselle says, and laughs. Then she throws away her lemon rind and squeezes Kayla's hands. "You'll always be my baby girl. You know that," she says to Kayla. I wish Giselle would squeeze my hands too.

"I know," Kayla says.

"Okay. I gotta get to work and you all do too," Giselle says. "Thanks for the lemon." Then she kisses Aubrey on the lips and walks toward the door. I run after her and wrap my arms around her waist and press my cheek into her uniform.

"Hey there," she says.

"Good job with the baby," I whisper. I realize after I say it that it was a weird thing to say, but Giselle doesn't laugh at me. She's the kind of grown-up who would never laugh at a kid. She rubs circles into my back like she did to Kayla.

"Thanks, Jack-Jack," she says. "Are you ready to babysit?" I nod into her shoulder. I can feel her start to pull away and I hold on tighter. I poke my finger into the fabric of her uniform. I think about how Kayla and I used to run through the Marriott lobby to her and she would swing us up into her arms—one girl on each side. Our chins would rest on her shoulders while she walked us through the golf course, showing us how birds of paradise look like real birds, and making them give us pokey kisses.

"Are you good?" Giselle says.

"I guess so," I say. She gives me another squeeze and I buzz her out the door. I walk back to the storeroom. Kayla is slumped against the safe with the jewelry inventory clipboard in her lap.

"What's wrong?" I say.

"Babies," she says, giving the safe a little kick.

"What's wrong with babies?" I say.

"They suck up everyone's money and energy like black holes and there's nothing left for anyone else."

"Isn't it worth it, though, because they're so cute and full of possibilities?" I say.

"They're not full of possibilities. They're full of drool and spit-up and poop," Kayla says, pressing the tip of a pencil into the clipboard so hard that it shatters. "There won't be any money for anything and my mom will be tired and sad all the time," Kayla says. I almost say that a tired and sad mom is better than no mom at all, but I don't.

Kayla opens a jewelry envelope and an eighteen-karat Cayman link chain slithers into her palm. She looks at it for a long time, like she's praying to it. Then she murmurs, still looking at the chain, "Let's do it. Your plan."

"What?" I whisper, even though I heard what she said. I want to hear her say it again. My heart starts to beat like I've done something wrong. "Are you serious?"

"Yeah. I want to go to St. Bridget's. I want to be rich." My throat is dry.

"We will be," I whisper. I hug Kayla and she hugs me back.

CHAPTER 10

DAD IS IN LOVE WITH THIS WOMAN NAMED CAMILLA. Pretty much every other guy in Cherry Beach is too. Camilla's skin is sparkly and she smells like a spa at a fancy hotel. Bankers, fishermen, carpenters, DJs, attorneys, scuba instructors, tourists—it doesn't matter who they are. They all take one look at Camilla and they want to spend money on her. They buy Cartier watches for Camilla, diamonds for Camilla, conch-pearl earrings for Camilla, and then, a few weeks later, she comes in and pawns them. "I only have ten fingers and one neck," she likes to say. Sometimes guys who bought stuff for Camilla come in and yell at us, asking what she pawned and how much she got for it. We hold our fingers over our panic buttons and say, "We're sorry, sir. That information is private."

Once, we had to call the police about one of Camilla's boyfriends because he said he had a machete in his car. When he left, Kayla said to me, "The thing guys don't understand about buying jewelry is that even if they buy the gold around a girl's neck or wrists or fingers, the skin underneath, what they really want, will always belong to her." It's one of the smartest things she's ever said, and she says a lot of smart things.

When Camilla's car pulls up in front of the store, we lock eyes. She's a perfect person for the plan since she never comes back for the stuff she pawns. Dad sees her too. He eats a breath freshener strip and unbuttons a button on his Paradise Pawn shirt. Then he opens his selfie camera and licks his fingers and smooths his hair down. We buzz the door open for Camilla and she glides past the appliances and TVs. The sound of her bright yellow shoes slices the air. Dad puts his phone away and looks at her like she's a wall and he is painting her with his eyes. I run to the bathroom, throw a jewelry cloth into the toilet, and flush.

"Dad!" I yell. "Some customer broke the toilet!" Kayla gives me a thumbs-up. I yank Dad to the bathroom by his sleeve. Camilla walks to the counter.

"How are you today, Camilla?" Kayla says, smiling a big smile.

"Good, baby," she says. I close the bathroom door behind Dad, run back to the counter, and stand beside Kayla. Kayla is testing a white-gold diamond bracelet that some man must have given to Camilla. The diamond tester flashes green, green, green. Kayla holds up her loupe to the diamonds and squints.

"They're VVS2, near colorless," she says. I pull on gloves, scrub the gold against the touchstone, and dribble acid on it.

"Eighteen karat," I say.

"I'll be back for it this time. I promise," Camilla says, blinking her long fake eyelashes.

I scroll through her customer history on MasterPawn—rings, necklaces, earrings, a nice wet suit, three iPhones—all defaults. She's never come back for a pawn in her life.

"Of course you will," Kayla says. We know Camilla is lying and she knows we are lying, but we keep smiling sweet, plated-gold smiles at each other. Kayla writes on a Post-it note: *loan her $300, say we loaned $400 in the computer?* I nod.

"That's fine," Camilla says, when we tell her $300. I stamp her pawn ticket. My hands are shaking. I want to give Camilla a hug, and to thank her for being the first participant in our plan, but instead I just smile at her and walk with Kayla to the cash drawer. Kayla stands on her toes, pretends to stretch, and brushes her hands in front of the security camera. I slip five $20 bills into my sleeve. Then we count out $300 for Camilla.

"See you next month, ma'am," we say.

"See you then," she says as she signs her loopy name on the pawn form, even though we all know she's going to default. I shake her soft, lotiony hand and the bills slide up and down my sleeve. We buzz the door for Camilla and I squeal. I run to Kayla to hug her and she ducks around the counter.

"Cameras," she coughs into her hand. "Don't act weird."

"Right," I say, and I keep running. I grab the Windex and run around Windexing everything so that anyone watching the cameras will think I am excited about cleaning and not about the fact that I have $100 in my sleeve. When I'm out of breath I walk back toward the counter, looking as relaxed as I can for the cameras.

"Where do we put it? The cash," I whisper. Kayla jerks her head toward the bathroom.

"Follow me," she says through her teeth, and I do. She locks the bathroom door behind us.

"It smells like throw-up in here," I say.

"Morning sickness," Kayla says. "That's why I'm never getting pregnant."

"What?" I say.

"That's what my mom was doing in here. She was throwing up. When you have a baby in you, it makes you throw up."

"That sucks," I say.

"Yeah. Babies suck. I told you," Kayla says.

"Why are we in here?" I say.

"Use your brain, Jackie. This is the only place in the store with no cameras." She crouches down and digs through the cabinet under the sink. She pulls out a box that says *Maxi Pads*.

"Hand me the money," she says. I slide the $20 bills out of my sleeve and hold them out to her like they're made of glass. She pulls an orange wrapper out of the box.

"Do you know what this is?" she says.

"No," I say.

"It's a pad. It's for your period. You put it in your underwear. Well, you don't. I do. You will someday. It catches the blood."

"That's cool," I say, even though I suddenly feel sick—sick from the smell of throw-up, sick from thinking about blood in my underwear, sick because Kayla always knows everything before I do, and sick because I'm worried that maybe God's eyes and God's heart will think we are stealing.

Kayla rips open the package and it makes a noise like cracking bones. She stacks the money inside the pad with Andrew Jackson face up, just like we're supposed to when we put cash in the register. Then she folds the package back up and seals it closed.

"I was thinking we could put a hundred dollars in each one so it'll be easy to count," she says.

"Good idea," I say. I put the box back under the sink. "Wow, Kayla. It's happening," I whisper.

"Wow to you too," she says. "Are you scared?"

"No," I say, even though I am a little scared. I press my face into her shoulder.

"Me neither," she says.

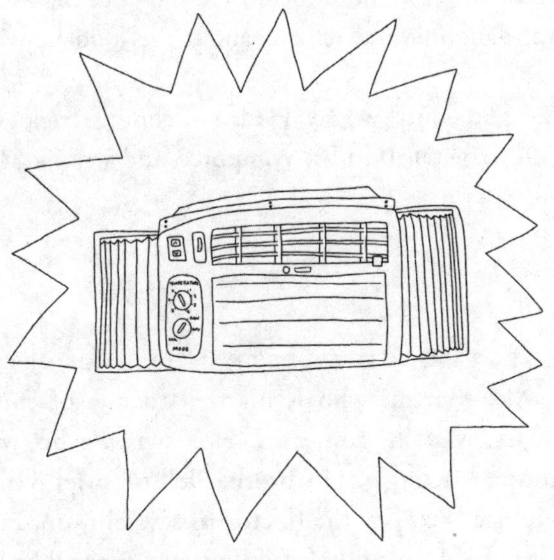

CHAPTER 11

THE PLAN IS LIKE A NEW PROCEDURE FROM CORporate, like cleaning the chains with a different cloth or making people fill out a new form to send to the police. It's a little bumpy for the first couple of days, but after a week we hardly have to think about it. It's all about N.E.H.A.—Need, Emotional attachment, History of paying us back, and Ability to pay. If we know people aren't coming back, we do the plan. If we know that they are, we don't.

A MAN WITH SKIN like pine tree bark brings in an air conditioner.

"How much do you need?" we ask.

"Enough for a plane ticket to Cuba," he says. "I'm going

to be an abuelo. I'm out of here." He shows us pictures of his pregnant daughter and tells us about the food he will cook for her.

"She's gorgeous," we say. He is not coming back. We give him $50, write $150 in the computer, and wrap a $100 bill in a pad.

ONE OF THE CUSTODIANS from our elementary school, Mr. Martin, who is married to one of the lunch ladies, Mrs. Martin, comes in. He's twisting his wedding ring around his finger. His brother fell off a Jet Ski onto a rock. He needs to pay the doctor to sew him up. His chin trembles as he slides off his wedding ring. He will be back to pick up the ring. We don't do the plan on him.

"MY HUSBAND DIED," a woman from Miami tells us. "I need to pawn his phone to buy his headstone. It keeps ringing and every time I pick it up and someone asks for Bill it's like he's died all over again." She will not be back for the phone. We give her $200, put $350 in the system, and wrap the extra $150 in pads.

MY LIFE NOW is like a corn husk. Every day I have to rip off stringy green handfuls of life to get to the pearly bright yellow part—the part where me and Kayla are St. Bridget's girls.

CHAPTER 12

CHRISTMAS IN JULY IS OVER. WE ALL LOOK A LITtle bare without our Santa hats. We unwind the tinsel from the bars on the windows and stuff the plastic tree in the storeroom until real Christmas. The phones ring their poor hearts out. People call and ask for one more day, one more week, two more weeks to make their layaway payments and we have to say, "September first was the deadline. I wish I could help you out, but that's company policy." We say it again and again, the way some people say prayers. As me and Kayla and Dad are peeling the Christmas in July banners off the jewelry cases, Dad says, "Girls, I've got some bad news, some more bad news, and some good news."

"What's the good news?" I say.

"Rob is taking us all scuba diving this weekend," Dad says.

"So the bad news is that Rob is coming?" Kayla says.

"Yeah, that's bad news number one. Bad news number two is that our numbers were crap last week. I don't know what's going on. In July, we were the top-performing Paradise Pawn, but last week Kissimmee beat us. Fort Lauderdale too. Even the Daytona Beach store, which has never beaten us before." I stick my head in a jewelry case and look in the mirrors at the infinite square Jackies with worried faces. Dad knocks on the top of the case.

"Hey! Come out of there. I'm talking to you," he says.

"Sorry," I say. I feel like ice cubes are sliding down my arms, into each of my fingers. I press my hands into the counter and try to take deep breaths. I try to look at Kayla but she is looking at the floor. Dad keeps talking. "Our loan book is high—really high, which is fine if people are coming back to pay their loans, but we're giving out tons of money to people who aren't coming back. We're not getting those fees in. We've got to be more careful about N.E.H.A." I nod at the floor. Dad keeps talking. "We have to N.E.H.A. every single customer who walks in that door. And we clearly aren't doing that right now or our numbers wouldn't be crap. Girls? I'm looking at you. Does that make sense?" Dad says.

"Look at Devon when he's talking to you, Kayla," Aubrey says, and Kayla looks up at Dad with a killer fake smile.

"Yes sir," she says.

"Jackie, got it?" Dad says. I nod.

What Dad doesn't know is that me and Kayla have been N.E.H.A.-ing better than we've ever N.E.H.A.-ed in our lives. We haven't messed it up once. Not a single person has come back for a pawn when we weren't expecting them to.

"Okay," Dad says. He's about to keep lecturing us when a tourist walks up to the door. Aubrey buzzes her in. She has sunburned ears, a bony face, and a windbreaker tied around her waist. Dad eats a breath freshener strip. He thinks she's pretty. Windbreaker Lady runs her fingers along the DVDs. Dad walks toward her.

"Hi, welcome," he says to her softly, breathing his fresh breath at her. She leans toward him, pulls the hairband out of her ponytail, and rocks her head back and forth so her hair swishes.

"Where you from?" Dad says.

"Denver," she says. Dad unbuttons a button on his Paradise Pawn shirt. They talk about movies and dogs.

"I have three cocker spaniels—Ford, Chevy, and Lincoln, but Lincoln lives with my ex-husband. It's hard on all of them," Windbreaker says.

"That must be hard," Dad says, nodding like it's the most interesting thing he's ever heard. He gets her to buy fourteen DVDs and a food processer. She writes her phone number down on a Post-it note. Then they keep talking about Ford, Chevy, and Lincoln, even though we need to close and go home. Me and Kayla rearrange the DVDs, then we walk around in circles and cough to try to get Dad to look at the clock and kick the lady out, but he doesn't take the hint. He starts fastening bracelets around her wrists. Then an Escalade pulls into the parking lot.

"Tell them we're closed. Be firm," Aubrey says to me and Kayla. We get ready to be firm, but the door to the Escalade opens and it's not a customer. It's Rob.

"Buzz the door! Buzz the door!" we yell. I lick my hand and smooth my hair and tuck in my shirt.

"We're closed!" Aubrey yells.

"It's Rob!" we scream.

"Jesus," Aubrey says under his breath. He runs around the counter and opens the door for Rob.

"Hello, sir! Welcome! Good to see you! You're a day early!" Aubrey says with a fake smile. Rob claps him on the back.

"My man!" Rob says. I fake smile, tense my arms, and get ready for Rob to hug me, but instead he leans toward Aubrey and whispers, "Who's the customer? Damn."

"Couldn't tell you," Aubrey says. He's trying not to sound annoyed, but he is. He wants to go home. I want to go home too. Rob waddles across the store and we follow him.

"What's this loser telling you?" Rob says to Windbreaker Lady. Rob squeezes Dad's shoulders and says, "What's up, pal? Good to see you." Dad turns around to shake Rob's hand, but Rob's hands are on Windbreaker Lady's windbreaker—on her hips.

"How are you, beautiful?" he says to her.

"Fine," she says, looking worried.

"What are you doing tonight?" Rob says to her.

"I've got to go, actually. I'm here for my friend's bachelorette party and we're meeting at seven." She wiggles out of Rob's hands. "Thank you. See you later maybe," she says to Dad. She walks away fast. I worry that she'll drop her DVDs and food processer, but she doesn't.

"What about me? Don't you want to see me later?" Rob calls after her. She laughs nervously and Dad buzzes her out the door. Rob glares at Dad. "Way to ruin my chances, pal," he says. Dad cracks his neck.

"Did you have a good trip up here, sir?" Aubrey says. Rob doesn't seem to hear him.

"God, she was cute," Rob says. "Jesus, it's good to be divorced." Dad fake laughs and then we do too. "I was just saying to this guy at the hotel that Gretchen, my ex-wife—God, I just love saying 'ex-wife' now. My ex-wife used to stop shaving her legs in the winter and it was like there were these two long, skinny porcupines rolling around in my bed. She stopped shaving everything else too, if you know what I mean. Mind you, it didn't stop her from wearing shorts, or even swimsuits sometimes. I couldn't handle it after a certain point. Who wants to sleep with a porcupine? Not me. I'll tell you that." Dad cracks his neck and looks at me and Kayla.

"Maybe this is a conversation for a different time," Aubrey says. I expect Rob to get mad, but he says, "God. Sorry, girls. I think I had one too many Bloody Marys at the hotel." Then he laughs.

"I hear Blake made the trip too?" Aubrey says.

"That's right! Blake's here. I can't wait for y'all to meet tomorrow."

"We're going scuba diving, right?" I say. Rob rolls some phlegm around in his throat.

"About that," he says, "The tickets all got sold, actually. There were only two left for me and Blake. I feel terrible." He puts his hand on my back and pats. "Honestly, I'm so sorry. Blake can tell you all about it, though. I'm gonna bring him in tomorrow afternoon after we dive and you girls can show him the ropes around here." The tickets did not sell out. Rob decided he didn't want to spend the $175 on tickets for us and we know it.

"That's okay," I say, with a golden fake smile.

"How old is Blake now?" Dad says.

"Gonna be a freshman in high school. God, they grow up so fast, don't they? Look at this—school picture," Rob says. He scrolls through his phone and holds it out to us. Dad and Aubrey look at it, then they pass it to Kayla, who passes it to me.

Blake is really cute. He has shiny skin and shiny hair with gel in it. There is a cleanness and a glow to him that Paxton and Hunter and the other boys we go to school with don't have. I look deep into the phone. I imagine crawling inside the picture and putting my head on Blake's chest beneath his golf shirt. I imagine touching the gel in his hair and touching his teeth with my fingers. Rob is still talking, but I am slow dancing with Blake. An end-of-the-movie song is playing. There's a disco ball and I am wearing a strapless dress. I have huge boobs and Blake can't stop looking at them. He's in love with me.

"Earth to Jackie!" I hear Rob say. He snaps his fingers at my nose.

"Sorry," I say.

We lock the safe, Dad sets the alarm, and we all walk out to the parking lot together. When I hug Kayla goodbye she says, "Are you okay? You look like a zombie." I'm a zombie in love, I want to tell her, but I'm worried the dads and Rob and Carter will hear, so I whisper, "I'll tell you later."

"What do you say we get a drink?" Rob says to Dad and not to Aubrey.

"Sure," Dad says. "I'll just drop Jackie off and then I'll meet you at Rackham's." Aubrey pretends not to hear them and he and Kayla get in their car.

"I'll miss you," I say to Kayla.

"I'll miss you too," she says. She opens her window and leans out and hugs me. Kayla hasn't been mad at me once since we started doing the plan together and I love it.

Dad gets Burger King for me and drops me off at home, then goes to Rackham's with Rob. I go into Dad's room and take off my clothes and look in his full-size mirror. I pull on my nipples to try to make my boobs look bigger. I arch my back to try and make my butt look fatter and my stomach look skinnier. Then I look at my legs and remember what Rob said about Gretchen—who wants to sleep with a porcupine? I comb my hands up and down my legs. They're porcupine legs. If Rob doesn't like Gretchen's hairy legs, Blake definitely won't like mine. I don't want to have sex with Blake, but I want him to want to have sex with me and he won't if my legs are hairy.

Giselle said Kayla can shave her legs when she starts high school, so my plan was to wait until then to learn from Kayla, but that's not an option anymore. Plus, Kayla hardly has any hair on her legs and the hair she does have is white blonde. The hair on my legs is brown and thick like yeti fur. I even have hair on my toes. I dig through Dad's medicine cabinet looking for a razor, but I can't find one. I find a pair of tweezers, put my foot up on the sink, and start to pull out hairs one by one. By the twelfth hair, I feel tears in my nose. There are over a thousand hairs left. I'll never be able to pull them all out.

Then I hear the gate open and I see Dad's headlights pulling into the garage. I scramble to the bathroom, dip my toothbrush under the faucet, then run to my room and turn off the lights.

I hear the sound of flip-flops and I hear a woman's voice say, "You're too funny!" with a snorty laugh. I punch my bed and pretend I'm punching the laughing, flip-flop–wearing woman. Most nights I am as nice as I can possibly be to the women in our house, but tonight is not going to be one of those nights. I need Dad tonight.

The woman starts whistling, loudly, and Dad says, "Shh, my daughter's asleep."

"Sorry, sorry," the woman whispers. Dad doesn't check to see if my toothbrush is wet to make sure I brushed my teeth like he usually does. He goes straight to his room. I watch his hairy bare feet and the woman's blue, scraggly toenails walk past the crack under my door. There is no hair on her feet. I hear the lock on Dad's door pop. Then I creep out of my room and into the kitchen. Fourteen DVDs and a food processer are splayed across the counter. The woman is Windbreaker Lady. I put my ear against Dad's door and I hear her laugh again. It's not quite a real laugh. It sounds like a seagull. After a few minutes it gets more real. Laughing is like yawning. If you fake it for a little bit, pretty soon you're doing it for real.

Dad turns on his fan and his air conditioner. He thinks that when he does that I can't hear anything that's happening in his room, but I still can.

I hear him and Windbreaker Lady kissing. She says, "Mmm-mm," like she's in a commercial for a restaurant, making noises to show how good the food is. It must be nice for her to touch Dad after only touching dogs and their poop since she got divorced. Dad starts smacking Windbreaker Lady's butt and she keeps mmm-mm-ing. I feel bad for ruining her night after all this work she's putting in, but I have no choice.

I knock on Dad's door. I hear his feet on the carpet. He pokes his head around the door. He's wearing boxers. He runs his hand all the way from his neck to his hair, mashing his nose like it's Play-Doh.

"Hi, baby girl. Are you okay?" he says. He's out of breath.

"No," I say. He slips out the door sideways and closes it behind him. We both pretend like I didn't just hear him slapping Windbreaker Lady's butt.

"What's wrong? What do you need?" he says. I press my fingernails into my palms and look at the carpet.

"Can you shave my legs?" I whisper.

"Can I what? Can I shave your legs?"

"Yeah."

"Aren't you a little bit young to be doing that? I thought girls did that in—what? In high school?"

"I'm basically in high school." I look straight into his eyes like he's a customer. He looks at the floor.

"Is this because of what Rob said? He shouldn't have said that. And he doesn't know what he's talking about. A lot of beautiful women have—I mean—just don't listen to Rob," Dad says.

"I thought Rob was the boss. I thought we have to listen to him," I say. I lock my eyes with Dad's eyes and I don't let him look away.

"Babe, just at Paradise Pawn. Not in the rest of your life. Jesus," he says, and starts to slide back behind the door.

"Stop!" I say. I clamp my hand on his arm. "It's not because of Rob. I just want to. I need to."

"Okay, but do you, I mean we—does it have to happen right this minute? You look really pretty just the way you are. And beauty is on the inside. Right? And I'm a little bit—tired right now." Normally I would back down. I would remember how hard Dad works to give me a nice life and I would let him have a nice life for a few hours, but this is too important.

"I really need to," I say.

"Did you think about asking Giselle how?" he says. I sigh dramatically. At Paradise Pawn, Dad says sometimes you have to go for a customer's emotional jugular. That is what I have to do.

"Dad, you're supposed to learn how to shave from your parents, not from your friend's parents, and since I don't have a mom, that leaves you," I say. Dad flinches a little. Then he pushes his thumbs so far into his eyes that I worry he will squash them. As soon as he opens his eyes, my eyes are ready to lock on to his again.

"Dammit," he says softly. He looks back toward his room.

"I don't want her help," I say. He lets out a deep breath and says, "Okay. Hang on just a sec." He goes back in his room and closes the door behind him. I lie on the floor and listen through the crack under the door.

"Howdy," I hear Windbreaker say. "I'm glad you're back."

"Listen," Dad says to her. "I am so sorry to do this, but my kid needs me."

"What does she need?" the lady says.

"She's sick. She's got a pretty bad fever," Dad says. I smile. I'm glad he didn't tell her that I'm shaving my legs. It's less embarrassing to have a fever than to have to shave your legs.

"Oh, you sweet man," the lady says. "I can wait. I've got nothing but time. I'm on vacation. Or I could make her some soup if you've got chicken broth in the house. I know a great—"

"No," Dad interrupts. "That's really nice, but it'd be better if you just leave. I wouldn't want you to get sick." I feel every muscle in my cheeks bloom into a big smile. I have won.

"Seriously?" Windbreaker says.

"Yeah. I'm really sorry."

"You're kicking me out right now?"

"Yeah, I mean it's not like that. You seem great, but—I've got to help my kid. I can pay for your Uber. I'm sorry—yeah, I'm sorry." I can tell Dad was going to say, "I'm sorry" and then her name, but he has no idea what her name is. Neither do I. It's probably something like Marcy. Poor Marcy.

"Did I do something wrong?" she says, sounding like she might cry.

"No, Jesus, of course not. You seem great. I just need you to leave," Dad says.

"This is unbelievable," she says. I hear the blankets moving and then Marcy slams the door open so hard that it bounces against the wall. She has smudges of blue makeup under her eyes. Her flip-flops are on the wrong feet and her shorts are unbuttoned. She almost steps on me, but I roll out of her way. She jumps when she notices me.

"Helllohh," I groan. I let some spit fall out of the side of my mouth and I roll my eyes back in my head so she'll think I have a terrible tropical disease. I cough a lot and I think some of my spit gets on her foot, because she wipes it on the carpet and looks worried.

"Feel better, honey," she says, backing away from me. I go into Dad's room and roll around in his bed. It smells like girly sunscreen.

“So,” Dad says, yawning. “Let’s get ’er done.” I follow him into his bathroom. He yawns again, opens a drawer, and takes out his razor and a shiny blue bottle that says *Shaving Cream for Men*. There’s a smiling guy in a white shirt on the bottle. He’s squinting, like he’s looking at a girl he wants to kiss.

“Dad! What is your problem? I can’t use shaving cream for men!” I say.

“Why not?” Dad says. I can tell that he’s deciding whether or not to argue with me. He puts both hands on the sink and looks down into it like it’s a wishing well. Then he looks up at himself in his mirror. He pulls down on his eyebrows and rubs circles into the sides of his head and twists his chain around his thumb. “Alright. Okay. God, this is a big deal, isn’t it, baby? Wow, okay. We should do this right, huh?”

“Yeah,” I say. I’ve closed my deal. He turns around and puts his hands on my shoulders and squeezes them.

“Waaoooh!” he yells in my face, the way he does when he runs up the beach with his surfboard. “Shaving!” I laugh a real laugh.

“Shaving!” I yell.

“Get dressed, baby girl. I think Mermaid’s is still open. We’re going to get you the nicest razor in Cherry Beach.”

“Okay!” I say. Mermaid’s is down the street from our house. It’s a little green shack with a big Heineken bottle painted on the side. It’s mainly a bar for tourists and old people, but they also have a gift shop that sells magnets and stomach medicine and razors. It also has a little tank of turtles for people to look at. Dad jogs to his room. His unbuttoned shirt flaps behind him like a cape. I run to my room and pull on a yellow lacy dress that’s a little too small for me.

Outside it is cool and the air is royal blue. The lights from a cruise ship crinkle on the waves. The tree frogs chirp, *Jack-ie, Jack, Jack, Jack-ie*.

"Stay on the side of the road," Dad says to me, and pushes me by my shoulders. It's muddy on the side.

"Don't push me," I say.

"You'll get run over," he says, and holds my hand. I like holding his hand. At Mermaid's, Dad pulls me through the dance floor—through sunburned tourist stomachs and vape clouds and slushy drinks. When we get to the bar, Dad sits down on a stool. I try to climb onto the stool beside him, but it's too tall, so he lifts me.

"Devon!" yells the lady behind the bar. Her name is Christine. She pawns her laptop a lot. "And Jackie? Daddy, she's a little young to be here right now, don't you think?"

"Special day!" Dad yells. Christine shakes her head.

"She should be in bed!"

"Listen, is the gift shop closed? We need a razor. A women's razor and women's shaving cream. For this one," Dad yells, pointing to me. "And a rum and Coke and a regular Coke."

"Oh, honey," Christine says, squeezing my hand. "This is a big day." She pours a rum and Coke for Dad and a plain Coke for me. Dad drinks half of his rum and Coke in one sip. "The gift shop is technically closed, but let me go get some razors from the back and I can put them on your tab," Christine yells. She pushes past a group of girls in sashes that say *Bride Tribe*.

"Watch it!" one of them yells.

"Well, move!" Christine yells. The bridesmaids lift their arms up to dance. Their armpits look like marble. I push a finger up through the sleeve of my dress and touch the hair on my armpit. Soon I will look like the bridesmaids—at least my legs and my armpits will. Dad glances at me and nods.

"You good?" he yells over the music.

"Yep!" I yell. I'm glad it's so loud. It means it isn't awkward if we don't talk. Maybe that's why people like loud bars. I blow bubbles in my Coke with my straw. Dad drums his fingers on the bar and follows the bridesmaids with his eyes. Some of them look at him too. He could dance with them if he wanted to, but he stays beside me.

Christine comes back with an armload of pink packages and bottles. She dumps them on the bar and slides peoples' drinks out of the way.

"Move. This is important," she says to a guy wandering around wearing a snorkel. She spreads everything out in front of me and yells, "Take your pick, baby!" Two guys with hairy chests order Coronas. I plug my ears so I can concentrate on reading the words on the razors and shaving cream. *ComfortGlide. Venus Sensitive. Lush Embrace. Hydro Silk. Vanilla Temptation.* Dad is getting impatient. He's done with his rum and Coke and he's chewing his nails. I choose a Venus Sensitive razor and Vanilla Temptation shaving cream.

"You set?" Dad says.

"Yeah," I say.

"Sweet," he says. He gives me a fist bump. "Christine! Can we get the bill?" The razors are expensive. Dad could have bought three rum and Cokes for the price of one razor.

"Good luck, baby cakes," Christine says to me. She blows me a kiss as Dad signs the receipt. "See you guys at Paradise."

"You bet," Dad says. We stop for a minute to watch the bridesmaids scream along to a song about finding love in a hopeless place. One of them pushes snorkel guy's snorkel out of his mouth and makes out with him. His arms wrap around her shoulders like hairy pythons.

When we're home, I march to my bathroom and Dad follows me. I poke the razors open with a barrette.

"Okay, how do I do this?" I say. "I want to do my armpits first." Dad bites the side of his thumb.

"Well," he says, "Can you roll up your sleeves?" He starts yawning and then stops himself. I push my sleeves as high as they will go, but they're too tight to go all the way up to my armpits.

"Frick," I whisper.

"Can you slide your dress off, maybe?" Dad says. "Would that be easier? I won't, you know, look at anything."

"Dad!" I say. "That's disgusting."

"Sorry. Sorry," he says. He cracks his neck. I push my sleeves up some more and they start to cut off my circulation.

"I didn't mean that you're disgusting. I'm just a little bit disgusting," I say.

"Babe, you're not disgusting," Dad says. "Don't say that." I hear my dress start to rip.

I look at Dad's reflection in my mirror. If he was anyone besides Dad, I would think that he was about to cry.

"I'm going to put my swimsuit on," I say.

"Sure. Good idea," Dad says. I run to my room and pry my arms out of the yellow dress. I put on my old red one-piece swimsuit. Dad doesn't like my two-piece one. He says it's too exposing. Dad is sitting on the side of the bathtub and blowing his nose when I get back.

"I'm ready," I say. He sniffs and says, "Cool. Me too. Let's do it." I lift my arms up. "Alright. You want to get your razor wet first, kind of like when you brush your teeth. Maybe I can do one armpit and you do the other? Does that sound good?"

"Yeah," I say. "Will it hurt?"

"I've never shaved my armpits before, but I don't think so. It doesn't hurt me when I shave my face. Sometimes you might cut yourself a little bit, but even that doesn't hurt too bad." I nod and try to take deep breaths.

"Maybe you should stand in the tub so we don't get hair all over the place," Dad says.

"Okay," I say. I pull back my shower curtain. It has pink fish on it. It's a little girl's shower curtain. I should get a more grown-up one. I stand in the tub facing the mirror and Dad stands with one foot on the floor and his knee on the side of the tub. In the mirror, I watch another Jackie lift her arms up. I watch another Dad lean toward her, looking afraid. Dad squirts some of the shaving cream into his hand.

"Ready?" he says. I nod. He pats shaving cream onto each of my armpits. It's cold. He runs the razor under the tap. Then he puts one hand on my hip and holds the razor with the other hand and slides it from the bottom of my armpit to the top. It tickles, but it doesn't hurt.

"There," he says softly.

"That's it?" I say.

"Well, no, but that's how you do it. You have to do that a few times." He taps the razor against the bottom of the bathtub. "This is how you unclog it if there's a lot of hair in it." He does it twice more, then I try it on the other armpit. It's pretty easy. The hair just falls off. That hair that I've been worried about all night just falls off and slips down the drain into the ocean. I wish everything I worry about could be shaved away. I wonder why Gretchen didn't just shave since Rob hated her hairy skin so much. Maybe they wouldn't be divorced if she had.

"You want to do your legs too?" Dad asks.

"Yes," I say. My legs are going to gleam like a tourist's legs. For once my legs will be prettier than Kayla's.

"I'm going to google it," Dad says. "Just to make sure we do it right." Dad sits down on the toilet and I stand beside him. My armpits feel wet and slimy.

YouTube is full of videos about moms helping their daughters shave for the first time, but none about dads and daughters. I click on one of the mom-and-daughter ones. The mom's name is Nicole and the daughter's name is Katie. They're in Minnesota. Katie looks a little bit like me. Her face is oily and she seems nervous. I bet she doesn't have many friends. Nicole is pretty. She's not nervous at all. She sings a song about shaving and dances around. She holds a hairbrush like it's a microphone as she sings. She calls Katie "lovey." Katie laughs at her mom's song in an embarrassed way, but not a mean way. Katie and Nicole go to buy razors at a big, empty store with shiny floors and bright lights. They blow kisses at the camera and hold hands. Katie skips around. Katie's dad is filming. His name is Craig. When they're back at home, they all go into the bathroom. Their house is big and white and pretty and so is their bathroom. Katie's dad holds the camera close to his face and says, "This is Mama's job now. It'd be creepy if I stick around. I'm outta here," and then he laughs. Katie's mom laughs too, and gives Katie a hug.

"God. Those people are sick in the head," Dad says, and turns the video off. "Why would they film that? Poor kid." I think they seem nice. "Come on," Dad says. "Let's do this. We don't need a video." I think what the dad said in the video made him mad. He seems like he's in a rush. He keeps twisting his chain around his thumb the way he does when he's uncomfortable. I sit on the edge of the tub and Dad rubs cold pink shaving cream all over my legs. I shiver.

"Will you do it?" I say.

"I think you should do it," he says. "Just like your armpits. Bottom to top." He's standing up to leave and I don't want him to leave, but if I follow him and make him stay, I'll get pink goo all over the bathroom. "You've got it. Right?" Dad says, yawning and not trying to stop himself anymore.

"I don't think I've got it," I say.

"You do. I know you do," he says. "Like they said in the video, this isn't really a dad thing."

"What? No, it can be a dad thing," I say.

"I just think it's more appropriate if you do it yourself," he says, not looking at me. He leans forward like he's going to kiss the top of my head, but he doesn't. He doesn't touch me. He leaves me stranded with my slimy pink legs in the tub. "Good job, baby. I love you," he says.

"I love you too," I say. I think about whining to make him stay with me, but I already made him spend money on my shaving stuff and I made him give up having sex with Windbreaker Lady, so I am quiet. When he's back in his room, I wobble to the living room with my slimy legs and I get Dad's laptop. I put the laptop on my bathroom counter and I pull up the YouTube video of Katie and Nicole. I turn the sound off so Dad won't hear it. I follow along as Nicole carves paths through the pink shaving cream on Katie's legs. When they wave to the camera, I wave back. When they move their mouths and no sound comes out, I imagine they're talking to me, telling me my legs look sexy, inviting me to come hang out with them and Craig in their big, white house in Minnesota.

I cut myself on my knee, but it doesn't hurt. I press some toilet paper into the cut while Katie and Nicole talk to me. I splash water onto my legs and the pink clouds of shaving cream slide down my skin and swirl into the drain. In the video, after Katie and her mom are done shaving her legs and Katie is wearing cozy-looking pajamas, Katie's dad comes inside wearing a big coat. He kisses Katie's mom. Then the screen goes dark.

I shave the hair on my arms and on my stomach. Then I take off my swimsuit and shave the hair on my vagina. I only get through one corner of it before the razor gets clogged with long hairs and I can't get it unclogged. When I try to pull them out of the razor blade with my fingers, I slice my thumb a little. I clip more hair off my vagina with scissors. I can't get all of it off, but I don't plan on showing Blake my vagina tomorrow. I pull my swimsuit back on and rinse all the sticky shaving cream off of me. Then I slide my fingers up and down my new legs and arms. *ComfortGlide. Venus Sensitive. Lush Embrace. Hydro Silk. Vanilla Temptation.* I slip into my bed and roll around. I feel as smooth as a dolphin.

Then I remember that Katie's mom put lotion on Katie's legs after she shaved them. I glide over to my dresser. I reach all the way to the back of my underwear drawer, where I keep my baby teeth and my pictures of Mom and my most special shells and the bottles of shampoo and body lotion from when Mom stayed at the Margaritaville Hotel. I unscrew the lid of the body lotion and I sit on the floor. I try to squeeze just a tiny bit of lotion onto my finger, but a huge glob falls out of the bottle and right onto my leg. It's like Mom is there, dumping her lotion on me like an angel.

I rub the lotion all over my arms and legs and armpits and stomach and the sides of my vagina. It stings a little, but then the stinging goes away. I peel off my swimsuit and fall into my bed feeling silky, lush, sensitive, glide, Venus. I think about Blake. I think about him touching my new skin and I feel like my heart has fallen down into my vagina and is beating there. I hope I can make Blake feel my legs tomorrow. I hope Kayla asks me to teach her to shave her legs. I will, but not right away, so my legs can be prettier and more grown-up than hers, just for a few days.

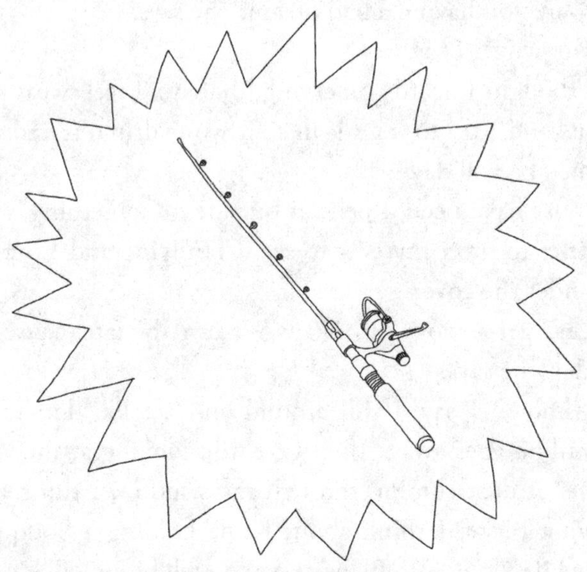

CHAPTER 13

IN THE MORNING, I SQUIRM AND TANGLE MY NEW plasticky body in my sheets. I start to think about Blake and pretty soon, thoughts about him flood my whole brain, like a drop of paint in water.

I pretend my palm is Blake's mouth. I lick my lips and push them into it. It doesn't make my hand feel anything special, like a kiss is supposed to. I google *how to kiss a boy* on Dad's laptop. I read an article called "12 Hot Guys on What Makes a Girl a Good (Or Bad!) Kisser."

I spit on my palm and lightly bite it and make little moans like the women who sleep with Dad do. Dad knocks on my door. I hide the laptop under my pillow and pretend to be asleep.

"Morning," he says. I yawn and blink like I am just waking up.

"Were you having a bad dream?" he says.

"No, why?" I say.

"I thought I heard you crying," he says. I feel sweat in my armpits and I try to hold it in so it won't drip out and make me smell bad all day.

"Must have been a pelican outside or something," I say. Dad tries to meet my eyes to see if I'm lying and I bury my face under the covers.

"Let's get a move on, okay? We can't be late 'cause it's a Rob day," he says.

"I know," I say. I roll around and act like I'm waking up until he goes away. Then I lie still, looking at the yellow streams of dust coming through my window. I think about marrying Blake. I think about Kayla holding a bouquet of roses while I look into Blake's eyes and tell him I will love him for richer and for poorer, except I won't mean the "for poorer" part, because Blake will own the whole Paradise Pawn empire when he grows up, so he will always be "for richer."

"Leaving in fifteen minutes, Jack-Jack!" Dad yells. My heart bashes against the inside of my chest.

I hurl myself out of bed. There is still so much I need to do to make myself pretty enough for Blake to like me. My hair is oily. My forehead and my nose are oily too. I scrape a dry towel against them. I yank off my pajamas and wiggle into the top of my two-piece swimsuit. I fill the boob cups with toilet paper. I tape the toilet paper to my skin so it won't fall out like at the Ritz-Carlton.

My legs that were so smooth and perfect last night have red bumps on them. My vagina has red bumps on it too, like a bloody chicken leg. I run my finger along the bumps and they start to itch. I'm worried I have a disease. I've never heard of getting a disease just from thinking about a boy, but maybe that can happen.

“Jackie, let’s move it!” Dad snaps, pounding on the door. I punch the wall and it hurts my hand. I don’t let myself cry, because if I do my eyes will get puffy and I’ll look even grosser.

“Don’t come in!” I yell. If Dad sees the red bumps, he’ll never let me shave again.

“Babe, I’m sure you look great. Let’s go. The car is pulling out in five minutes whether you’re in it or not.” Dad normally doesn’t talk to me like that—like a mean dad in a movie—but he’s nervous about Rob.

I yank my Paradise Pawn shirt over my head and sculpt my toilet paper boobs underneath it. The tape pokes my skin, but they look pretty good.

I wiggle into a skirt and roll it a few times to make it shorter. Then I unroll it because the bunched-up fabric makes me look fat, and I don’t want to draw too much attention to my legs, because they still have the weird red bumps on them. I jam my toes into flip-flops and run to the car. Dad’s eyes bounce from my chest to my face. He coughs, deciding whether or not to say something. He stays quiet and pulls the truck out into the road. I forgot to brush my teeth so I chew on my tongue to try to get the bad breath out of it.

“You want some gum?” Dad says, like he can read my mind.

“Thanks,” I say, even though I’m mad at him for rushing me. Aubrey’s car and Rob’s car are already in the parking lot when we pull in.

“Shit,” Dad whispers.

“Hey-hey! Look who decided to show up!” Rob bellows when we walk in.

“Good morning, sir. Sorry we’re late,” Dad says. I catch Kayla’s eye and point to my boobs. I expect her to smile and say I look good, but she rolls her eyes at me.

“Where’s Blake?” I say.

"On the john," Rob says. His eyes don't meet mine. They rest on the toilet paper in my swimsuit top. "They sure grow up fast, don't they?" he says to the dads, still looking at my chest. Dad tugs me away from Rob. "I guess they do," Dad says.

"You're looking like a young lady," Rob says to me. He laughs, even though no one said anything funny. I feel Dad's fingers drill into my shoulders.

"Thank you," I say, feeling weird that toilet paper can change how someone sees you if they think it's skin and fat attached to you.

"Should we get down to business?" Aubrey says, stepping between me and Rob. Rob's smile fades. He looks up from my chest and says, "Yeah, so I think y'all are all aware we've got issues here. Major issues."

"Yes sir," we say like we're in the army. I watch Kayla chew her fingernails. Rob leans over the computer and clicks through the numbers on MasterPawn, saying, "This is not what I like to see. Not good, people. We're giving out too much cash to customers who aren't coming back." I'm so nervous and shivery that I almost forget about Blake until I hear the toilet flush.

He walks out of the bathroom toward me. I feel like I'm seeing a famous person. I've spent so much time looking at pictures of him, but now he's not a picture. He's a moving, breathing, sweating body. He's playing a game on his phone. It's the iPhone model that just came out. We haven't gotten any of them into the store yet. The light from his phone glows purple on his face like he's at a club. It catches on his shiny hair and on his braces when he smiles. I can almost feel his skin underneath his gray shirt.

"How we doing, my man?" Rob says to him. Blake shrugs. "Can you say hi to our employees?" Rob says.

"Hey," Blake says, still not looking up from his phone. I

expect Rob to yell at Blake and make him look at us and be respectful and shake our hands, but he doesn't.

"Hi!" I say in his face. I hold out my hand for him to shake. He pulls out his AirPods and looks up. His eyes are blue and shiny, like a Pepsi can. He just looks at my face, not at my legs or my chest. My face is ugly and oily and no more grown-up-looking than it was yesterday. I wish he would look at other parts of me. I tug my shirt down my chest and try to bounce my breasts like a girl in a music video, but he still doesn't look at them. "Hi," I say again in a soft, sexy voice.

"What's up?" Blake says. His voice is deep and quiet. I want him to keep talking, but Rob is talking instead. Rob bends over the computer awkwardly, squinting at MasterPawn. He taps the numbers on the screen with the end of a pen. His voice is getting louder and angrier, but I am not listening. I want to lean into Blake and kiss him. I want my tongue to lick his tongue.

In the middle of Rob's speech, a customer buzzes and we all fake smile, except for Blake, who looks down at his phone. The customer is a carpenter from Haiti with a band saw. We chat with him a little about how hot it's been, and then we get him to tell us that he just bought a new band saw. That means he's probably not coming back for the one he's pawning. Normally me and Kayla would do the plan on him, but Rob leans over the computer and breathes on us as we do the transaction, so we let money that should have gone in our maxi pads go into Rob's bank account.

"That's the way you gotta do it," Rob says when the customer leaves. "Just treat the money like it's your own. Think carefully. Use those brains." Rob taps Kayla's forehead with his pen.

"Yes sir," we say. Then Rob claps his hand against Blake's back and Blake jumps.

"Ow, Dad," Blake mutters.

"Oh, grow a pair," Rob says. Blake hunches his shoulders. "Time to scuba, buddy," Rob says. Blake rolls his eyes. They both walk out to the parking lot and get in Rob's Escalade. If I married Blake, I would never clap him on the back like that. I would be so gentle with him. I would skim my fingers all over his skin as gently as a bug walking on water.

If I married Blake, I would get to leave people to polish my gold chains and dust my TVs and Windex my windows while Blake and I went scuba diving. I would wear a bikini on the boat, and my hair would blow in the wind, and Blake would gaze at me. My bikini would be filled with fake boobs made of expensive silicone instead of toilet paper.

Kayla and I decide not to do the plan at all today, since Rob will probably check every transaction when he gets back. There are some perfect opportunities—Russian tourists pawning a telescope, an old lady selling a ring from a broken-off engagement, a dad selling a baby necklace for a baby who died before she was born. I don't mind not doing the plan as much as I usually would. I'm busy dreaming about Blake.

"You're in love with him, aren't you? Blake, I mean," Kayla says as we're sticking price tags on fishing poles.

"No," I say. Then I burst out laughing and say, "Okay, fine. Yes, I am. I'm totally in love."

"I knew it!" she says. She pokes me in the stomach and then hugs me. I hug her back.

"You shaved your legs, didn't you?" she says. I nod into her shoulder. "We should write him a note. I'll give it to him. Harley says it's bad luck to give a note to your crush. You have to have a friend do it to show him you have friends." Harley is a girl from our class last year who doesn't like me because she wishes she was Kayla's best friend instead of me.

"When were you talking to Harley?" I say.

"At orientation for high school. Doesn't matter. Let's write this note," she says.

"Oh," I say, and for a minute, all I can think about is Kayla and Harley talking about crushes without me. I didn't even know that Kayla went to orientation. She didn't tell me. Kayla holds me by the shoulders and looks at my face. She can tell I'm sad.

"Hey," she says. "What's wrong? Don't you think it's a good idea? I'll show you how to do it." She digs an old lay-away contract out of the trash and writes: *Blake—Do you like me? From, Jackie.* Then she draws two boxes—one marked *yes* and one *no*.

"Wow," I breathe. I imagine how easy my life would be if I could pass a *Do you like me?* note to every person I've ever known—to Kayla, to Dad, to Giselle.

Kayla folds the note into a complicated triangle that she probably learned how to fold from Harley. She slips it into her pocket and squeezes my hand.

"The answer is going to be yes," she says.

"Do you like me?" I say to her.

"What?" she says.

"Do you like me?" I say again.

"What kind of a question is that? Of course I like you," she says.

"Do you like Harley more?" I say.

"Don't be dumb, Jackie," she says. Then she leans toward me and fits her *Best* necklace and my *Friends* necklace together. "If I liked Harley more than you, why would I be wearing this?"

"You're not lying, are you?" I say.

"Obviously not," Kayla says. She sighs like she's annoyed with me.

"Okay, sorry," I say quietly. It has felt so good to have Kayla not mad at me for the past few weeks, and I want to keep it that way.

"If I marry Blake and I get a bunch of money, I'll give half of it to you," I say.

"That's okay. I'm going to make my own money," she says, walking to the supply cabinet to get more price stickers.

"Well, yeah, obviously, but if I had infinite money from marrying Blake, wouldn't you want me to give you some of it?" I say, running after her.

"It wouldn't really be your money. I'm sure he'd make you sign a prenup," she says.

"Whatever," I say, and we stick the rest of the stickers onto the fishing poles in silence.

AT 4:30, Rob and Blake get back from scuba diving. They drip water all over the floor and Carter mops it up. Blake's hair is wet, his swimsuit is wet, and his T-shirt is wet. He looks like a cologne commercial. Rob shows us pictures of himself squeezed into a shiny wet suit like a cockroach. He shows us a picture of Blake kissing a turtle. I try to think of a joke to make about how I would be better at kissing than a turtle, but I can't think of anything that wouldn't sound weird. Rob has been drinking beer on the scuba diving boat. We can smell it.

"I'm gonna go talk to your no-good dads in the office," Rob says, and chuckles. "You girls show Blakey how it's done."

"How was scuba diving?" Kayla says. Blake shrugs.

"Okay," he says. "I got really cold."

"Did you see any cool fish?" I say.

"Not really," Blake says. "It wasn't as good as Hawaii."

"Oh," I say. Kayla nudges me.

"Ask him more questions," she whispers. "When boys talk about themselves to you, it makes them like you more." I nod.

"What do you like to do?" I ask. It's a stupid question that only lame grown-ups ask kids, but I can't think of anything better.

"Play video games. *Fortnite*, mostly," he says.

"Yeah, *Fortnite* is awesome," I say, even though I don't know anything about *Fortnite*. I wait for him to ask me what I like to do. I plan to say that I like clubbing, even though I've never been clubbing. But he doesn't ask. He doesn't say anything. He just leans against the counter like a model. Then he puts in his AirPods. Someday he will buy me AirPods. I poke Kayla and whisper, "Should you give him the note?" She nods and slides the note out of her pocket and walks toward Blake.

"How's it going?" she says. He can't hear her with his AirPods in. "How's it going?" she yells. He still doesn't look up from his phone. A customer bangs on the door and we buzz her in. Me and Kayla slap on smiles. Blake scrolls through Instagram. He's not smiling or even making eye contact with the customer. I step on his foot and whisper, "Smile."

"Huh?" Blake says. He takes out one of his AirPods.

"You have to smile when a customer comes in," I say.

"You're not the boss of me," he says, which is true. He is technically the boss of us. He's the boss of Aubrey and Dad too. He is the boss of all of Paradise Pawn. When I marry him, I will be the boss of Paradise Pawn too.

"You're right," I say, and I smile at him and wiggle my chest. He doesn't smile back, or look at my fake boobs or my shaved legs.

The customer walks to the counter. She has tears in her eyes. She's missing one of her front teeth. Me and Kayla soften our smiles from fake and cheerful to fake and sympathetic.

"I need a thousand dollars," the customer whispers, her chin twitching. "This morning at breakfast my daughter dropped her toast on the ground and then she reached for it and our pit bull, Freddy, got on top of her and bit her. She's at the hospital now—tubes all over her little body. We're going to kill the dog. I just need my baby to be okay. I don't have money for the bill." She fumbles with the chain around her neck. Blake backs away from the counter and presses himself against the wall like he's scared. I guess most of the people he hangs out with in Miami have all their teeth. You can't act scared of a customer, no matter how weird they look. If you act scared, they'll never trust you.

"Let me help you," Kayla says. The lady leans forward and Kayla unhooks the chain. It gleams orange-yellow in the light above the touchstone. It's either eighteen karat or plated.

"Want to learn how to test gold, Blake?" Kayla says.

"Okay," he says. Kayla nudges me and whispers, "Go!" I squeeze her hand. Then I turn to Blake.

"Come over here," I say, in what I hope is a sexy voice. I am the boss of him now. I give him the gloves. I put my hand over his hand and show him how to scrub the gold against the touchstone. It's like we are in a movie and the boy is showing the girl how to play pool, except that the girl is showing the boy how to test gold. I pull gloves over his fingers and tell him to drip the fourteen-karat acid onto the lines. It holds. I tell him to drip the eighteen-karat acid. He does, but then he doesn't put the top back on the bottle. He reaches for his phone and knocks the bottle off the counter and spills a bunch of it. He's basically spilling money on the ground, because acid is expensive, but it's his money, so no one can get mad at him. I dive to the ground and grab the acid before all of it spills. My fingers sting. I shouldn't have given Blake the gloves. Soon my fingers will be yellow and blistered. I hope Blake won't notice if he holds my hand.

"Whoops," he says, like he's stepped on an ant or stubbed his toe, not like he's just spilled money on the floor.

"It's okay," I say patiently. "Scrub it on the touchstone again." He does. I drip the eighteen-karat acid on his line so he doesn't spill it again and it holds.

"Now weigh it," I tell Blake, and he does, then hands it back to me. The customer leans against the counter and watches us. Tears are pooling in her eyes. Kayla puts a Kleenex box on the counter for her.

"We'll have a price for you shortly," Kayla says. I bounce the chain up and down in my palm. It doesn't press into my skin the way gold should. I squint at it through my loupe. Just like I thought, there are scribbles of tungsten where we scratched away the gold. Kayla asks me with her eyes if it's plated, and I nod.

"I'll tell her," Kayla whispers. We both look at Blake, who is looking at his phone again. Kayla puts on her kindest fake smile and leans toward the woman.

"I'm so sorry, ma'am, but unfortunately we're not going to be able to take this today. It's beautiful, but it's not solid gold." Tears teeter on the edges of the woman's eyes, but she doesn't let them fall.

"How about this?" she says, throwing a cracked Samsung phone on the counter. "Or this? Or these?" she says, yanking fake diamonds out of her ears, pulling an umbrella and a half-empty bottle of perfume out of her purse. We can't give her money for any of it. Blake looks nervous, like a baby animal. I wonder if I should tell him to go into the storeroom, so he doesn't have to see where the money for his Jordans and Air-Pods and scuba diving comes from, but I don't. Rob told us to show him how it's done.

"Please?" the woman whispers. A line is building up behind her.

"We could give you twenty dollars for the phone, to help you out," Kayla says, which is what we say when we want people to get mad and leave. Right on cue, the lady says, "I would never sell my phone for twenty bucks. That's insulting, you know that? I have dignity. You think I have no dignity, is that it?" She grabs her chain and paces around by the TVs. Blake elbows me.

"Can't we just loan her some money? Isn't that what we do?" he says. His voice isn't as deep as it was earlier. I shake my head.

"We can't do anything without good collateral," I say. I can tell he doesn't know what "collateral" means, but I don't have time to explain it to him. "The chain isn't real gold," I whisper.

"But look how upset she is. Shouldn't we make an exception?" Blake says, way too loudly. You should never let customers hear you talking about them. I want to shush Blake, but I don't.

"She could be lying," I say.

"Look at her. She's not lying," Blake says. I look at Blake's pale, shiny face and realize he has probably never had to lie in his life—maybe tiny lies about homework, but nothing big. If you've never had to lie, you don't know easy it is if you have no other choice. His face seems to morph from something sexy into something vulnerable and soft.

"You have no way of knowing that she isn't lying," I say to Blake.

"But it's not fair!" he says, so loudly that people in line peer over each other's shoulders at us.

"Shut up," I hiss.

"You shut up," Blake says. "You don't know what you're doing. Give that woman some money, or I'll tell my dad." His chin is quivering.

"Are you crying?" I say.

"No," he says, even though he's clearly about to cry.

"Dude, you can't cry in front of customers. Bite your tongue and breathe in through your nose and out through your mouth. It works," I say.

"Don't tell me what to do!" Blake yells. He wipes his nose with the back of his hand and walks toward the lady with the plated chain. He taps her on the shoulder and she jumps. You should never surprise a customer like that. He leans too close to her and says, too loudly, "My dad owns this whole place. I'm going to get you your money so you can help your daughter, okay?" He smiles at me like he thinks he's a hero. I want to slap him. Then he runs into Dad's office with the chain and I follow him.

"Hey, pal. We're a little busy," Rob says.

"They're cheating people!" Blake sniffles. "Dad, you have to do something!" My dad stands up.

"Woah woah. Slow down. Jackie, what's happening?" Dad says.

"Somebody wants a thousand-dollar loan on a plated chain and we're not giving it to her," I say flatly.

"Sounds fair enough," Dad says.

"But we're cheating her!" Blake says again. His voice is squeaky. "Her daughter is sick."

"You can't know that, buddy. Sometimes people lie about that sort of thing to try to get our emotions on their side," Dad says.

"What if Jackie's lying?" Blake says.

"Jackie doesn't lie. She's got integrity," Dad says. I feel my face getting hot. I do have integrity, but I lie all the time.

"All you have to do is look at it through a loupe," I say. I grab the chain from Blake and hand it and my loupe to Rob. "Right there," I say, pointing to the scratches. Rob grips the loupe and narrows his fat eyes.

"Yep, that's plated alright. No can do, amigo," Rob says. Dad gives me a thumbs-up under the table.

"This is so unfair," Blake mutters.

"Sorry, pal. That's business. Gotta man up," Rob says, and laughs. Dad and Aubrey and I laugh too, because we have to laugh when Rob laughs at his own jokes. He is the boss. I take the chain and my loupe and walk back out to the floor. Blake follows me. His shoulders are hunched. The after-work rush is starting. Kayla is running from counter to counter, trying to help everyone.

"Geez. Welcome back. Way to strand me," she says. "Test that amplifier. Then test that drill. Then get that Gucci link chain out of the safe and clean it 'cause the guy called and he's picking it up and he sounded mad." I look for Blake to tell him to help us. He's sitting on the floor behind the counter, looking at his phone.

"Didn't your dad say you're supposed to help us?" I say.

"I'm taking a break," he says. I have to fold my lips into my mouth to keep from laughing. He didn't do anything useful and now he's decided that he gets a break.

"Okay, enjoy your break," I say. I can feel my crush on him drying up like water on sand. I start testing the drill. Then I feel Blake tapping me on the ankle.

"Don't you think this whole place is kinda messed up?" he says. His eyes are wide and shiny, like a baby seal's.

"Well, this whole place pays for your life," I say. He blinks, stunned. It's like I've just told him that Santa doesn't exist.

He puts his AirPods in and I go back to testing the drill. Then I try to pick up the amplifier that needs to be tested, but it's too big and I stumble and fall, so I slide it across the floor to the outlet. Blake doesn't offer to help. I tell Kayla to throw away the *Do you like me?* note, and she does.

AS WE PACK the jewelry into the safe for the night, Rob watches every move we make.

"I want you to know that stealing is not the way to success," he says.

"Absolutely," we say. It's almost funny that he thinks we'd be dumb enough to slip jewelry into our pockets right in front of him. He would never guess that we're smart enough to have almost $5,000 of his money hidden in maxi pads in the bathroom.

As I'm wrapping the chains in paper towels before they go in the safe, I hear Blake scream. We run to the storeroom. My heart beats in my throat.

Blake is holding Cheri. She's still wearing Kayla's sweater. His arm is around her waist. Her boobs are jiggling in his face. Her hair is swishing against his shoulders. We run toward him.

"Sorry," Blake says. "I found this and I thought it was a dead body for a second." Rob starts to laugh. He roars and claps his hands. The dads stare at me and Kayla.

"Priceless!" Rob hoots. He gets out his phone and takes a picture of Blake holding Cheri. Blake slides her down his body so her feet touch the ground. He blinks like a deer. I don't think he knows what Cheri is for.

"Somebody pawned that? How much did you get for it?" Rob asks, looking at the dads.

"I don't know anything about that item," Dad says, cracking his neck.

"Don't be embarrassed, Devon. She's beautiful," Rob says. He takes Cheri from Blake and holds her up to Dad's face and makes kissing noises. It makes me queasy.

"It wasn't Devon. We helped the customer who pawned her," Kayla says.

"God. Hilarious," Rob says. He takes a selfie with Cheri. Dad looks at me. His face is pale.

"How much did you lend on it?" Rob asks us.

"We lent five hundred on her," Kayla says. "The guy never came back." Rob laughs and laughs. He can't get a hold of himself. Even when he stops laughing, his belly keeps jiggling and then he starts laughing again.

"My God, and it'll sell for what, eight hundred?" He runs his fingers up and down Cheri's legs.

"What else are you girls hiding from us? Huh?" he says, still laughing.

"Nothing!" We say in unison.

"I don't know if I believe that," Rob says, taking a step closer to us. I breathe in and out and then he says, "I'm just messing with you." Then he touches my hair. "You know what?"

"What?" we say.

"I'm going to a bachelor party for my buddy Steve in a couple of weeks. Third time's the charm with wives, they say. I might just have to make this be his wedding present. Blakey, what do you think?" Blake shrugs. He looks confused. "We're doing it," Rob says. "You wanna ring me up, Devon my man?" Dad picks at the side of his thumbnail.

"Yes sir," he says. Dad rings Rob up and hands him a receipt like a zombie.

"Woo!" Rob yells, and slaps Cheri's butt. "Blakey, you wanna carry the merchandise?" Blake shakes his head. Rob heaves Cheri over his shoulder. "Come here, you," he says. Cheri's hair drags on the floor and Rob steps on it.

"I'll carry her!" Kayla says, and takes Cheri from Rob.

"Be my guest," Rob says. Kayla carries Cheri on her back, the way she carries me. Cheri's eyes open and she looks relieved. Rob snaps a picture of Kayla carrying Cheri and says, "Priceless," again.

"Delete that," Aubrey says sharply. Nobody ever tells Rob what to do, not even Dad. I wait for Rob to get mad, but he doesn't. He just says, "You're right, man. My bad." He twists up his face like he really does feel bad.

We walk to Rob's car in silence. I touch Cheri's legs. My legs feel a lot like her legs now, even with the red bumps. I suddenly wish all the hair I shaved off of me would grow back and I would have legs like a gross little kid again. Kayla slips her sweater off Cheri and puts it on.

Rob takes Cheri from Kayla when we get to his car. He shoves Cheri face down in the back seat and squeezes her butt. I hope Steve is kind to her, whoever Steve is. I hope Rob didn't just make Steve up so that he could have sex with Cheri.

When Dad and I get home later, he stands in the kitchen. He cracks his neck so much it sounds like he's popping bubble wrap. I can tell he wants to talk to me so I sit on the floor and watch TV until he's ready. Finally, he says, "Baby, do you have any questions about anything?"

"I know about what Cheri is for, if that's what you mean," I say.

"Cheri?"

"The doll."

"You named her?"

"No, she came with that name. That's what the manual said." Dad pushes his fingers deep into his eyes.

"You read her manual?" he asks. I nod. I hear him whisper, "Shit," but I pretend not to hear. "So you know about what happens when a man and a woman love each other?"

"You mean do I know about sex?" I say. He cracks his neck and I say, "Yeah, I know about it." He blinks his eyes like he's trying to wake up from a bad dream.

"And you know you never need to do that before you're ready. Right? If a guy tries to touch you and you don't want it, you call me and he's dead. He's dead in the street. I would go to jail for life before I would let that happen to you." The veins in Dad's head are bulging.

"I know," I say, though it's scary to think about someone making me have sex with them, and it's even scarier thinking about Dad killing someone and going to jail. Dad looks scared too. I think about hugging him, but I don't.

"Do you have any questions?" he asks again in a small voice.

"No," I say. "Do you have any questions?"

"Jackie, if I had a dollar for every question I have, I would, God, I would buy you a yacht. I'd buy you a horse. I'd buy you this whole world." Then he laughs, but it sounds more like crying.

"Do you want a hug?" I say. He opens his arms and I sink into his Paradise Pawn shirt. I can hear his heartbeat. He smooths my hair hard, like he's trying to scoop something out of my brain. I feel a drop of water sliding down my hair and the back of my neck. I look up at his face. He is crying. I pretend not to notice and I put my head back on his chest.

"I'm just so sorry," he says.

"It's okay," I say, even though I don't know what he's saying sorry for. I put my feet on top of his feet the way I used to when I was little. Dad laughs and marches me around on his feet. He can't lift his feet as high as he used to when I was little, but he shuffles back and forth across the living room. He sings the marines' song, just like he always used to when I was a kid and I marched on his feet. I don't know how he knows the song. He was never a marine.

"First to fight for right and freedom and to keep our honor clean. We are proud to claim the title of United States Marine," we sing together.

Then he says, "Okay, bedtime." I climb off his feet and he salutes me.

"I love you," I say.

"Love you too," he says, and kisses my hair.

CHAPTER 14

ON MONDAY MORNING, THE DADS ACT LIKE SCARED fish around us. They dart away when we look at them. They make us do safe inventory so we're not out on the floor, like they think that just because we read Cheri's manual, we're going to kiss every construction worker and banker who comes in the store. Since we're not on the floor, the sales numbers for the day will be terrible, and Rob will have even more to yell at us about when he and Blake get back from the aquarium. What's even worse is that when we're not on the floor with customers we can't do the plan and we're already way behind on our numbers for the week.

"I'm not mad at you. I'm mad at myself," Dad keeps saying.

"Don't be mad at yourself, Devon. It's fine," Kayla says.

"It's not fine," Dad says, kneading his eyebrows.

"Just let us be out in the store. Please, Dad," I whine. "We're so bored."

"Not gonna happen. Not today. Get the safe open and do some inventory," he says. He hands us clipboards and highlighters, then leaves us.

"I'm going to die of boredom," I say, banging my head against the safe.

"No, you're not. Come on. Put in your code," Kayla says, so I do. To open the safe, two people have to put in a code. Then you have to wait for two minutes so that in case someone is standing beside you with a gun and trying to rob the store, you can press your panic button and there's time for the police to arrive. All the Paradise Pawns have the same kind of safes. They're so strong that once, in Orlando, someone tried to break into the safe with dynamite and they couldn't.

In the safe are hundreds of doll-sized envelopes. They have dates scrawled on them in black Sharpie. The top shelf is where the oldest envelopes go. Some of the stuff in them was pawned before Kayla and I were born. They're all things that people don't want to give up, like wedding rings and lockets with hair in them and tiny boxes of dead people's ashes. People come back and pay interest on them month after month. Even though they know they may never have the money to get them out, they'll keep paying us, just so we don't sell their items to someone else. Lifers—that's what the dads call the people with envelopes on the top shelf.

We do inventory on a box of chains, then a box of earrings. I check the time on a rose-gold Versace watch in the safe. It's not even 11:00.

"Ugh," I say. I flop on the ground and drop my clipboard. It slides across the floor and bangs against the filing cabinet. I roll onto my stomach. The cement is cold against my cheek.

"Oh, stop." Kayla says, yanking my shirt.

"I'm dead. Let me rest in peace," I say. I flutter my eyelashes and roll my eyes way back so that only the white part is showing.

"Ew," Kayla squeals. She grabs my ankle and drags me across the floor. "I guess I'd better bury you. Where do you want to be buried?" I put a hand on my forehead.

"The beach," I say.

"You got it," Kayla says. Then she lets go of my leg and lies down next to me and we are quiet.

"What do you think it's like to be dead?" Kayla says finally.

"Probably boring," I say. "Even heaven sounds kind of boring to me."

"Don't say that," Kayla says, and crosses herself. "I bet you can pick if it's boring or not. Like hot and cold knobs on a bathtub. You can pick boring or exciting. Kid or grown-up. Take care of people or be taken care of, and you can have it be totally different every day if you want," Kayla says.

"Wouldn't that still be boring, if you just knew you could always turn your excitement knob down if things got too exciting?" I say.

"I think it would be nice," Kayla says.

"We'd better die on the same day so we'll be able to find each other in heaven. I bet it's like an airport up there when you first arrive."

"We'll find each other," Kayla says. "It's heaven, remember?" Our stomachs rise and fall in the same rhythm.

"We'll go to heaven, right?" I say.

"I think so," Kayla says. I close my eyes. If heaven turned out to be just lying on a floor talking to Kayla, I would like heaven a lot. I reach for her hand and squeeze it. Then she says, "Well, since we have to finish inventory and you're dead, that leaves me no choice."

"What?" I say.

"I have to tickle you." She sticks her fingers into my armpits. I scream and tickle her back. I'm laughing so hard I can barely breathe.

"Okay, stop!" I gasp, and she stops. I catch my breath and we brush the dust off our pants. "Can it be like this forever?" I sigh.

"You sound so cheesy. You're like a girl in a bad movie talking to her boyfriend who is, like, going to war," Kayla says.

"I mean it," I say. Kayla wraps her arms around my shoulders. "Can it?"

"If it's like this forever, then how will we go to heaven? How will we get rich? It's not supposed to be like this forever. Nothing is supposed to be one way forever," Kayla says.

I want to tell her that my version of heaven would be being fourteen, or maybe twelve, with her forever, but I don't want her to make fun of me, so I just say, "Yeah, good point."

CHAPTER 15

ON THE LAST DAY OF SUMMER, THE DADS LET US leave before the lunch rush to bike downtown and buy our school uniforms at Uniform Depot. I pedal and Kayla sits on my handlebars. I weave through a cruise ship family with ice cream dripping down their chins, then through a crowd of Haitian construction guys, and then I turn into the strip mall parking lot. We lock my bike and go inside. Uniform Depot is thick with crinkling plastic and little kid sweat. Moms tug on hems and tighten belts. Kids shiver and bounce in new plaid skirts and stiff shoes. Two girls from our grade are huddled around the mirror—Harley and Addison. When no grown-ups are watching, they fold over each other's skirts so the hems slide up their legs. I don't want them to notice us, but they do.

"Kayla!" Harley squeals. Harley was the third-prettiest girl in our grade last year and she's gotten prettier over the summer. Her skin has cleared up and the ends of her hair are dyed purple. Kayla runs to her. They cling to each other and rock back and forth, hugging the way you should only hug your best friend. The girls swallow Kayla. They touch her hair and her arms and her face. She laughs with them.

"Where have you been? I freaking miss you," Addison wails.

"Just working," Kayla says. "I'm so excited for school to start. I've missed you girls too." I hope she's lying. She must be lying. I know she didn't miss them. She had me.

I wait for her to reach her hand out from the swirl of girls and pull me into it, but she doesn't, so I pretend to be very interested in my fingernails. I wait some more and when I can't wait any longer, I find the rack of St. Bridget's uniforms—the green skirts and white shirts and silk scarves we have been dreaming about since fourth grade. I press each scarf on the rack into my cheek. Harley and Addison will never get to wear a St. Bridget's scarf.

I choose the two softest scarves and a small skirt and shirt for me and a medium skirt and shirt for Kayla. I push through a crowd of elementary school kids trying on shoes to get back to Kayla. She's already zipped into a public school uniform and Harley is folding over her skirt.

"Hey," I say, but no one hears me over the kids screaming about their shoes. I duck into the changing rooms. I unbutton my Paradise Pawn shirt and slide into my St. Bridget's skirt and shirt.

The shirt is thick and buttery like it's made of the inside of a croissant. I fold the collar around my necklace so my broken heart pendant is centered. I spin and the skirt twirls more perfectly than any skirt that has ever touched my legs. I watch the body of a St. Bridget's girl with my face on top swirling in the mirror until I am dizzy.

I wish my face was a little prettier to match the pretty uniform, but someday it will be, when I know how to do my makeup and I don't have pimples. Kayla is already pretty enough for a St. Bridget's uniform. I march out of the dressing room, back to the clump of girls.

"Kayla!" I yell. Harley's head whips around.

"Jackie!" Harley croons, pretending like she didn't see me when I walked in with Kayla. "What's good?" Kayla's eyes fall on the medium St. Bridget's skirt and shirt on hangers in my hand. She pulls away from Harley and says to me, "Are you trying on the medium too? I think the small looks good on you." Then she gives me a look that I don't understand.

"No, the medium is—"

"You might grow. Maybe you should get both," Kayla interrupts.

"Yeah I hear the food is really good at St. whatever it's called—maybe you should get a large, just in case," Addison says. Everyone laughs, even Kayla. I laugh too, so that they're laughing with me, not at me.

I didn't expect that going to St. Bridget's would make girls like Harley and Addison decide to like me, but I hoped it would make them jealous of me or scared of me, or at least make me less scared of them. When the laughter dies down, I say, "Your uniforms really look good," even though they don't. They look cheap and scratchy. My uniform looks like cursive writing, like money, like pearls. Their uniforms look like grocery bags.

"True that," Harley says. "Girls, we do look good." She wraps her arms around Kayla and Addison and they all pose in front of the mirror. I wait for someone to tell me that my uniform looks good too, but no one does, not even Kayla. When Harley and Addison go to look at shoes, Kayla whispers to me, "Put that medium back! Are you crazy?"

"You have to get it today. Otherwise the price goes up," I say.

"Just put it back," she says. "And whatever you do, don't say anything to the other girls about me going to St. Bridget's."

"Why?" I say.

"Um, I don't know, maybe because we're stealing the money to pay for it and I already told them I couldn't afford it, so if all of a sudden I can afford it they could get suspicious?" she hisses.

"Oh, yeah. Good point," I say.

"Use your head, Jackie," she says. I nod and follow her as she walks toward the other girls. "Give me a little space," she whispers.

Then she follows Harley and Addison to the shoe rack and doesn't invite me. I pretend to look out the window. Then I go back in the dressing room. I carefully unbutton and fold my skirt and shirt. They don't feel as special as they did ten minutes ago.

As we're leaving, Harley and the other girls kiss and hug Kayla.

"See you so soon!" Kayla chirps at them.

On the bike ride back to Paradise, Kayla pedals and I sit on the handlebars with our folded uniforms against my chest. Kayla only got a public school one.

"You were being super mean in there," I say.

"You were too," she says.

"How the heck was I being mean?" I say.

"You were rubbing it in everyone's face that you're going to St. Bridget's."

"No, I wasn't," I say. "Plus, those girls wouldn't even want to go to St. Bridget's. They're trashy."

"Don't say that. Of course they would want to go to St. Bridget's if they could. It's not like they don't care about their futures, but they can't even start to want that kind of thing. Addison lives in a motel and Harley's dad is in jail. Did you know that?"

"No," I say.

"Yeah. Her whole family has to drive four hours to see him on the weekends. So for her mom to even think about spending money on St. Bridget's—no way. But that doesn't mean she doesn't wish she could go. It doesn't mean she doesn't resent people with money for that kind of thing."

"What does 'resent' mean?" I say.

"Well, it's like us looking at those kids at the breakfast buffet at the Ritz-Carlton. We can't even really start to want what they have, or understand what it would be like to have it, but we still hate them a little bit for having it, you know?" Kayla says.

"So you think Harley and them will resent you if you tell them you're going to St. Bridget's? That's why you didn't want me to tell them. It wasn't really about keeping the plan secret, right? It was about you not wanting to be resented," I say.

"Yeah, kind of," she says. "I need allies."

"I'm your ally," I say.

"Yeah, but you won't be at school with me tomorrow." The reality of going to school without Kayla sinks into my skin like something cold and awful. I've thought about it before but it always seemed far away. Now it's really happening.

"Well, it won't be like that for long," I say.

"Yeah, I know," Kayla says, but she doesn't sound like she believes what she's saying. I turn around on the handlebars to hug her and I almost tip us over. She laughs and I laugh and I try to feel like everything is okay even though it isn't.

CHAPTER 16

A RADIO AD ABOUT PARADISE PAWN'S BACK-TO-school sale on laptops and tablets ran this morning and the store is bubbling. People buying laptops are like people buying cars. They get mad if we tell them a laptop has problems, but they get just as mad if we tell them it works perfectly, because they think we're lying to them. The solution is usually to make up a tiny problem the laptop has, fake smile, and say "bandwidth" and "firewall" and "gigabyte" like we know what we're talking about until they buy it.

Kayla and I dump our school uniforms in the storeroom and run to the case where we keep the laptops. I sell laptops to a tugboat captain, a banker, and a man with a parakeet in a cage.

As I'm spreading out the tablets we have left to fill the empty space, I watch a customer walk toward the engagement ring case and drum his fingers on it.

"Looking for something special?" I ask him.

"Yes, really special," he says, almost in a whisper. "I'm asking my girlfriend to marry me. She thinks I cheated on her, but I didn't. This is the only thing that will fix it. I have the hotel room and the roses already. I need a diamond, though. Something big. Something that says—'Trust me.'"

"You've come to the right place," I say. I unlock the case and pull out three diamond rings. I place them on a display pad and hold them up to him.

"What's your name?" I ask.

"Marcello," he says.

"Great to meet you, Marcello. I'm Jackie," I say.

"Put that one on," Marcello says, pointing to a yellow-gold princess-cut ring. I slip the ring onto my finger. It's too big for me. Marcello reaches for my hand and holds it up to the light.

"How about that one?" he says, pointing to a pear-cut white-gold one. I try on fourteen more rings for him. Each time he grabs my wrist and twists it around to see the diamonds in different kinds of light.

"Let me see that one in a box," he says when I try on a marquise-cut rose-gold one. I stack all the rings on my thumb so he doesn't steal them and I reach under the counter for a black velvet box. I peel off the *Made in China* sticker and tuck the ring inside. I hold the box in my palm, then I open and close it a few times while he watches.

"It's gorgeous!" I gasp, pretending to be his girlfriend. "Of course I'll marry you!" I expect him to laugh but he doesn't. He chews off his pinky fingernail.

"Put this one on," he says, reaching for another marquise-cut ring that a divorced tourist just sold to us. I slip the ring on my finger. It's a size eight. It's too big for me. "Now put it in the box," he says, and I do. I hand the box to him. He opens and shuts it three times. I need to get him to commit. I need to make buying this ring feel inevitable.

"What are you going to say to her when you propose?" I ask.

"You want to hear?" he says.

"Yes sir," I say. Marcello takes his phone out of his pocket and reads, "Maria, baby, the first time I saw you, I knew I wanted you forever. I love you. I love your smile. I love the way—hang on," he says. "I'll skip that part. That's just for her. And this part." It's probably something about how he likes having sex with her. I hope it will make her feel respected and not weird. He scrolls through his phone, then says, "Okay, this is the last part: I'll love you when you're mad. I'll love you when you're sad. I'll love you even when you hate me and I hate you."

"That's the end?" I say.

"Yeah. What do you think?" he says, biting his nails again. I watch Kayla lift a TV over the counter. I love her even when I hate her and even when she hates me. I watch Dad clipping a bracelet to an old man's wrist. I love him even when I hate him and even when he hates me.

"I think it's beautiful. I think she'll say yes," I say. He takes the marquise-cut ring out of the box.

"Put it on again," he says, and I do. "Can you polish it for me?" he says.

"Of course, sir," I say.

"What's the price on that one?" he says.

"Two thousand three hundred," I say.

"Are you serious?" he says, and presses his fingers into the sides of his head. "Damn."

"I mean, if you're not sure how much you love her, I could show you some smaller diamonds," I say.

"No, God no. I love this girl to death. I'll do it. I'll do it," he says. He pulls out his credit card and hands it to me. I shake his hand, still wearing the ring.

“I’ll get it all buffed and shined for you. She won’t know what hit her,” I say, which is what Dad always says when he sells engagement rings. I scan Marcello’s ID and fingerprint him and swipe his card. “It’ll be just a moment while I get this cleaned for you,” I say. “We’re having a sale on laptops and tablets. My colleagues would be glad to show you some.”

“I think I’ve given you enough of my money for one day,” he says, but his eyes drift to the tablet case and Kayla swoops in.

“Feel how light this iPad is,” she says to him, and he curls his hands around it.

I take the engagement ring to the jewelry cleaning room and dust it with red chalk. Then I turn on the buffer and hold the ring up to it with the tips of my fingers. If you hold your fingers too close to a buffer, it will buff your skin off. Then I heat up the ultrasonic, dump solvent in it, and let the ring soak. I glance back at the tablet case. Kayla is showing Marcello a mini iPad. He’s going to give us more of his money. Dad always says that customers don’t stop buying unless we stop selling, so we can never stop selling.

I flip off the ultrasonic and blast the ring with steam. Then I go into the bathroom, lock the door, and squirt soap on the diamond toothbrush. I put the ring on my left hand and scrub with my right hand. I imagine Maria’s finger sliding into the ring. I imagine her whispering to Marcello, after she’s said yes and they’ve kissed and had sex and they’re lying in the hotel bed together, “How much did it cost?” and Marcello telling her, “Two thousand three hundred,” and her kissing him again and him thinking that he’s glad he gave us so much of his money.

I close my eyes and keep scrubbing. I watch Marcello and Maria kissing like a movie in my head. Then I hear something clink against the bottom of the sink. I open my eyes. On my finger is a ring with four naked prongs poking out of it. The diamond is somewhere in the bubbles at the bottom of the sink. I paw through the bubbles, popping them as fast and as carefully as I can so I don't push the diamond down the drain, but there's nothing but crusty white porcelain beneath them.

I poke my fingers down the drain. It is cold and empty. I slip out the door and grab a flashlight and shine it down the drain, but all I can see is mold. I poke my head out the door again. Camilla is standing by the TVs and Dad is flirting with her. He's sliding his fingers up and down her arm. He'll be mad if I interrupt him. I run back to the jewelry cleaning room. Next to the buffer is a bag of CZ stones—little glassy stones that look just like diamonds. There's a marquise-cut one. I wedge it into the ring. It's the perfect size. I think about setting it and giving it back to Marcello, but I decide it's better to get in trouble with Dad than for Maria to wear a fake engagement ring for the rest of her life. I pull the CZ stone out of the prongs and run behind the counter and poke Dad in the back.

"Can I talk to you?" I ask, tugging him away from Camilla.

"What?" he groans. Marcello looks up from a laptop Kayla is showing him.

"How's my girl's ring doing?" he says, grinning.

"Great," I say, and give him a shaky thumbs-up.

"I dropped a diamond down the drain," I whisper to Dad. He fake smiles at Camilla and says, "I'll be right back." He follows me into the bathroom and whisper-yells, "You did what?" I hold up the empty ring.

"It went down the drain," I say. Dad mashes his thumbs into his eyes.

"Come on, Jackie. Why do you do this to me?" he says. He reaches for a wrench and sticks his head under the sink. His nose is inches from our box of pads filled with money. I can't believe I forgot to hide it. My lungs feel like they're full of sand.

"Jack-Jack," Dad says to me, his head still under the sink.

"Yes?" I say, trying not to let my voice shake. He crawls out from under the sink and stands up, holding the box of pads. I feel like the blood in my stomach is turning to cement.

"Are these yours?" he asks

"They're Kayla's," I say, grabbing the box from him. He nods.

"Tell me if you ever need that stuff, right? Like, if you get your period?"

"Ew," I say. He laughs a little and reaches for my hair with his wet hands. I try to make myself breathe.

"I'll buy you whatever you need, whenever you need it, as far as tampons and all that," he says. "Do you know how it works? Like, how it comes once a month? Unless you're pregnant, which you won't be for a long time?"

"Yeah, I know how it works," I say.

"And do you know how to use these? I think this is the kind that you don't stick inside you, right?" He reaches for box of pads and I jerk it away from him. I shout, "Look!" I crouch by the sink and I hold up the CZ stone. "It didn't go down the drain! It's right here."

"Thank God," Dad says. "Good eyes."

"I'll put it back in the ring," I say. Dad will know it's a CZ stone if he looks at it under his loupe. Usually he doesn't let me set stones, but he wants to get back to flirting with Camilla.

"Okay," he says. "Just be careful, and don't forget to polish the prongs when you're done."

"I will," I say. Slowly, blood seeps back into my limbs.

"You know you can talk to me about that stuff, right?" he says.

"What stuff?" I say. He looks at my shaking hands.

"Period stuff. I know it's a little scary," he says. He thinks I'm shaking because he's talking about periods.

"Yeah. Really scary," I say.

"I get it. It's a weird time, puberty. But I'm here for you, okay? It happened to me too. Not, like, girl puberty and periods, but other stuff. Boy puberty. I get it. Or at least I'll try to get it," he says. He pulls my head against his chest and kisses my hair. "Love you," he says.

"I love you too," I say. When he leaves, I pump air back into my lungs and tuck our pads back under the sink. I look for the diamond one more time, but it's probably in the ocean by now.

As I set the CZ stone in the ring, I hope God is busy helping people get out of a burning building or blessing a baby at a baptism or doing anything besides paying attention to me. I wonder if God would love me even when he hates me.

Maria will never know that her ring is fake. She will know that Marcello paid $2,300 for it—that she is worth a lot of money to him, which is the most important part of an engagement ring. A ring is meant to convince people that someone's love for them is real, and a fake ring can do that just as well as a real ring, as long as nobody has a jewelry loupe.

I finish setting the stone, I polish the prongs, and I blow dust off everything. I close my eyes and whisper to God, "Look, I know I'm doing something wrong. I get it, but it's a small wrong thing that is part of a much bigger right thing. If Dad had found our money, our whole plan would have been ruined. Do you get it? I hope you get it." I breathe in and out and wait to see if maybe I'll hear God talking back to me. "If I'm a bad person for doing this, will you give me a sign or something?" I say. I watch the big grandfather clock on pawn tick for one minute. God doesn't send me any kind of sign, so I push the ring into a box and walk back out to Marcello. Kayla has sold him an iPad to give to Maria along with her ring. I give her a subtle fist bump.

"Here's your ring," I say to Marcello. "She's a lucky woman."

"Thank you," Marcello says, his eyes shining. I feel guilt sloshing around in my stomach. I hope it's not a sign from God that I'm a bad person. I decide it's not.

✷

USUALLY, WHEN WE CLOSE THE STORE on the night before the first day of school, there's a nervous shimmer in the air. Me and Kayla go over our plans for where we will sit at lunch and assembly, which pockets of our backpacks will be for pencils, which will be for gum, what we will do with our hair. Tonight we are quiet. Once we've packed up the safe, we meet in the bathroom to count our money from the day.

"Are you okay?" Kayla asks me. "You've been acting kind of weird."

"Yeah, are you?" I say. She nods.

"Sorry for the stuff at Uniform Depot," she says.

"It's okay," I say. I want to tell her about the diamond in the drain, to cry into her Paradise Pawn shirt and tell her I'm worried I'm turning into a bad person, but I can't. If I tell her, she will say that I should tell the dads. They would call Marcello, he would have to tell Maria, and everything would turn into a huge mess.

"It's insane that I won't see you at school tomorrow," Kayla says. I nod. I'm worried that if I say anything I'll start crying. "Don't worry, though," Kayla says. "It'll be okay. You'll have fun." I wrap my arms around her like she's a paper bag of groceries about to rip and spill. I don't want to have fun tomorrow. I don't want her to have fun either. If either of us has fun, we could trick ourselves into thinking we don't need each other anymore. I grab Kayla's broken heart necklace and fit it together with mine.

"Best friends," I whisper.

"Obviously," she says. I hold on to her for a few minutes longer until Aubrey knocks on the bathroom door.

"Hey, Kayla, your mom has dinner on the table. Let's get a move on," he says.

"Coming," Kayla says. She squeezes me and then lets go. My necklace lands back on my chest with a thud. Carter sets the alarm and we walk out to the parking lot. It's starting to get darker in the evenings. It smells like fall.

"I'll miss you," Kayla says.

"I'll miss you too," I say. I'm worried that I mean it more than she does.

When Dad and I get in the truck, he turns on the radio and brushes his fingers through my hair. His hand is warm.

"Nervous?" he says.

"About tomorrow? No," I say.

"Are you going to be okay without Kayla?" he says.

"Yeah," I say.

He opens his mouth to say something else and I say, "Can you just shut up?" It comes out way meaner than I want it to.

"Geez," he says. The skin on his face seems to wilt. He takes his hand off my head and puts it back on the steering wheel. "I feel like something is wrong. Is something wrong?"

"Nothing is wrong," I snap.

"Please don't lie to me, Jack-Jack. It scares the bejesus out of me."

"I'm not lying!" I say.

"Well, I can tell something is wrong. You don't have to talk to me about it, but don't lie," he says.

"I'm not lying," I say through my teeth.

"Honestly I think it'll be good for you to go to school without Kayla. You can put yourself out there a little."

"I don't want to put myself out there!" I yell, louder than I mean to. Dad fiddles with his chain and cracks his neck.

"Okay, well, I think you're going to do great tomorrow."

"Whatever," I say. "I'm done talking to you." I feel bad as soon as I say it. I shouldn't be so mean to him, but I can't help it. There are too many worries ricocheting around inside me. I look at myself in the mirror on the back of the sun visor and mash white gunk out of the pimples on my forehead. I can tell Dad thinks it's gross, but he doesn't say anything.

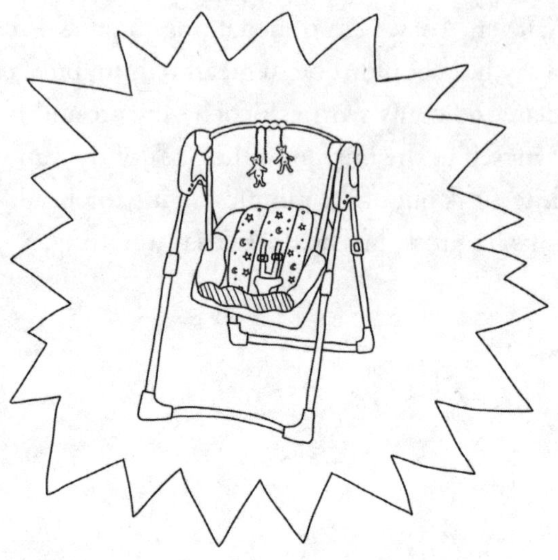

CHAPTER 17

WHEN I WAKE UP, DAD IS ALL EXCITED ABOUT MY first day of school. He says I can put chocolate milk on my cereal like I do on my birthday, but I don't feel like eating and I'm worried the chocolate milk will make me gassy, and I already have a stomachache.

"Thanks, but no thanks," I say. He squeezes my shoulder and looks a little sad.

"Hey, you know you're going to crush it today, right? You're going to knock their fancy knee socks off." He reaches for my hair to smooth it and I slap his hand away harder than I mean to. "Ow," he says.

"Sorry," I say. "I just can't have the grease from your fingers on my hair. It's already too greasy."

"Well, it looks great to me," he says. I roll my eyes at him without meaning to.

"Sorry," he says in a small voice. I want to say sorry too, but he gets up and goes to the bathroom. I smash my Cheerios and regular milk into a pulp and pour them down the sink.

Then I go into my room and look in the mirror. My St. Bridget's uniform doesn't feel like it did in the dressing room. It's tight in all the wrong places and loose in all the wrong places, because it's designed for a girl with actual boobs and a bra. I think about wearing my bikini top with toilet paper in it, but I might have to hug people, and when you hug someone, you can tell if you're hugging real boobs or a bunch of toilet paper in a swimsuit. I scrape oil off my forehead with a scratchy towel until my skin turns red. I pull my hair into a ponytail six times and it looks worse each time. Kayla would have done it perfectly the first time. Dad knocks on my door.

"How's it going in here? You about ready?" he says.

"Leave me alone!" I yell.

"You need to get there on time, Jack-Jack. And if you're early you're on time, right? So we gotta leave in about ten minutes, okay?" he says. I kick the wall and hurt my toe. I can't bear to look at myself in the mirror again, so I march out of my room.

"You look gorgeous," Dad says. He reaches for my hair and then stops himself.

"Don't lie," I say.

"I'm not. Why would I lie to you?" he says, blinking at me like a confused dog.

"Whatever," I say. We drive to St. Bridget's in silence. Dad doesn't even turn on the radio. My stomach feels like someone poured candle wax into it and it's starting to harden. I should have eaten something, but it's too late now. Kayla always has packages of peanut butter crackers in her backpack. For a minute, my brain forgets that she won't be at school. I imagine eating peanut butter crackers in the bathroom with her and my stomach starts to feel better just thinking about it, but then I remember that I won't see her for an entire school day and I feel even worse.

There's a wall around all of St. Bridget's with curls of barbed wire on top. It's like a prison, except they're trying to keep people out, not keep people in. Dad pulls up to the guardhouse. The guard is an old lady. She has dangly earrings and a pin shaped like an apple that says *I'm a teacher. What's your superpower?* She's not even a real guard. She's just a teacher. Her superpower definitely wouldn't help if someone tried to rob St. Bridget's.

"Welcome, sweetheart," she says to me. I don't know what to say back and she chuckles at me. I glare at her and she stops. The school building is shiny and white, like a wedding cake. The parking lot is made of creamy cement with no cracks in it. Dad pulls the truck in between a Bentley and a Land Rover. I watch through the windshield as the St. Bridget's girls pose on the glossy white steps while their moms and nannies take their pictures. They know how to smile and pop their hips like girls in catalogs. Their nannies are Filipina. Their moms are white and wrinkled and hold yoga mats or paper cups of coffee or both. There are no other dads. Not even one.

"Let's get your picture!" Dad says, unbuckling his seat belt.

"Don't get out. Are you crazy?" I say through my teeth. Dad looks through the windshield. Then he blinks like he's trying to get something out of his eye and whispers, "Jesus."

"Sorry," I say. "Bye." I kick open the door of the truck, get out, and then slam it shut. I hide behind the Land Rover until Dad pulls away, so people won't see that I got out of a falling-apart truck with Paradise Pawn junk in the back. I feel an ache for Kayla in my veins. Dad waves goodbye out the window and I pretend not to see him. I look in the Land Rover's side-view mirror and try to arrange my face into a bored, relaxed smile.

Then I walk toward the steps, bouncing myself up and down the way a girl who thinks she's pretty would walk.

"Hey!" someone yells at me. I turn around and smile, ready to make my first St. Bridget's friend. Then, like a bad dream, one of the nannies steps out of the crowd, reaches for my hand, and shakes it.

"You're from Paradise Pawn, aren't you?" she says. She holds her wrist in front of my face. On it is a rose-gold watch that I sold to her on layaway last year. "I love it there! Such great deals!" She puts her hands on my shoulders. One of the St. Bridget's girls laughs at me with her eyes.

"I've never been to Paradise Pawn. You must be thinking of someone else who looks like me. Sorry," I say. The nanny looks confused. I pull away from her and run inside.

The hallway is swarming. The other St. Bridget's girls have faces and hair and bodies that are pretty enough to match our uniforms. Some of them are wearing lace bras. I can see the outlines of the bras beneath their uniform shirts. The girls all know each other's names. They have been at tennis camp and sailing camp and surfing camp and horse camp together all summer. Their moms are friends. Their nannies are friends. Their dads work at the same banks and golf at the same golf places. I stand close to groups of them and try to laugh when they laugh like I know what they're talking about.

We are herded into a big room with dark wooden benches in it. An old man in a suit gives a speech, telling us we can be whatever we want to be. I am the only girl listening to him, because everyone else has someone's hair to play with or someone to split a stick of gum with or someone to whisper to. They don't need anyone to tell them they can be whatever they want to be. They already know, because they are rich.

At lunch, there are quinoa burgers and soup that smells like feet and nothing but fruit cups for dessert. I wander around with my quinoa burger, pretending to look for a friend. I half expect someone to tell me I can sit down with them, but no one does, so once I've walked past every table, I stand in the corner and pretend to be really interested in the bulletin board. There are still twenty more minutes of lunch left. I eat a few bites of my quinoa burger. It's like swallowing gravel.

I feel a swelling ache in my chest for Kayla. When the bell rings, I am swept up in a river of plaid and blonde. Everyone is too busy giving each other piggyback rides and passing around a bag of sour Skittles to notice that I am alone.

In math, the teacher passes out calculators the size of shoes. Everyone pokes at the buttons and makes graphs on the screens. I get so confused that I ask to go to the bathroom so I don't cry in front of everyone. I sit on the floor, rolling toilet paper into bracelets until the end of the period.

When Kayla gets here, she will understand how to use the calculators and she can explain it to me. She will make friends here too. Making friends is like breathing for Kayla. When she gets here and makes friends, her friends will have to be nice to me because I am her best friend.

When the day is over, the other girls wrestle violin cases and squash rackets and horse-riding helmets out of their lockers.

"What is that?" I ask a girl dragging an instrument the size of a surfboard.

"A harp," she says. "Do you do any after-school activities?"

"I'll probably just go on my dad's boat," I say.

"Ooh, invite me!" she says. "My brother barfed in the hold of our boat last weekend and now it smells weird. Which marina is your boat in?"

"I have to pee," I say, and I run away and hide in an empty classroom for a while.

When I go outside, I see Dad waving at me in a crowd of moms and nannies. There are a few other dads, but they're all wearing fancy shirts and talking on their phones. Dad is wearing his Paradise Pawn shirt, grinning at me and waving like he's trying to tell an airplane where to land.

"Why aren't you in the car?" I hiss at him.

"Wow," he says. "Are we going to do this until you're eighteen?"

"Do what?" I say.

"Are you going to keep acting like you're embarrassed to be seen with me?" he says. I'm not just acting like I'm embarrassed to be seen with him, I really am embarrassed to be seen with him.

"I don't know," I say quietly.

"Well, this doesn't feel like a very fun way to go through life for either of us, so we need to figure something out," Dad says.

"Whatever," I say quietly. Dad opens his mouth to tell me to be respectful, but then he is quiet. He cracks his neck and says, "Was it a hard day? Were they nice to you?"

"It was great," I say, trying hard to sound like I mean it.

"Okay. Whatever you say," he says, even though I don't think he believes me. I wish he would ask me more questions, but he's probably scared that I'll keep being rude to him. He turns on the radio. I hunch against the window. My skirt itches.

"HOW WAS SCHOOL?" I ask Kayla as we change out of our school shirts and into our Paradise Pawn shirts in the storeroom. It's the first time we've ever had different school uniform buttons to unbutton or zippers to unzip. It's the first time I've had to ask her, "How was school?" because every other day of school has been the same for us. I want her to say school was miserable, but she talks about Harley and Addison and some boys I don't know and about how someone threw a pencil at the ceiling tiles and it stuck and about how she's going to try out for a play and she has to prepare a song and she's thinking of running for ninth-grade student council president and she has to design posters by Friday. I stop listening.

"How was it for you?" she says.

"Awesome," I say, and I walk out behind the counter. When it starts raining and traffic gets slow, Kayla takes a piece of paper out of the printer. She writes *Kayla McCabe for Ninth Grade President* on it. She shades the letters with pencil so it looks like they're three-dimensional. Then she draws a picture of herself talking into a microphone and an American flag flying behind her. It's a good drawing.

"Why do you want to be president if you're just going to leave to go to St. Bridget's next semester?" I say.

"Why is it your business?" she snaps.

"Geez," I say.

"Sorry," she says. "I'm not trying to be mean. Just, you don't have to stick your nose into everything I'm doing all the time. Okay?" she says.

"Fine," I say, and I walk away. When it gets busy again, Kayla puts her poster design away in the storeroom. I look at it when I'm getting a necklace out of layaway. It looks really good. She'll probably win. Part of me wants to crumple it up, but I don't.

As I'm putting a laptop on layaway for a family from Honduras, I see Harley and her mom get off a bus in front of the store. Harley skips toward the door, flinging her hair around. Her mom follows behind her, carrying a baby swing. I buzz them in. Harley runs to Kayla and they hold each other by the shoulders and jump up and down. I stamp the family's layaway contract, then I crouch behind the counter. Harley's mom pushes the baby swing across the floor. I don't stand up.

"Hello?" Harley's mom says, sounding annoying, just like Harley. Harley's mom has a double chin and she smells like onions and cigarettes. Dad comes out of the storeroom holding a stack of video games.

"Jackie! Look alive! Help this woman out!" he says, and jabs me with his knee. "Sorry, ma'am," he says to Harley's mom. My face is burning but I stand up and slap on a smile.

"How may I help?" I say.

"Hey, Jackie," Harley says in a fake-nice voice with a fake-nice smile. "Get my mom a good deal on her swing, okay?" Then she leans over the counter and wraps her arms around Kayla again.

"May I see your ID please, ma'am?" I say to Harley's mom. She looks more like Harley in her ID picture—prettier and meaner. I type in her birthday. She is forty-seven. She probably won't have any more babies who need a baby swing.

"Friday? Maybe," I hear Kayla say. Harley looks at me and fake smiles. Then she says, loudly, to make sure I can hear, that on Friday night her brother and his friends are going to Rum Beach and one of them has a jet ski and one of them has a crush on Kayla and Kayla *has* to come and she can borrow one of Harley's bikinis.

Harley's mom doesn't hear them. She passes the baby swing over the counter to me.

"I'll be back for it," she says. I know she won't. She's a perfect target for the plan. Kayla peels herself away from Harley and jogs over to me.

Give her the full amount. Don't do the plan, she writes on a Post-it note. I shake my head.

Not fair, I write.

Come to the beach with us on Friday. We can meet high school guys! she writes.

"I don't want to! I don't want you to go either. It sounds dangerous," I whisper. "I'll only not do the plan if you promise you won't go to the beach with her."

"Jackie, that's not a fair trade," Kayla whispers. There's a line forming behind Harley's mom.

"What's going on?" yells a guy in a construction hat. Aubrey and Dad come out of the storeroom. I crumple the Post-it note and fake smile at them.

"Girls, what's with you? Chop-chop!" Dad says. "I can help you over here," he says to the construction worker.

"Whatever. Do it," Kayla whispers. "I'm going to Rum Beach." My hands are shaking and I'm too mad and sad to do math without messing it up, so I just write $50 in the computer and get $50 out of the cash drawer. I test the baby swing. It is rusty and it whines with each swing, like there's a ghost baby in it.

"Sign here," I say to Harley's mom. Harley and Kayla are giggling again. Harley digs through her backpack and hands Kayla something. It's a gold bikini. Kayla holds it up to her boobs and they glint like they are eighteen karat.

"So hot," Harley says.

"Thanks," Kayla says. They whisper some more until Harley's mom tells her it's time to leave.

"Love you," Harley says to Kayla, loud enough so I can hear.

"You too," Kayla says.

"Bye, Jackie," Harley says. I don't say anything. She and her mom get back on the bus and I put the baby swing in the storeroom. Kayla tries to catch my eye and smile at me, but I glare at her.

"Jackie, you should come on Friday," Kayla says, draping her arm over my shoulders, like that's going to make me stop being mad at her.

"No way," I say, and shake her off of me.

"Harley invited you. She's honestly so much nicer than she was when we were little," Kayla says.

"She's only nice to you," I say.

"She was trying to be nice to you but you were acting all rude and shy," Kayla says.

"She doesn't like me," I say.

"Just give her a chance," Kayla says.

"I don't know why you want to be friends with her. You're only going to be at that school for like another three months." Kayla sighs and starts Windexing the jewelry cases.

"Can I be honest for a second?" Kayla says.

"Okay," I say.

"School was fun today. It wouldn't be the worst thing ever if I didn't go to St. Bridget's," Kayla says.

"Don't say that!" I say, slamming my hand against the counter.

"I mean, obviously I missed you, but other than that it was pretty cool. High school is a lot bigger than middle school. There are tons of people all rushing around doing different things. It's exciting," she says. I kick the wall.

"Don't you care about your future?" I say.

"Yeah, but if you think about it, the plan could be bad for my future too. Don't you think? With Rob snooping around so much recently, it just makes me nervous."

"Is this 'cause Harley is your new best friend now?" I say. Kayla sets down the Windex like it is very heavy. She breathes a long breath out of her nose and I feel it on my shoulder.

"No, Jackie. It's not about that. You're still my best friend. I'm just trying to think about the big picture of my life and whether or not this thing we're doing is worth it," she says.

"It's obviously worth it," I say. I walk away from her toward the appliances, and I start rearranging the coffee makers.

Later, when we're wiping phones in the storeroom, Kayla says, "I'm going to try on this swimsuit Harley loaned me. Will you tell me how it looks?"

"Ew, no," I say.

"Don't say ew. Why are you saying ew? That's mean," she says. She turns her back to me, pulls her Paradise Pawn shirt down around her waist, and starts twisting the gold strings of the bikini over her shoulders. She looks so beautiful.

"I'm not trying to be mean," I say.

"Then what are you trying to be?" she says. I don't know what I'm trying to be. She stands up tall and looks at her reflection in the shiny deep fryer on pawn. Her reflection is blurry, like an Impressionist painting of a girl in a bikini.

"I just want us to be the same," I say, my voice squeaky. Kayla turns away from the deep fryer and breathes out another deep breath.

"Well, that's not realistic. We're different. And we're probably going to keep getting more different as we get older. But that's not a bad thing," she says. "And I'm really not trying to leave you out. You can come to Rum Beach too. I keep saying that."

"But you know I don't want to go to Rum Beach, so by going you are leaving me out!" I say.

"Well, sorry, but I'm fourteen and you are too, and if you don't want to be left out, all you have to do is stop acting like a kid and being so scared and weird about everything," Kayla says.

"All you have to do is stop acting like a grown-up!" I yell. Kayla laughs a mean laugh.

"I couldn't stop acting like a grown-up if I tried," she says. "Look at me." She stares at her boobs and her stomach reflected in the deep fryer. She stands up tall at first. Then she hunches. She looks a little confused and sad, like something ended before she was able to say goodbye. I crawl across the floor. I sit on her feet and wrap my arms and my knees around her calves.

"You're trapped," I say. I mean it jokingly, but she just sighs and says, "Yeah."

*

KAYLA GOES TO RUM BEACH with Harley once, and then twice, and then more times than I can count. She goes to parties in people's apartments with no parents. Sometimes her jeans smell like cigarette smoke.

I stop calling her on Friday nights to come over and make English muffin pizzas or make ant houses or ride on my bike or do any of the things we used to do, because whenever I call, she invites me to do something else with a bunch of her new friends, and I say no.

I tell myself that as long as we stay on budget for the plan it will be better soon, because we will be at St. Bridget's together. The pads under the sink are getting fat with bills, like Easter-egg–colored wallets. Sometimes, I sit on the bathroom floor and open the pads and gaze at the presidents on the bills the way girls in movies gaze at pictures of their boyfriends. I whisper to the presidents, "Kayla and I will be the same again soon, right?" and I pretend they tell me we will.

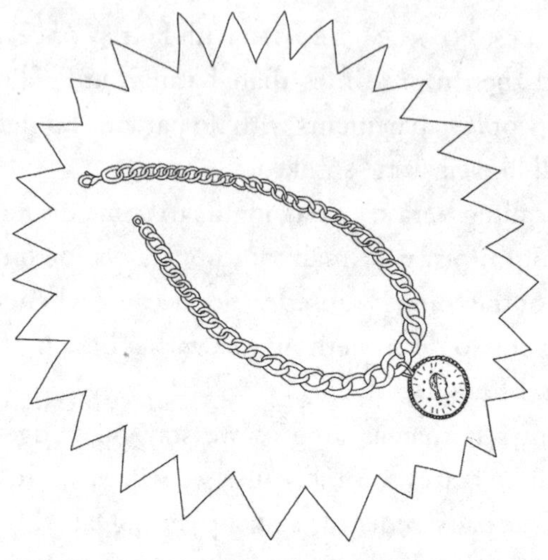

CHAPTER 18

I HAVE NO ONE IN THE WHOLE WORLD TO TALK TO. I barely talk to Kayla anymore. I want to, but she doesn't seem to want to talk to me. No one at school knows who I am, so no one talks to me, including the teachers. I don't like talking to Dad anymore, even though he wants to talk to me. I still love him, obviously, but I feel like every time I'm in a room with him for more than ten minutes, I accidentally get annoyed by him and then I say something mean. It's like sometimes I turn into an evil daughter who yells and knows the perfect thing to say to make him sad. Because of that, I talk to him as little as possible.

It's getting colder up north, which means there are plenty of cruise ship moms for him to bring home. He used to tell me funny stories about them, but he doesn't anymore.

I don't eat breakfast with them anymore either. I hear him waking them up and sending them home before I get out of bed.

The box of pads at the store gets so full that Kayla and I start taking cash home in little bits each day.

One night, I lay all my bills out in a huge, metallic-smelling quilt on my floor. When Dad knocks on my door, I expect him to say he's going out, so I open the door a crack and press my nose through it and say, "Have fun!" He laughs a little.

"I'm not leaving you," he says.

"What do you want, then?" I say. I try not to make my voice sound mean, but it still does.

"Well, I was hoping I could talk to my daughter quick, if there's time in her schedule," he says. He puts his hand on the door and starts to press.

"Stop!" I say, shoving my shoulder into the door. "Sorry, I just have some private stuff in here," I say from behind the closed door. I can picture his sad face and I don't want to open the door and look at it.

"That's cool. I get it. We all have our private stuff," Dad says.

"Thanks," I say.

"Would you want to clean it up and then we could talk in your room, or would you want to come out here and talk? I just have something to tell you."

"I'll come out there," I say, trying my best to sound like a nice, not-annoyed daughter. I slide through the door and leave it a crack open so I don't seem suspicious.

"Is it any kind of private stuff that a dad could help with? Or someone else could help with?" he says.

"Nope," I say, giving him a big, fake smile. He's so skittish around me these days, like he expects me to yell at him at any moment. I reach out and hug him. Something about the hug feels different. Usually the pendant on his chain presses into my cheek when I hug him, but it's not there. "Dad, where's your chain?" I say.

"Oh, don't worry about it," he says.

"No, what's wrong?" I say. "Something's wrong."

"Nothing is wrong. I just don't want you to get mad at me," he says. It's like I'm the father and he's the daughter. I take a deep breath and say, "I'm not going to get mad." He blinks at me for a while.

"You sound like you're mad already," he says.

"Well, I'm not. Okay? What were you going to tell me?" I say.

"Yes, sorry. I made an orthodontist appointment for you," he says.

"A what?" I say.

"To get braces." I think he's joking and waiting to tell me something worse, but he's quiet.

"That's it? Dad, why would I be mad at you about that? That's fine," I say. His shoulders relax and he rubs my arm like a kid rubbing a blanket to feel safe.

"Oh, okay. I'm so relieved. See, I'm just not very good at knowing about these kinds of things, but when I went to Parents Night at St. Bridget's, I couldn't get over everybody else's teeth. I know that sounds weird, but I had this realization like, 'Jackie can't have teeth like me when she's older. She's got to have teeth like these people.' So I made the appointment. It's at a place called Snyder Smiles. Supposed to be the best in Cherry Beach. That's why I don't have my chain on right now. I pawned it so we can pay for the braces."

"Oh, okay," I say. "Thanks."

"It's not that your teeth aren't beautiful just the way they are. You know that, right? It's just a weird way that people signal that they're high class—having straight teeth—and I want you to be able to send the right signals."

"Okay," I say. I wish I could smooth his hair to make him stop worrying, the way he smooths my hair, but that would be weird. "Is that it? That's what you were going to tell me?" I say.

"That's it," he says. He leans close to me like he's going to kiss my forehead and I get worried he'll see the money on the floor of my room through the crack in the door.

"Don't!" I scream. I shove the door closed and stand in front of it. Dad looks down at the floor and kicks one foot with the other.

"This is what I mean," he says softly. "I feel like I never know when you're going to be mad at me these days."

"I'm obviously going to be mad when you look in my room without asking!" I say. I slip through the door backward and slam it shut. I feel bad as soon as the noise of the slam leaves my ears. I sit on the floor and watch Dad's toes curl nervously into the carpet. I take a few deep breaths and I say, "Thank you for the braces," but he's gone.

I START TO STARE AT PEOPLE'S TEETH, even when they aren't smiling. It's true what Dad said—rich people have big, shiny teeth in rows like airplane seats. Poor people have brown teeth and yellow teeth, huddled together in the corners of their mouths, like craggy rocks.

I don't have to go to school on the morning of my orthodontist appointment and Dad is taking the morning off from Paradise. When I walk into the kitchen, he's not wearing his uniform shirt. He's wearing an ironed white shirt with all the buttons buttoned. He's trying to look like a St. Bridget's dad. His shirt kind of looks like the other dads' shirts, but the rest of him—his hair and his skin and his teeth—look like they always do. There's beef jerky, a package of peanut brittle, a bag of popcorn, a plate of apples and licorice, and three packets of gum laid out on the table.

"Ta-da!" Dad sings.

"What is this?" I say.

"It's all the foods you can't eat when you have braces. A last hurrah, kind of." I think about him walking around the empty grocery store last night, all by himself, with a list from the internet of all these things, piling them into a cart, hoping I will stop being so mad at him if he buys them for me.

"Thanks, Dad," I say. "You're really nice." He looks surprised.

"Oh, I don't know about that," he says, smiling. "I guess I get it from my daughter." We lean against the counter eating beef jerky with our jagged teeth. It's the last time my teeth will ever look like his.

In the car, I cross my fingers and make a promise to myself that I won't be mean to Dad, but I'm worried I won't be able to keep it—not because I'll be mean to him intentionally, but because I do mean things by accident when I'm nervous.

We pull into the Snyder Smiles parking lot. All the cars are way nicer than our truck, just like at St. Bridget's. The Snyder Smiles sign says *Parents Trust Us. Kids Love Us.* The part about kids is probably a lie.

Everything inside Snyder Smiles is white and shiny, like a spaceship, but instead of people floating around, it's like gravity is pulling everyone down even more than usual. Kids and parents yawn and look at their phones. I sit across from a girl with a red streak in her hair and rubber bands in her mouth. I watch them stretch when she yawns. She must be rich if she has braces, but she doesn't look rich. She's older than me and she's wearing makeup on her eyes, but she isn't very pretty. She'll never be pretty no matter how straight her teeth are. The girl takes a pen from the reception desk and draws a skull on the side of her shorts. Then she draws a winking emoji on her hand. She's pretty good at drawing. I look at her until she looks up at me and then I turn my head and pretend to be looking at the fish tank.

A nurse with pink pants and a pink shirt says, "Jacqueline?" Dad and I walk with her down a hallway. The drawing girl follows me with her eyes and then gives me a rubber-band-y smile. I'm so surprised that I forget to smile back until it's too late.

The nurse is named Abbie. Her name tag says so. It's shaped like a big, smiling tooth. The tooth's smile has teeth too. Someone should have realized that is weird.

"Have a seat right here, my friend," says Abbie. I wonder how many kids say, "I'm not your friend," when she says that. I don't say it, I just think it. She's fake smiling. I wonder if Abbie has a boyfriend. I wonder how she smiles at her boyfriend. She has one silver tooth at the back of her mouth. I wonder if she gets embarrassed by it, hanging out with all of these people who care so much about teeth. Abbie sits me in a cold chair and gives me a bright orange too-big T-shirt.

"This is for you, my friend," she says. On the front, the shirt says *Snyder Smiles: Parents Trust Us. Kids Love Us.*, just like the sign. On the back is a picture of a penguin.

"Let me tell you something super cool. Are you ready?" she keeps talking without waiting for me to say if I'm ready. "Every time you wear your shirt to your appointment, you get twenty Snyder bucks!"

"What are Snyder bucks?" I ask.

"Great question," Abbie says. "Snyder bucks earn you prizes. You can get them by wearing the shirt, like I said, and by filling out your brushing and flossing log that we'll get for you here in just a sec."

"But is it actual money? What's the conversion rate?" I ask. Abbie laughs and so does an older, uglier nurse with her fingers in somebody's mouth.

"That's my girl," Dad says, and laughs a little too. I feel myself starting to get mad at him. I wasn't trying to be funny.

"Well, hon, you get prizes," Abbie says. "For instance, if you earn two hundred Snyder bucks, you get a Smoothie King gift card," she says.

"Wow," I say, to be polite. Abbie fake smiles at me.

"You also get to take home your very own state-of-the-art electric toothbrush today," she says, handing me a toothbrush in a package the size of a shoebox.

"Thanks," I say.

Then Dr. Snyder himself saunters toward my chair. He smiles like he thinks he's handsome because he eats a lot of Caesar salads and goes to the gym, but he's not. He has badly dyed hair and two pimples on his chin.

"I'm glad you got the memo," he says to me.

"What memo?" I say

"That it's no smiling day." He gives me a dopey clown frown. I give him a weak smile to shut him up. He puts on blue gloves and pokes his fingers around the insides of my cheeks. I think about biting him, but I don't. I don't want to embarrass Dad, not when he's gone to all the trouble of ironing his shirt and taking off work.

Dr. Snyder's watch knocks into my ear. I twist my head to get a better look at it.

"Oops, hold still for me now, Jaqueline," he says. His watch is an Omega from the Prestige collection. It's definitely real.

"How many Snyder bucks did that watch cost?" I ask, but nobody understands me because my mouth is all clogged up with Dr. Snyder's blue fingers.

"What's that now?" he asks, with his fingers still in my mouth.

"Never mind," I say, and he smiles—a Snyder smile. The ugly nurse clips a bib around my neck to catch my saliva. Her name is Miranda. It's too pretty of a name for a person who spends her days clipping on saliva bibs. They all lean over my face with blue masks and blue fingers. Dad holds my hand, which is embarrassing, but I let him.

About an hour later, I have braces. They claw the inside of my mouth like a cheese grater grating wet, fleshy cheese. Yesterday, when Dad showed me the different colors on the Snyder Smiles website, I picked "sea green." I liked the color on the website, but I didn't think about how sea green would look on my teeth. It looks disgusting. I bet no girls ever choose sea green. Probably not many boys do either, unless they're the weird kind of boys who like Legos and books about frogs.

"Wow, look at you, baby!" Dad says, squeezing my hand. I pull my hand away from his. He should have told me sea green was a bad idea. I look terrible. My whole face aches.

Abbie leads us into a little room with no windows and a poster that says *Today is the first day of the rest of your life* with a tooth on it. She says I look great, and I was so brave. I don't look great and I've done much braver things than open my mouth and let people mess with my teeth. She hands Dad some forms on a clipboard.

"Oh-kay," Abbie sings. "That's the payment plan for you to look over, Dad," she says.

"He's not your dad," I say under my breath.

"And for you, Jaqueline, let's talk about taking care of your beautiful new smile." She holds up a giant plastic model of a mouth with braces on the teeth. The mouth is open, like it's screaming for help. "Meet my friend here," Abbie says. Dad fake laughs. Then his phone buzzes and he answers it.

"Aubrey?" he says. "I'm so sorry," he mouths to Abbie.

"You're fine," she says. Her teeth are smiling, but her eyes are annoyed. While Dad plugs one ear and says, "Okay" and "Got it" into the phone, Abbie leans toward me.

"So, Jaqueline, what do you do for fun?" she asks.

"Ride horses," I lie.

"Oh, that's amazing. Do you have your own horse?" Abbie says.

"I have three," I say. On the phone, Dad says, "Was he drunk or just high?" Abbie's smile tightens.

"What are your horses' names?" she says.

"And the police found the bracelet in his underwear?" Dad says. Abbie's face twists. She pretends like she's not listening to Dad, and like she still believes that I have three horses.

"I'm so sorry. Little crisis at work," Dad says. "Do you mind if I just run over there and come back in twenty minutes?"

"Certainly," Abbie says, "though you'll need to pay for the braces first." Dad cracks his knuckles.

"Can't I leave her and the braces here and come back?" Dad says. "I'll be right back."

"That's not really our normal protocol," Abbie says. Dad tugs on the collar of his fancy shirt. I realize that normally when he's annoyed, he twists his chain around his thumb, but his chain is in the safe at the shop now, racking up interest on the money that paid for my sea-green braces.

"I certainly understand that, ma'am, but this is an emergency. I'll be right back, okay?" he says. "Jack-Jack, you and your teeth stay here." Before Abbie can argue, he's jogging out to the truck. Abbie throws her hands up and says, "Just wait in the lobby then, I guess, and don't go anywhere." She's annoyed at us and she's done talking to me about my fake horses. I sit in a cold chair in the lobby and read an article in a women's magazine about "12 Sneaky Secrets to Trick Yourself into Losing Weight." They're all pretty depressing, like "Sit in front of a mirror while you eat dinner so you'll notice if you're overindulging." Then I hear someone say, "What's up?" It's the girl with the rubber bands in her mouth. She's sitting at the tiny table in the children's play area, building an Eiffel Tower out of the blocks.

"Hi," I say, and walk toward her. I wait for her to say something, but she doesn't, so I ask, "What did they do to your teeth?"

"Who knows?" the girl says. "It only took about twenty minutes, but I always tell my mom to come back in two hours so I can miss school and chill here for a while."

"Wow," I say.

"I'm kind of a vigilante," she says.

"Okay," I say.

"Have a seat," she says, as if it's not weird for us to be sitting on tiny chairs with teddy bears on them when there's a whole room full of grown-up chairs. I sit. "I'm Beth," she says.

"Jackie," I say.

"Well, Jackie, let's have a look," Beth says, and points to my mouth. I part my lips and the braces scrape against my cheeks. "Sea green," Beth says, nodding. "Dope."

"Seriously?" I say. I smile, even though it hurts to smile.

"Yeah, the sea green works for you. With your eyes. It's unique. Not many people pick sea green."

"Thanks," I say, still smiling. Beth's braces are hot pink and black. I decide I will get that next time they tighten mine and I get to change the colors.

"Do they hurt?" Beth says. I nod. "Can I show you a magic trick?"

"Okay," I say.

"Well, I can't actually show you, but I'll tell you about it. See that toothbrush?"

"Yeah, they told me about it. State-of-the-art, right?" I say.

"No, they didn't tell you about it. Abbie and Miranda and all of them did not tell you what you need to do with that toothbrush. If you're only using that thing on your teeth, that's a crime against yourself and against women everywhere," Beth says.

"What are you talking about?" I say. Beth leans across the tiny table.

"That toothbrush works as a vibrator—like the world's best vibrator ever," she whispers.

"What's a vibrator?" I whisper.

"Wow, seriously? How old are you? You are so lucky I'm explaining this to you. This is going to change your life. A vibrator helps you masturbate."

"You mean like what boys do?" I say.

"Oh dear God," she says, not whispering anymore. She slaps the table and the Eiffel Tower wobbles. "See, this is the problem with our society. I wrote a paper on this for my debate class. Boys get to talk about masturbating all they want, but everybody freaks out when girls talk about it. Everyone freaked out when I wrote my paper about it, even. It's completely unfair. It's like—what is this, the Stone Age?"

"Wow," I breathe. I have goose bumps. I'm half grossed out and half amazed. The receptionist gives Beth a quiet round of applause and Beth salutes her with two fingers. They must know each other well if Beth hangs out in the waiting room for two hours after every appointment.

"Alright, logistically speaking, you've never done this before, right?" Beth says.

"You mean masturbated?" I say, as quietly as I possibly can.

"Yeah," says Beth. I shake my head. Beth puts her hands on my shoulders.

"Okay. This day is going to go down in the history of your life," she says.

"Okay," I say. Beth clears her throat.

"Basically, you put the batteries in your toothbrush, wash it off with soap and warm water so you don't get an infection, then go to town on your private parts," she says.

"How?" I whisper.

"However you want. Just try a bunch of stuff. It might not work the first time, but if you practice a little bit, you'll get it.

And when you get it, you'll know." I nod and try to act like I talk about masturbating all the time. "Trust me. It makes the whole braces thing totally worth it," Beth says.

"Okay," I say quietly. "But doesn't, like, God say you're not supposed to do that? Even for boys?"

"No, Jackie, that's where you're wrong, and where a lot of people are wrong. This toothbrush is why I believe in God. He definitely wanted us to do this, or he wouldn't have made it feel so good." She doesn't seem like she knows very much about God, but I don't want to be rude.

"Okay," I say.

"Where do you go to school?" she says.

"St. Bridget's," I say.

"Ha!" she says. "Then you need this even more than I thought. My condolences."

"What does that mean?" I say.

"It means I feel bad for you. I go there too."

"You do?" I feel like a little helium balloon has attached to the top of my head—like maybe I'll have someone to talk to at school and I won't have to feel heavy and scared all day. I say, "I've never seen you before. I feel like I would have because you're—" I don't know how to say what I'm trying to say without sounding mean.

"Because I don't look like all the other clones?"

"Well, yeah," I say.

"Thank you. I guess I keep kind of a low profile. I'm not really an extracurriculars kind of person. But I'm there, unfortunately."

"Cool," I say.

"For the record, you don't look like the clones either," Beth says. In a way, she's saying that I'm not pretty, because the clones are pretty. If she were a different person saying that, it would feel mean, but I can tell she means it as a compliment.

"Thank you," I say.

"You're welcome," she says. "You a freshman?" I nod.

"What are you?" I ask.

"Sophomore," she says. "Are you in A lunch?" I nod again. "I'm missing lunch today, 'cause I'm hanging out here, but you should sit with me tomorrow," she says. I feel like the balloon will lift me up through the ceiling of Snyder Smiles and into the clouds. I will have someone to sit with at lunch—a weird someone, but a weird someone is a million times better than no one.

"Thank you," I whisper. Without thinking, I lean across the table and hug her. She hugs me back. She doesn't make me feel weird. I feel her fingers pat my shoulder blades and her warm breath on my neck. I feel like I could cry from happiness.

"Don't mention it," she says. Then we sit quietly, adding to her Eiffel Tower. Beth puts two Lego people on top of it.

"Oh no, Pierre, I'm scared of heights!" she says in a French accent. "Me too, Marie!" she says in some other kind of accent. I laugh with my whole body. It feels like I'm breathing air after being underwater for too long.

"Let's get down from here and eat some escargots!" I say. Beth smiles.

"Oui oui," she says, and I laugh some more. I look out the window and see Dad jogging across the parking lot. He runs through the door, panting.

"Hey, baby," he says. He has pawnshop dust streaked across his white shirt and his collar is crumpled. I wait to feel embarrassed the way I usually do when Dad is around St. Bridget's people, but I don't feel embarrassed in front of Beth.

"This is my dad," I say.

"Hi, sir," Beth says.

"Mornin'," Dad says. I don't want to leave Beth and go back into the room with Abbie.

"Jackie, what's your number?" Beth says.

"Oh, I don't have a phone," I say, and somehow I don't feel embarrassed about that either.

"Old school. I like it," she says. I laugh for no reason. "How about if I meet you by the lunch line tomorrow?"

"Okay," I whisper.

"Don't forget what I told you about that toothbrush, okay?" Beth says, and winks. I've never seen someone my age actually wink.

"Okay," I say, feeling jittery in a good way.

"Hasta mañana," Beth says, giving me a two-finger salute. I giggle.

"Should we go pay an arm and a leg for these braces now?" Dad says. Beth laughs at Dad's joke and I smile.

"I guess so," I say. I stare at Beth for a few more seconds and then I say, "Thank you."

"Give 'em hell," she says.

"Did you make a friend?" Dad says.

"Yeah, she goes to St. Bridget's," I say. I watch Dad breathe in and out with his shoulders, like he's feeling the balloon feeling, too.

"That's fantastic, baby," he says. "I told you you'd be okay without Kayla. You're both finding your own way," he says. I feel something bristle inside me.

"No!" I say too loudly. "It's not like that." Dad's shoulders tense again.

"I didn't mean it as a bad thing. You can have more than one friend, baby," Dad says.

"But Kayla is my *best* friend," I say.

"I know that. I didn't say she isn't," Dad says. I glare at him, even though I don't mean to. "Sorry. I was just trying to say I'm proud of you for making a friend."

"Whatever," I say. I march ahead of him into the windowless room where Abbie is waiting for us.

"Where were we?" Abbie says in an annoyed way.

"I was going to give you a chunk of change for these things on my daughter's teeth, I think, unless you want to give them to us for free," Dad says. He's trying to make a joke, but Abbie doesn't laugh. She looks at us like we're not the kind of people who are supposed to be at Snyder Smiles.

"That's correct," she says. "We were going over the payment plan." When Abbie ducks her head under the desk to fish for some papers, I say, in what I hope is a nice voice, "Was everything okay at the store?"

"Drunk guy tried to steal that big Gucci link bracelet in the display case. Carter tackled him and got it. Then he threw up on the cello and some tourist called the cops. No biggie. The cello can be cleaned up. I know a guy," Dad says. Abbie pokes her head out from under the desk like she's afraid to come out. Dad looks a little embarrassed that she heard him. I wonder how much money Abbie makes. I wonder if it's more than Dad.

"So what we've got here is the payment plan," Abbie says. "I'll need you to sign and date a few of these." I pull my chair up to the desk so I can see. I add up the payments in my head. Then I add them up again with a pen and a Post-it note shaped like a tooth and I get the same number both times—$6,000, enough for a whole semester of tuition at St. Bridget's.

"Dad," I whisper while Abbie is talking about scheduling my next appointment to get the braces tightened.

"Don't interrupt, please," Dad says, but I have to interrupt.

"This is a total rip-off!" I whisper. "There's no way these things are worth six thousand dollars. That's, like, half a year of tuition at St. Bridget's." Dad puts a finger to his lips and says, "Quiet, Jackie." He looks embarrassed. Abbie keeps talking. I kick Dad's calf and he pretends not to notice. I elbow him and whisper, "Dad, you have to bargain. Come on." He shakes his head and puts a hand on my knee to tell me to stop. I pinch the skin on the top of his hand. He flinches, but he still doesn't say anything. I turn to Abbie. I look right in her eyes.

"Gosh, Abbie," I say. "Six thousand is pretty steep. What would you say to one thousand?" Abbie opens her mouth but doesn't say anything, so I keep talking. I stand up and lean across the table and take her hand. I try not to think about how many thousands of teeth her hand has touched. "We just aren't in a position to pay six thousand dollars for these braces. I like you, Abbie, so let's make a deal. One thousand dollars in cash. Final offer. I don't think you'll get a better offer than that."

"Jackie, stop!" Dad says. "This isn't that kind of place." I look at Abbie, and she's laughing at me. Dad still looks embarrassed, but he starts laughing, too. It's not fake laughing to be polite to Abbie. It's real laughing.

"There's nothing funny about this," I say.

"Baby, it's okay. We have the money," Dad says, putting his hand on my shoulder and trying to get me to sit down.

"Well, first of all, we don't actually have the money, because you pawned your chain," I say. Dad turns red and cracks his neck.

"Jackie, stop," he says.

"If you'd told me braces cost six thousand dollars, I never would have said yes! I don't even want braces. I just did this to be nice to you. I want you to use the money for Kayla's tuition," I say.

"Kayla's tuition has nothing to do with this," Dad says.

"Yes, it does!" I say. I don't want to yell, but it's hard not to. Dad bites his thumbnail.

"Listen, hon," Abbie says, leaning toward me with her Snyder Smile. "You're really lucky that Dad cares about you so much. A beautiful smile is priceless, so you're actually getting a great deal." I glare at her.

"Braces don't make beautiful smiles. Happiness makes beautiful smiles," I say. It's a good line. It sounds like a poem. It's the kind of thing Kayla would say. I watch Abbie cover her mouth because she's laughing at me again. I wish I could smack her teeth out of her mouth.

"Are we done here?" Dad says.

"She has to do the brushing and flossing tutorial," Abbie says, still laughing at me with her eyes.

"Fine. Do the tutorial. I'll finish this up," Dad says, gesturing to the paperwork. Then he turns to me. "I know it doesn't make sense right now. We'll talk about it later, okay?" I don't say anything. "Can I hug you?" he says.

"Fine," I say. I sit down finally and I let Dad hug me. He presses my sore chin into his chest. "You're hurting me," I say.

"Oh God, sorry," he says. He recoils away from me like I'm a hot stove. I should say, "It's okay," because he looks so worried, but I don't.

A different nurse named Bryn shows me how to brush my teeth with my braces. She has white hair and an empty nose piercing hole. I don't listen to anything she says. When she stops talking, I say thank you and walk out to the parking lot with Dad. I feel like a zombie—like everything that used to make the world make sense has been wrung out of me like water out of a washcloth. The truck feels shabby and broken compared to the sleek office.

"Look," Dad says. He turns on the engine and starts driving for a long time without saying anything.

"What?"

"I don't know how to say what I want to say. I think it's because I wish I didn't have to say it, but life isn't fair. I'm spending my money on your teeth instead of Kayla's school, and I know you don't think that's fair."

"Yeah, it's not," I say. I want him to say that he's going to change his mind, or at least that he's sorry, but he just keeps driving and cracking his neck. When we pull into the parking lot at St. Bridget's, he says, "I don't know what to say. I'm just sorry." I get out and slam the door. My teeth ache, and I wish I could cry, but I can't cry at school. At lunch I sit by myself, but I conjure up a little of the balloon feeling, knowing that tomorrow I will be sitting with Beth.

When I get to Paradise after school, Kayla is arranging pulled gold chains on the fuzzy plastic necks.

"Look at you, braces girl!" she says. "You look like you belong on a cruise ship."

"That's not really a compliment," I say.

"I mean it like a compliment. You look rich," Kayla says. I want to tell her how mad I am that $6,000 is glued to my teeth, scraping the insides of my cheeks whenever I talk, instead of in a bank account waiting to pay her tuition, but instead I just say, "Thanks," and I smile, and it hurts.

"I would love to get braces," she says.

"No, you wouldn't. They hurt really bad," I say.

"I wouldn't care if it meant I would have classy-looking teeth for the rest of my life," Kayla says. I have the feeling that I'm watching a movie I've already seen. Then I realize it wasn't a movie—it was a talk we've had before.

"This is like when we talk about bras, except now I have what you want instead of you having what I want," I say. Kayla stares at me.

"Yeah, good for you," she says. She slams the jewelry case shut and all the plastic necks inside tremble.

"Wait, I'm sorry," I say. "That sounded mean."

"It's whatever," she says, walking away from me to get more chains. I sit on the floor and pinch my finger in the door of a jewelry case to try to distract myself from how much my teeth hurt and how bad I feel for saying what I said to Kayla.

When the after-work rush starts at 5:30, I do the plan harder than I ever have. Grown-ups steal from each other every day of their lives—Dr. Snyder, Dad, Rob. They all steal from people, and they're not even stealing to make the world fairer. They're stealing so they can buy golf clubs and gold and stuff to give to women they want to have sex with. I put away more money in two hours than we usually do in two days.

"Slow down," Kayla whispers as I put a $1,000 loan on a fishing rod in the computer and give the guy pawning it $100.

"You're not the boss of me," I whisper back. By the end of the day, I'm sweaty and my teeth are throbbing. I run to the bathroom and start counting the money we made from the plan and folding the bills into pads. I hear a knock on the door.

"Don't come in," I say.

"It's Kayla."

"Oh," I say, and unlock the door. Kayla looks at the piles of bills on the sink.

"We're going to get caught," she says. "What's wrong with you?"

"Nothing's wrong with me. There's a lot wrong with the world, though, and we're fixing it," I say. I sound like a grown-up. I look at myself in the mirror and smile.

"I don't really think we're fixing it. I don't think we can," she says.

"Of course we can," I say. "We can't fix the entire world, but we can fix this little part by paying your St. Bridget's tuition."

"Can I tell you something?" Kayla says.

"What?" I say.

"I won student council president yesterday."

"Why do you look so nervous?" I say. She shrugs.

"I thought you'd be mad," she says. I am a little mad, but I try to smile a real smile.

"No, that's great," I say. "You can be student council president at St. Bridget's next semester," I say.

"Don't you not even like St. Bridget's that much?" she says.

"Of course I like it. It's the best school in Cherry Beach. Plus, education is the key to a good future," I say, which is something they said to us at an assembly in the room with the wooden benches.

"Yeah, but if having a good future means turning into a bitch along the way, I don't think I want that. No offense. I'm not calling you a bitch. It just seems like you don't have many friends there, and if people don't want to be friends with you, they probably suck."

"I do have friends!" I say. "I have this amazing friend named Beth. I sit with her at lunch."

"That's good," Kayla says. "I was worried you were, like, super lonely. I kinda got that impression. But I'm glad you have a friend. We're both finding our ways."

"No, we're not!" I say. "Why does everyone keep saying that? Our way is doing the plan. That's our way. We're not finding it. We know what it is."

"But what if there's a better way? One that's not illegal?" Kayla says.

"There's not!" I yell. Dad knocks on the door.

"What's happening in there?" he says.

"Nothing," we say together.

"Well, if nothing's happening, then let's get a move on. We need help closing out here."

"We can talk about it later," Kayla says, helping me arrange the pads in their box and hide it under the sink.

"Fine," I say. "Congratulations on being president, though."

"Yeah, thanks. I'm super excited about it," she says. I can tell she wants to talk about it more, but I walk out the door and I don't look at her as we pack up.

✷

DAD MAKES ME a smoothie bowl for dinner because I can't chew anything hard. I'm still mad at him, but I say thank you.

"I put the special toothbrush in your bathroom," he says. "Don't forget to do that, right?"

I feel my face get hot, even though Dad has no idea what Beth said to me about the toothbrush.

"I won't forget," I say. I eat the rest of the smoothie bowl too fast and then I run to my bathroom and sit on the edge of the bathtub and stare at the toothbrush. On the box, there's a picture of the toothbrush with blue light shining from it, like the light coming off of Jesus in the pictures of him walking around with lambs on the walls of Kayla's church. I open the box carefully and snip the plastic around the toothbrush with my fingernail clippers. The toothbrush is smooth and sleek, just like everything in Snyder Smiles is. It looks out of place in my crusty bathroom.

I wiggle out of my pants and stand up and scrub the toothbrush around on my underwear like I'm brushing my teeth, but I don't feel anything special. Then I press the button on the side and it hums. It feels itchy, but not in a special way. Then I hold the toothbrush by the thin part and press the handle against my underwear. I move it down underneath the elastic. My underwear is green with little strawberries on it. It came in a ten-pack of underwear with different fruits on each one. I remember buying it with Dad last year. All my fruit underwear is a little too small this year, but I'm embarrassed to ask Dad to buy me new underwear. I slip my other hand down under the elastic. My vagina is slimy. The slime is clear and stretchy. I keep moving the toothbrush handle back and forth. I think I'm doing it right. I feel like my whole body is smiling. I poke my finger into the hole where the slime is coming out. It's warm and soft inside, like an orange in the sun. I wiggle my finger around in the warmth and mash the toothbrush handle deeper into my skin. My heart is beating in my vagina. I'm out of breath. I feel like I'm swimming in a river of honey with jewels in it. It's getting thicker and the jewels are getting brighter until *whoosh*, a wave pushes me out into a honey ocean, and I float there. I sink down, but I can still breathe. I see the jewels falling slowly through the honey around me, and I am falling slowly, too. I feel like God is holding me in that Jesus-y light coming off the toothbrush.

It's the best feeling I have ever felt in my life. I can't believe nobody ever told me about it until now. I sit down on the floor. Then I lie down and press my hot cheek against the cold tile. I close my eyes and swim in a half sleep. Then I hear a knock on the door.

"Don't come in!" I scream, yanking my underwear back up. I open the door and glare at Dad.

"Sorry to bug you. It sounded like you were crying while you brushed your teeth, and I wanted to make sure your teeth weren't hurting."

"I wasn't crying," I say.

"Okay, well, I know it's been a really weird day, and I can imagine your teeth might be sore. Plenty of reasons to cry, if you were."

"Well, I wasn't," I snap.

"Okay," he says. "I brought you an Advil, if you want." He holds out a little orange pill and a plastic cup of water. It's my Clifford the Big Red Dog cup that I used to love. The water is cold, and I swish it around in my cheeks. Dad reaches out to touch my hair and I back away from him. "Sorry," he says. I swallow the water and say, "It's okay."

"Are you worried about something? You seem worried," he says.

"Geez, no, just leave me alone," I say, pushing him out into the hallway and shutting the door.

"Okay, okay, sorry," he says.

I sit down on the side of the tub, holding my Clifford cup. Part of me wishes I could tell Dad what I was doing with the toothbrush. Part of me wishes I could tell him about the plan. Part of me wishes I could tell Kayla that I've been miserable at St. Bridget's even though I think she already knows. I feel like everything I do these days is a secret from someone. Maybe that's what growing up is—having more and more secrets to keep from people until the only person you can really talk to is yourself.

CHAPTER 19

I START EATING LUNCH WITH BETH. I THINK SHE ate lunch by herself every day before she met me. Sometimes we talk and sometimes she reads comic books and I read them over her shoulder. I thank her for telling me about the toothbrush and she says, "It's my duty as a feminist." I don't really know what she means by that, but I don't feel dumb for not knowing. She never makes me feel dumb. Beth doesn't eat the cafeteria lunch. She brings her lunch from home—fancy stuff like sparkling water and sushi that comes in a little box. She shares her desserts with me since the school desserts are always healthy and weird. We have contests to see who can scrape the cream out of her Oreos the fastest. Being with Beth isn't as good as being with Kayla, but compared to being alone, it's like heaven.

“Want to come over to my house?” Beth says one day at the end of lunch.

“Are you joking?” I say.

“No. Why would I joke about that?” she says.

“When?” I say.

“How about today?” she says. “My nanny can pick us up.” It’s the first of the month, which is payday for a lot of people, which means Paradise will be crazy this afternoon with sales and loan pickups. Kayla wasn’t at the store last payday because of a student council meeting. I should get to miss a payday, too.

“Can I use your phone?” I ask Beth.

“Sure,” she says, handing it to me. It’s the new iPhone. I call the store, and Dad answers.

“Thank you for calling Paradise Pawn. How can I help?” he says in his customer voice.

“Dad? It’s Jackie,” I say.

“Hi, baby. Are you okay?” he says. I take a deep breath.

“Can I go over to a friend’s house this afternoon?” I say.

“It’s payday. Store’s going to be nuts,” he says.

“I know,” I say. “Please?” He clears his throat.

“Okay. I guess that’s fine. We’ll manage without you.”

“Are you sure?” I say.

“Yes. I’m glad you’re making friends,” he says. He sounds stressed, but I don’t really care.

“Thank you,” I say. When I hang up, I expect to feel a little guilty for abandoning everyone on payday, but I don’t. I just feel jumpy and excited. Beth grins, and the rubber bands on her braces stretch.

“Yay!” she squeals. Usually her voice is deep, but she sounds like an excited little girl on Christmas. I think Beth needs this as much as I do. That must be part of the reason why people become friends—when they need each other at the same time. Beth leans across the table and hugs my shoulders. It feels different from hugging Kayla. Beth's arms are more muscly. Kayla smells like sweat and body mist. Beth smells like a fancy candle.

In language arts after lunch, I watch the other girls giggling to each other, and I don't feel the wad of loneliness crumpled inside me like I usually do. I have someone to giggle with, too, and I'm going over to her house today. When I felt lonely before, I used to try to remind myself that I had Kayla, but it doesn't feel the same to have a friend at a school halfway across town as it does to have a friend down the hall.

Beth's nanny picks us up in a Land Rover. I've seen her in Paradise Pawn, but I don't think she recognizes me in my St. Bridget's uniform. Beth doesn't talk to her in the car. She only talks to me. I think Beth is a little nervous. Kayla is never nervous around me, but I'm nervous around Kayla a lot. It feels kind of good to have someone be nervous around me.

"So, I was thinking, if you want, we could go in the pool and the hot tub," Beth says.

"You have a pool and a hot tub?" I say.

"Yeah," Beth says.

"That's awesome," I say.

"Thanks," Beth says. Then it gets quiet and a little awkward. It's never awkward to be quiet with Kayla. I weave my seat belt in between my fingers. As we drive, the houses get bigger and bigger. They all have pools. Some of the pools have little waterslides. I hope Beth's has a waterslide. We pull up to a gate, and Beth's nanny types in a code. We drive down a street lined with trees dripping Spanish moss, toward a big cul-de-sac.

"Here we are!" the nanny says. It's the first thing she's said since we got in the car.

"Thanks," I say. We walk inside, and Beth's nanny carries our backpacks. There's a sparkly chandelier in the hallway. The floor is made of shiny stone. It looks like the whole house is an ice-skating rink with furniture. On the walls are pictures of Beth and her family standing on the beach wearing white shirts and white pants. She has an older sister who is prettier than she is.

"Your family looks nice," I say.

"Looks can be deceiving," Beth says.

"What does that mean?"

"It means they look nice, but they aren't."

"Oh. I'm sorry," I say.

"It's okay. It's mainly my dad who's not nice, but he makes everyone else not nice too." I nod and expect her to stop talking, but she doesn't. "He doesn't even live here anymore. He's dating this girl who used to be my mom's yoga teacher. She's, like, twenty. Her name is Maya. He cares way more about her than about any of us." I try to imagine what it would feel like for Dad to care about someone he was dating more than me, and I can't.

"That sucks," I say.

"It is what it is," Beth says. Then she looks at me like I should tell her some kind of secret. She doesn't really know anything about me. She doesn't know about Paradise. She doesn't know that I don't have a mom. She doesn't know that I have a best friend named Kayla. I could tell her, but I don't want to. With Kayla, it's always me listening to her talking about how awesome her family is and me feeling sad that my family is just me and Dad. It's weirdly nice to feel like my family is better than Beth's.

"At least you have these pictures," I say.

"When my braces are off, my mom says we're going to get new pictures taken without Dad," Beth says.

"Oh," I say. I think about telling her about how me and Kayla took pictures of the people on the beach, but to tell her that I would have to explain a bunch of other things.

"Want a tour of the house?" Beth says.

"Sure," I say. I follow Beth through room after room of puffy furniture. Beth's family's stuff would be worth so much money at Paradise Pawn. In the kitchen, I start to add up what they could get for their fancy coffee maker and their fancy blender and their fancy toaster, and I get dizzy. It's pretty unfair that the people who have expensive things to pawn are also the people who never need loans from pawnshops.

"What are you doing?" Beth says when she sees me counting on my fingers.

"Nothing," I say, and I stop. We go upstairs. I peek into Beth's parents' room. It's the size of Kayla's entire apartment. There's a big sign above the king bed that says *Always kiss me good night*, which makes me feel a little like crying. Beth's dad is kissing the yoga teacher good night now, not her mom, but her mom still has to look at the sign. Without thinking, I give Beth a hug. She hugs me back, hard.

"I'm really glad you're here," she says.

"Me too," I say.

"It hasn't been the best time for me friend-wise. My friends from last year kind of ditched me," she says. It's a little weird that she keeps telling me so much embarrassing stuff about her life, but it also makes me feel like we're really friends. "A few of them got boyfriends over the summer and got obsessed with them, and the ones who didn't get boyfriends got obsessed with the idea of boyfriends."

"That sucks," I say. "I don't have a boyfriend, for the record," I say.

"Oh, I know. I can kind of tell," Beth says.

"Oh," I say.

"It's because you actually listen to what I'm saying. You're not constantly wishing I would stop talking so you can start talking about your boyfriend," she says.

"Thanks," I say. "Yeah, it's nice to listen to you." She nods. We are quiet, and it isn't awkward like it was in the car. It's a friend-to-friend quietness.

"Want to swim?" she says.

"Sure!" I say. "I don't have a suit, though."

"You can borrow one of mine," Beth says. We walk into her room. Her room doesn't match her at all. The walls are pink. There are black-and-white pictures of old movie stars with big eyes hanging on the walls. It looks like the set for a play about a teenage girl's room. Beth digs through a dresser.

"I know my room is cringey. Blame my mom," she says.

"It's nice," I say, thinking about what it would be like to have a mom who picks out pictures for the walls of your room.

"FYI, I swim in swim shirts," Beth says. She tosses me an orange long-sleeved swim shirt and bottoms. I hold them up to my body. They look like what a three-year-old girl would wear if her parents were crazy about sun protection. I almost laugh, but I don't. Beth takes off her uniform and pulls a turquoise swim shirt over her head.

"I figure, swimming, at its core, is fun," she says. "But feeling like everyone is looking at your stomach and your boobs and judging you is not fun. So, why would you wear a bikini and make yourself do something not-fun while you're trying to do something fun?"

"Wow," I say. Sometimes Beth says things that make complete sense but that I don't think anyone else in the world has ever said. "I guess for some people, who have perfect boobs and stuff, the bikini part is fun," I say.

"That's what you would think, right? But I don't think that's how it is. I had to do this terrible girls' day with my sister and Maya. We got pedicures and then we went to the beach, and Maya kept saying she looked fat and she missed being a teenager. And she's literally a yoga teacher Instagram model person. She's like a skeleton."

"Weird," I say. I wonder if Kayla likes the bikini part of swimming. She certainly seems to like it, but maybe she just thinks she's supposed to like it. I don't know how I would ask her. It's weird to be talking to Beth about something that I might not be able to talk to Kayla about, even though I know Kayla so much better than I know Beth. I turn my back to Beth and change into the swim shirt she gave me.

"Companies want us to feel terrible about ourselves—women at least—like Victoria's Secret and diet pill companies and those places that freeze off your wrinkles. The worse people feel about themselves, the more stuff they buy. Like orthodontists! That's a perfect example," Beth says.

"Not all companies are like that," I say. I don't think Paradise Pawn wants people to feel terrible about themselves.

"Name one company that doesn't make people feel bad about themselves," Beth says. I don't want to tell her about my job, so I say, "I don't know." Then, the more I think about it, the more I wonder if maybe Paradise does want people to feel terrible about themselves. We make customers feel like they should have more money than they do. We make them walk past cases of gold chains as they're coming in to get loans so they'll take out more money that they don't have to buy the chains. We take things they love, then make them feel bad for pawning those things so that they'll pay interest on them for years. "Maybe you're right," I say.

"It's a hypothesis, at least," Beth says. She can use big words without sounding like a snob. "Do you want to stay for dinner?"

"Sure!" I say.

"What do you want?" Beth says.

"Whatever your parents are making is fine." Beth laughs.

"They're not going to be here. My dad's with Maya, and my mom is doing who knows what. I'll just order us delivery. Maybe Thai food?" I've never had Thai food, but I say, "Sure."

"I always get pad see ew. What do you want?"

"I'll have that, too," I say, even though I don't know what she's saying.

"Cool," Beth says, typing on her phone. "I'm going to get us some fried chicken and spring rolls too."

"Okay," I say. Beth gets towels from the bathroom and I follow her down the stairs through a sliding glass door out to the pool.

"This is really nice," I say.

"Thanks," she says. The water is a perfect blue and a perfect temperature. Beth does a cannonball, and I do, too. I haven't done a cannonball since I was little. Then we dive for plastic pirate coins. Then we have an underwater handstand contest, just like me and Kayla used to do. I laugh when I'm underwater as Beth does a silly dance on her hands. I feel water get in my nose and I realize I can't remember the last time I laughed underwater. It feels great. I'm having more fun with Beth than I've had with Kayla in a long time. It's a sad thought, and I try to stop thinking it, but I can't. I come up for air. My chest is tight. Beth splashes out of the water, grinning.

"Have you tried to get your old friends back?" I ask her.

"Huh?" she says.

"Your friends who ditched you. Have you tried to become friends with them again?"

"Why?" she says, looking a little panicked.

"I'm not saying I'm going to stop being friends with you. Don't worry," I say. "It's just that you're nice and fun to be with, and it's weird that people who were your friends would stop being your friends. How does that happen?" I'm not really talking about Beth's friends. I'm talking about Kayla, even though I don't want to admit it to myself.

"Yeah, it sucks. People just change. It'd be so much easier if they didn't, but they do."

"How do you make them change back?"

"You can't. You try, of course, but after a while it just gets sad and you have to stop. It's like with my dad. After he met Maya, and we all figured out what was going on, my mom set up this huge surprise party for his sixtieth birthday. She got an Elvis impersonator and a magician and all this other desperate stuff, and he never showed up. He was at Maya's apartment. My mom kept trying to do other stuff—we all did. My sister wrote him a bunch of dumb poetry. We went on this family hiking trip to Switzerland. It just made everything sadder in the end. If we hadn't tried, we could have pretended like we didn't care." I can't believe Beth can say everything she's saying without crying. It's making me feel like crying just listening to her.

"So you think it's better to just try to stop caring? Like, if you can tell that you're losing somebody?" I say.

"I don't know. Maybe you just have to find other things to care about. Like, I care about you," she says. I think she really means it. It's pretty weird to say that you care about someone after knowing them for two weeks, but maybe it only seems weird because I don't know anyone like Beth.

"I care about you, too," I say. I tell customers that I care about them all the time and I don't mean it, but I do mean it for Beth. My smile isn't forced and tight. I'm just smiling.

Beth hugs me and I hug her back. Our swim shirts stick together. I feel like I'm cheating on Kayla, but I don't really feel bad about it. I wonder if this is what Beth's dad felt like when he cheated on her mom.

"I think our food's here," Beth says, pulling away from our hug. She paddles to the side of the pool and types on her phone. A car pulls up in the driveway and a man gets out and hands Beth two white plastic bags that say *Have a nice day*.

"Dinner is served!" she says. She drags a little pink boat out of a shed and puts it in the water. "I use this for a table," she says. She arranges the white boxes of food on the boat, gets in the water, and pushes the boat toward me.

"This is awesome," I say. Beth hands me a pair of chopsticks. I've seen people use chopsticks on TV, but I've never used them before. I try to pinch the noodles with them, but they're too slippery. I feel my face get hot with embarrassment. I try to lift a big bite of noodles to my mouth, but I drop them in the pool. I scramble to fish them out. I'm worried Beth will get mad at me, but she just laughs—not a mean laugh, a nice laugh.

"Don't worry. The pool cleaning guys will take care of it. I drop food in the pool all the time. Once, I knocked over a whole plate of nachos in here." Beth giggles. I know she's trying to make me feel better, but she's coming off as a little spoiled. The pool cleaning guys probably didn't think cleaning up soggy nachos was very funny. "Want me to get you a fork from inside?" Beth says.

"Sure," I say. "Thank you." The noodles drift in the clear blue water like eels. I catch a few of them and put them on the side of the pool. I let the rest of them drift down to the bottom. It's funny how money can make some problems into nonproblems right away. The problem of spilling food in your pool isn't a problem if you're rich enough to have pool cleaning people. But if you're trying to fix other problems, like your husband not being in love with you or your friends ditching you, money might as well be wet, useless Kleenex.

Beth comes back with a fork.

"I'm a merman, and this is my trident. Fear me!" she says, splashing into the water. She just says things without worrying whether or not she sounds cool.

"Thanks," I say. The noodles are warm and tangy. We shovel them into our mouths. The fried chicken is buttery and the spring rolls are slimy in a good way. "This might be the best food I've ever had," I say.

"Are you kidding?" Beth says. "You need to get out more." I could be offended by her saying that, but she's so clueless and well meaning that I'm not.

"I get out," I say. "Just not to fancy restaurants."

"That's true," Beth says. "You do get out. You seem like you know about the world more than pretty much anybody."

"That's nice of you," I say. It's nice because it's actually true. I do know more about the world than most people—especially St. Bridget's people.

"You should come the next time my dad takes me and my sister out for dinner," Beth says. "It's his way of trying to get us to like him again. He takes us to really good restaurants. The only downside is you have to hang out with him and Maya, but you get to eat yummy food."

"Okay," I say. That's another way that money can't fix big problems. Beth's dad could buy her the nicest food in the world, and it wouldn't make her feel better about him leaving her mom.

When we're done with the food, we get out of the pool and into the hot tub. The hot water laps at our swim shirts. Steam rises off our skin.

"I'm a wizard," Beth says in a funny voice, waving her steaming hands around. I laugh. She gathers bubbles off the top of the water and makes them into a beard. I laugh some more. "Do you want to be a wizard, too?" she says.

"Sure," I giggle. Sometimes Beth acts like she's five years old. If I don't think too hard about how weird it is, it's fun to act like I'm five years old with her. Beth scoops up a pile of bubbles and pats them onto my chin. Then she dabs a bubble mustache above my lip. I hear the crinkly noise of bubbles popping in my ears.

"Perfect," she says.

"So can we do magic and spells and stuff?" I say.

"Duh. We're wizards," she says.

"What kind of magic?" I say.

"Whatever kind we want. We can do friendship spells." I almost laugh at Beth, but I stop myself because she looks serious. She leans her bubble-covered face toward mine until our foreheads are touching. "Hmmm," she hums. "We will be friends forever hmmmm." Beth closes her eyes. I feel her bubble beard dripping and connecting to mine. It doesn't feel silly anymore. It feels real. Like maybe something magic really is happening. It seems crazy to be fourteen and pretending to be wizards with magic, but it also feels right. I close my eyes, too. When I open them, Beth is smiling at me.

"Well, I guess we solved it. How to make sure you don't lose people, I mean. We just have to cast spells on them." I laugh a little, even though it's actually heartbreaking that in real life we can't cast spells on people to hold on to them. The difference between being five and playing magic and being fourteen is that when you're fourteen you know for sure that it's fake.

The sky is starting to turn orange, and my skin is getting raisiny.

"I should probably go home," I say. Beth's eyebrows crinkle with worry. "Our friendship is sealed in magic now, so you don't have to worry that we won't hang out again." Beth smiles.

"Thank God," she says.

CHAPTER 20

SCHOOL FEELS DIFFERENT NOW THAT I'M FRIENDS with Beth. My whole life feels different. Even just seeing Beth for five minutes in the hallway can make a day good when it would have been bad before I met her. I go to her house a lot. I don't tell her very much about me. I don't tell her about Kayla or Paradise, but I tell her about Dad going on dates and she understands what I'm talking about. Beth's mom, Christina, loves me. I think she's really happy that Beth has a friend. She takes us to Sephora and buys me bright pink lip gloss. Kayla says it looks trashy when I wear it to the store, but I think she's just jealous. She's jealous that I have a new friend, and she's jealous of how good the lip gloss looks.

One afternoon, Beth and I are sitting outside on the lawn waiting to be picked up. She's waiting for her nanny and I'm waiting for Dad. St. Bridget's has the greenest, smoothest lawns of anywhere I've ever seen. They're so green that they're almost blue. The grounds people water them with sprinklers constantly, so there are only a few places you can sit and not get wet. Beth and I are sitting in one of those places. The whole tennis team is sitting in another non-wet place. They're all wearing their tennis skirts and they all have their hair in big, swinging braids. They're eating sandwiches. Some of them are drinking iced coffees. The tennis team, I've observed, is the second-prettiest team at St. Bridget's. Soccer is the prettiest. Squash and volleyball are tied for third prettiest.

A pelican is washing itself in the drip of one of the sprinklers. One of the tennis girls has a ham sandwich. She rips off a piece of bread and tosses it at the pelican. The pelican gobbles it up immediately and the tennis girls laugh.

"Give it some more!" yells another girl. The girl pulls a big piece of ham out of her sandwich, folds it into a ball, and throws it at the pelican. It hits the pelican's wing. Then the pelican snatches it.

"They shouldn't do that," Beth whispers. "It'll get sick." I like that Beth wants to make the world a better place, but I don't want her to do it here, in front of the whole tennis team.

"It's probably fine," I say, putting my hand on Beth's knee. I need to distract her. I try to think of a question to ask her about one of her comic books.

"It's definitely not fine. That pelican doesn't know what's good for him. Bread and ham probably taste amazing now, but they'll get stuck in his digestive system and kill him," Beth says.

"Survival of the fittest, though, right?" I say.

"No. That's not how it should be," Beth says.

"Well, it is, though. If that pelican was smart enough to not eat the ham, it would survive," I say. Beth isn't listening to me anymore. She's standing up. She's ducking under the sprinkler, walking straight toward the tennis team. I do a quick calculation. I could stay here and pretend not to know her, or I could go with her and try to soften whatever she is saying to make it less embarrassing for her and for me. I decide to go with her. I don't duck under the sprinkler in time, so I get wet.

Beth is talking to the girl with the sandwich, Agnes. It's super impressive that she's able to be as popular as she is with a name as ugly as Agnes.

"They can only digest fish," Beth is saying. I expect Agnes to get mad, but she just says, "Oh, okay. Sorry, pelican!" and she keeps eating her sandwich. Beth and I walk back to our spot. I'm amazed.

"You were so brave," I whisper to Beth.

"What, you're scared of pelicans?" Beth says.

"No, scared of tennis girls," I say. Beth scoffs.

"The clones are harmless. Annoying, but harmless." She's technically right. The pelican looks at Agnes expectantly, hoping for more ham.

"I can't feed you. Beth said it's bad for you!" Agnes calls out to the pelican. I'm surprised she knows Beth's name. Sometimes I forget that Beth really could be part of the clones if she wanted to be. She's gone to all the same ballet classes and golf lessons that they have. It makes it even more impressive that she stands up to them to protect pelicans. I couldn't join them even if I wanted to. They don't know my name. I don't have golf clubs or leotards or hair that would swing in a braid the way theirs does. If I did have all of that, I don't know if I would be as brave as Beth is. I might just join them.

Sometimes I wonder if Beth sees me as another pelican to protect—if she is becoming friends with me because she feels like it's the right thing to do, like recycling. But then other times I get the sense that she has no idea how much richer than me she is, and she needs me just as much as I need her.

Either way, I'm lucky to have her. I wrap my arms around her and hug her.

"Want to hear a cool fact about pelicans?" Beth says.

"That's a classic Beth thing to say," I say. She smiles. "Yes, I want to hear it."

"So I saw an art history YouTube video about this. Pelicans are a symbol for Jesus. You see them on a bunch of stained-glass windows from the Middle Ages. And it's because people used to think that mom pelicans fed their babies their own blood. They thought the moms were sacrificing themselves to feed their babies, just like Jesus. But actually, the moms were just eating food and barfing it up for the babies to eat and the barf was reddish. So they weren't really sacrificing their blood. So it makes no sense for pelicans to represent Jesus."

"Making yourself throw up for your babies is still a sacrifice, though," I say. I think of Giselle throwing up in the bathroom of Paradise because of her baby. "In a way, throwing up is more of a sacrifice than bleeding. It's more embarrassing. It's more human. Like, I know the point of God sending Jesus to Earth was so that he could experience human suffering, and he could sacrifice himself for us. But getting nailed to a cross when you know you're the Son of God isn't actually a normal kind of human sacrifice and suffering, you know? It's kind of elegant, perfect suffering, because it's so extreme. But imagine if every time you saw a statue of Jesus in a church, instead of him being nailed to a cross, he was throwing up. I think that would make him seem more relatable. You know? Most sacrifice isn't bleeding and looking cool. It's messy and gross." I realize I have been talking nonstop and probably sounding pretty weird, but I'm not embarrassed. Beth is listening to everything I'm saying and nodding. I want to keep talking while Beth listens to me, but her nanny pulls into the parking lot.

"Bethy!" her nanny calls out the window.

"You should come over!" Beth says. Rob is coming to the store today. They'll need me. I'm about to say no, but Beth looks so excited. And it would be so much more fun to sit in Beth's hot tub and order takeout than to get yelled at by Rob.

"Can I use your phone to call my dad?" I ask. Beth hands me her phone and I dial the number for Paradise. Dad answers after one ring.

"Thank you for calling Paradise Pawn, this is Devon," he says.

"Dad, it's Jackie. Can I go over to Beth's house?" I say. The line is quiet.

"Baby, I hate to say no, but Rob's coming this afternoon. Remember?" he says.

"I know. All the more reason to go to Beth's," I say. I can hear Dad cracking his neck.

"We just really need to do a good job for him this time, with the numbers being what they are." The numbers are what they are because of the plan, but I say, "Well, that's not my fault."

"Jackie," Dad says. His voice is weirdly pleading. "You also need to understand there are a lot of other kids Rob could hire to do your job. We've been covering for you and Kayla as you get settled into school, but you know you get paid to be at the store. It's your job. You don't make any money when you're hanging out at your friend's house."

"Well, maybe I like hanging out with my friends more than I like being in the store. Did you ever think of that?" I yell into Beth's phone.

"Yes, Jackie. Obviously. That's kind of the point of a job. It's something you don't like doing, but the money makes it worth it."

"No one else in this whole school has a job," I say. I sound like a brat. I feel bad. I hear Dad crack his neck both ways.

"I know that," he says. I listen to him breathing.

"Okay, fine. I'll come in. I'm sorry," I say.

"Thank you," he says quietly. "Carter will pick you up from school because I'll be busy getting ready for Rob."

"Carter's picking me up? Seriously?" I say. Carter's car barely runs. The back window is broken so there's a garbage bag duct-taped over it, and the muffler is busted. Getting picked up at St. Bridget's in Dad's truck is bad enough, but getting picked up in Carter's car, especially if the tennis girls are still sitting by the parking lot, will be mortifying.

"Yeah, I won't be able to get away from the store. He's picking up Kayla, too. Is that okay?" It's not okay. I want to whine and make Dad come get me instead, but I can tell Dad is already annoyed with me, so I just say, "Fine," and hang up. I hand Beth her phone.

"What store do you have to go to?" she says. "I thought you never went shopping." I blink at her and realize how little she understands me. It crosses my mind that I could just tell her about Paradise. I could try to make her understand that her life is so different from mine because she has so much money, but I don't want to. "So can you come over?" she says.

"No. My dad says I can't," I say. She looks sad, but I don't have the energy to come up with something to say to make her feel better. "Bye," I say.

"I'll miss you," she says.

"Uh-huh," I say. She gets into her nanny's car and they drive away.

Carter will be here any minute. The tennis girls don't appear to be leaving. I cannot let them see me getting picked up by a guy with a neck tattoo in a busted car. I decide to hide inside until I see Carter pull up, then run out the back door and around the edge of the parking lot to his car. I wait and wait. I watch as the tennis girls massage their calves with a little buzzing machine. I watch them drop ice from their iced coffees down each other's shirts. They have no idea how stressed they are making me by sitting there. I wish they would go play tennis. Then I see a girl wander into the parking lot. It's Kayla. I almost don't believe it. She looks small in the giant parking lot. I run out the door and I throw my arms around her.

"Kayla! Oh my God, you're at St. Bridget's!" I squeal. I pull her toward the steps. "I want to give you a tour," I say. Her body is rigid.

"No," she says. "You have to go to the principal's office. They took Carter there."

"What? Why?" I say. She shakes her head, and I realize she looks scared. Kayla almost never looks scared.

"We went in the wrong entrance or something. They thought he was trespassing. They got super mad at him and they said they would call the police before he told them he was getting you. He's supposed to have some kind of paper signed by your dad to be able to pick you up."

"What should we do?"

"You tell me. You're the one who goes here," she says.

I can feel my face getting hot. A group of nannies is staring at us. I try to breathe in through my nose and out through my mouth. "Follow me," I say, trying to sound calm.

Me and Kayla walk up the stairs of St. Bridget's together, just like we used to dream about from behind the fence, but nothing about it is right. We're not glamorous and beautiful. We're sweaty and afraid and mad at each other. As we walk through the dark hallway, I wave to everyone we pass and say, "Hey," even if I've never seen them before. Most of them say hey back. I hope Kayla thinks they're all my friends.

"Isn't it pretty in here?" I say to her.

"I'm not really worried about if it's pretty right now. I'm worried about Carter and about getting back to the store before Rob arrives."

"Sorry," I say.

On the dark wooden door of the principal's office is a poster that says *All are welcome here* with a picture of a box of crayons on it. I push it open with my shoulder.

"Hi," I say to the receptionist, trying not to let my voice shake. She has big yellow glasses that make her look like an unfriendly bug. "Is Carter here? He was supposed to pick me up."

"Who?" she says.

"Carter Harris. He was supposed to pick her up, but the guard thought he was trespassing," Kayla says. I'm grateful and annoyed at the same time that she's taking over.

"Did he have a pass signed by her legal guardian?" the receptionist says in a monotone voice.

"No, I don't believe so," Kayla says.

"Have a seat. I'll go see what's going on," the receptionist says. We sit on a wooden bench that feels like it's made of ice. Kayla jiggles her knee nervously.

Then a lady with a long, tight ponytail who looks like she's had Botox sticks her head out another door and says, "Jaqueline?" I grab Kayla's hand.

"Will you come with me?" I whisper.

"Fine," she says. Carter is sitting in a fancy office. He's kneading the sleeve of his Paradise Pawn shirt. His eyes are wide. I've watched him handcuff people and shoot guns and cut down trees with chainsaws. I have never seen him look scared before today. I want to give him a hug.

"Hi, sweetheart. I'm Mrs. Polk. I just need to talk to you briefly about our pickup policy here at St. Bridget's, okay?" the lady says. Her voice sounds like a fire alarm. Her bright red mouth droops down like a frog's mouth. "I've just called your dad, and we're going to make an exception today because you guys are new here, but going forward, we only allow a parent or designated caregiver, like a nanny, to do pickups. It's just about keeping our community safe, okay? We can't have random people walking around on the grounds, or parents get worried." She glances at Carter like he smells bad.

"I don't have a nanny," I say.

"Then you'll need to be picked up by your mom or your dad," she says. I look at Kayla.

"I don't have a mom," I say.

"Oh, sweetheart," she says. I watch her eyebrows try to slant down and then get stuck because of the Botox. She leans over her desk and for a minute I can't tell what she's doing, so I back away. Then I realize she's trying to hug me. Her hands are cold even through the sleeves of my uniform. "I'm so sorry," she says too loudly into my ear.

"It's okay," I say, wiggling out of her hands. "She's dead, but I didn't know her very well." Mrs. Polk shifts nervously in her chair.

"Tissue?" she says, handing me a box.

"I'm not going to cry about it," I say.

"You're very strong," she says.

I blink and try to think of what to say next. Mrs. Polk's mouth is stuck in a grin. She clears her throat and says, "Unfortunately, we're not going to be able to make an exception to our pickup policy, even with the unique family situation, so if we can all just keep in mind that only Dad should be picking you up, that would be great. Okay?"

"You got it, ma'am," Carter mutters.

"Great," the woman chirps.

"Let's get out of here, girls," Carter says, looking at the floor. The lady puts her hands together and bows to us. "Thanks everybody. Namaste," she says.

We walk through the hall together, then out the front door. Kayla's and Carter's hands are trembling. Mine are too.

The tennis girls are still on the lawn and I turn my face away from them as we walk to Carter's car.

"Seat belts," Carter says when we get in. His voice is shaky. I want to say something to make him feel better. I don't know what to say.

"Hey, I'm so sorry," I say. It comes out sounding weird and gushy like the lady in the office. "Sorry," I say again.

"It's all good," Carter says, though he sounds kind of mad.

"That was super weird. I don't know why they freaked out like that," I say. I actually do know why. It's because everyone walking around St. Bridget's looks rich and Carter doesn't, but I can't say that. I look to Kayla for help, but she's looking out the window.

I FEEL WEIRD ALL AFTERNOON and I can tell that Kayla does too. A guy from Miami comes in with a surfboard. Kayla does the plan on him and we get $300. I write it down in the unicorn notebook.

"Kayla," I whisper when surfboard guy leaves. "That was twelve thousand. We just hit twelve thousand."

Kayla blinks at the numbers in the notebook.

"Oh my God," she breathes.

"Is that a good or a bad 'Oh my God'?" I say.

"I don't know. Yeah. It's just like, wow. It feels real. I'm gonna go to that school. I guess I haven't totally believed it until now." My stomach lurches in a happy way.

"Believe it," I say. "It's happening." I squeeze Kayla's shoulders and she squeezes my arms.

"It's happening," she repeats.

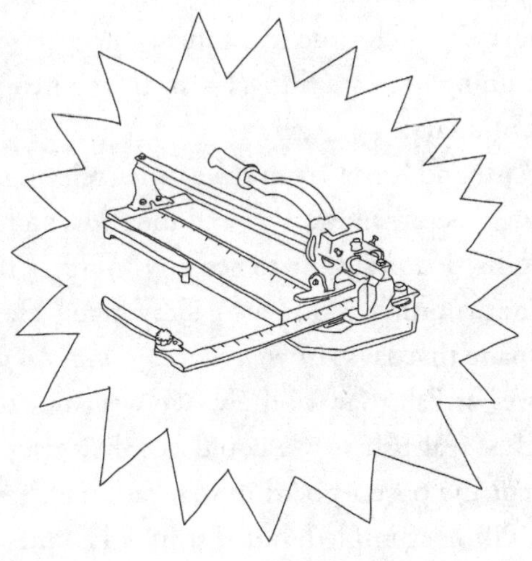

CHAPTER 21

ROB CALLS TO TELL DAD THAT HE'S COMING FROM the hotel and he'll be late. He's always late for us.

"Be extra nice to him, okay?" Dad whispers to us when he gets off the phone. I make a barfing noise and I expect Dad to laugh a little, but he just says, "No, I'm serious."

"Why?" I ask. Dad pulls on his fingers and cracks them. I can tell there's something secret he doesn't think he should tell us. "We shouldn't have to be extra nice if you don't tell us why," I say.

"He's just had too much to drink, okay?" Dad says, "So be nice. Got it?"

"Fine," I say, and roll my eyes.

When Rob gets to the store, he goes right to the bathroom. He pees and it gets everywhere. Carter cleans it up. Then Rob runs his fat fingers over all the TVs and wiggles his fingers in our faces to show us that they're dusty. Me and Kayla have been working fewer hours since school started, so we don't have as much time to clean.

"Who's going to buy a filthy TV from you people? I know I wouldn't," he says.

"Sorry," me and Kayla say, and we turn a pile of paper towels black wiping dust off all the TVs and monitors and Xboxes.

"Also, girls, I don't want to see any more of these junky signs. I'm not running a kids' art gallery here." He rips down a sign we made that says *Ask us about discounts on fishing reels!* with pictures of fish that we drew. We went out to the dock and looked at real fish so we could get their eyes and scales right. We cut the poster board into a starburst shape and the points got a little crumpled, but it still looked pretty cool.

"Got it. No more signs," Dad says. We nod, even though customers love our signs. While Rob is looking through the computer, we take down the *Please flush* sign we made for the bathroom with a picture of a mermaid on it, and the *We do loans on boats* sign with a picture of Noah's ark and all the animals.

"Your loan numbers are shit," Rob says, clicking through the computer. He kneads the sides of his big pink head with his thumbs. "I expected so much from you people this quarter. I really can't figure it out. You're going to bleed me dry if this keeps up." He mops sweat off his forehead and his nose. Then he puts his hands over his whole face like he's crying.

"I sure do apologize, sir," Dad says. He lifts his hand like he's thinking about putting it on Rob's shoulder, but he doesn't. He just holds it in the air for a while.

"They'll get better soon. We promise," I say. Rob pushes his face up out of his hands.

"What if they don't, though?" he says, looking right at me. I look at the floor. Rob keeps talking, almost in a whisper. "I can't keep this up. If the numbers don't get better, I'm sunk. They'll take my car. They'll take my house." Rob puts his face in his hands again, gasps in a breath like he's going to sneeze, but then, instead of sneezing, he starts to cry. Watching Rob cry is like a weird dream. Nobody knows what to do.

"Go ahead and cry, sir," Aubrey says gently. Rob looks up from his hands. I feel my shoulders tense, thinking he's going to yell at us again, but he just keeps crying. His body quivers like Jell-O. We back away from him. We turn up the radio and pretend to be busy. He puts his head down on the counter, where so many other people have cried over interest payments and layaway deposits that went into his bank account, and he sobs. Something must be very wrong with his finances. Me and Kayla pretend to rearrange the home security systems, but we can't stop staring at Rob. After a few minutes, he peels his hands off his face and looks at himself in his selfie camera. He blinks, combs his fingers through his hair, drives his thumb into one of his eyes, and then stands up.

"All good," he says, and drums a little song on his thighs. Then he strolls around the perimeter of the store like a kid with no one to talk to trying not to look awkward. He is never this quiet, and it makes us sweaty. After an hour of Rob being quiet and weird, Kayla has to leave to go to a student council meeting, and I am left alone with Rob and the dads.

A MAN IN SUNGLASSES who doesn't speak English comes in and hands Dad his passport. Then he draws a picture of a tile cutter on a Post-it and puts his hand over his heart like he's saying he loves his tile cutter. Dad gives him a thumbs-up and finds his profile in the system. The man pushes his sunglasses up onto his head, and I realize that I recognize his eyes and his face. He waves at me. I wave back a little, then pretend to be busy arranging ring boxes.

A month ago, the man and I had a conversation in pictures on the back of pawn tickets because we couldn't talk to each other. He only spoke Spanish. He drew an ocean and an airplane and stick-figure kids and a stick-figure lady with long eyelashes. He drew something about soccer that I couldn't understand, and we laughed about it. Then he gave me his tile cutter and I did the plan on him. I was sure he was going to get on an airplane to be with the stick-figure family and never come back. It seemed so obvious. I gave him $300 for the tile cutter and put $1,200 into the computer and drew a happy face on his picture, and arrows pointing to the kids and the lady. He smiled and took the picture with him and walked away with his $300. I thought he was never coming back, but now he's here, rubbing a crinkled $100 bill between his fingers. That's the interest he thinks he owes, because he thinks he got a $300 loan, but the computer says he owes $400. I just N.E.H.A.-ed him wrong. I feel blood surging through my body like a pack of wolves running as fast as they can.

"Are you picking up the item or extending the loan?" Dad asks the man. The man looks confused, so Dad acts out paying money or taking something home. He makes his arms into a roof over his head to show "home." The man makes his hands into a roof and shakes his head no.

"So just paying interest?" Dad says. The man nods his head, smiles, and hands Dad the $100 bill. Dad looks at the computer and shakes his head and holds up four fingers. The man laughs and then looks worried.

"No, no," he says.

"My system says you owe four hundred. Can you pay that?" Dad says in a soft voice. Rob, who has been drunkenly inventorying phones, waddles over and watches.

"One hundred," the man says.

"No, you owe four hundred," Dad says. The man points at me. I stand up, and he smiles. He reaches for my hand and squeezes it. His hand is warm and wet. "Jackie, did you do this transaction?"

"I don't remember," I say. The man nods. He can tell what we're saying. "I mean yeah, I think so," I say.

"You gave him twelve hundred dollars?" I feel like all the blood in me has stopped in its tracks. I look at the guy. His eyes are bright. The stick figures he drew were a real family who needs money. If he loses his tile cutter, he won't be able to find work and then he won't be able to afford a plane ticket to go be with them. Dad snaps his fingers. A line of people is forming behind the man, and Rob is watching. "Chop-chop, Jackie. Did you give him one thousand two hundred?"

"Yeah," I say, looking at the ground.

"No, no," the man says again. He reaches for my hand again, but I keep it tucked behind my back. "Mistake, mistake," he says. I shrug.

"I'm awfully sorry, sir, but it looks like if you don't have money for the four-hundred-dollar payment, we're going to have to take your tile cutter." The man narrows his eyes at me. He knows what I've done, but he can't say it in English. Behind him, the line of people is getting restless. "Do you have four hundred?" Dad says. The man shakes his head.

"This isn't kumbaya time, Devon. We're running a business. Default and get on with it. I don't like to see a line like this," Rob says.

"Yes sir," Dad says. Dad clicks through the man's customer history. He can tell something isn't right. My hands are slick with sweat.

"I'll do it," I say. I click *default* on the spreadsheet and say, "Have a nice day." The man gives me a last, pleading look.

"Have a nice day," I say again. The man's shoulders rise for a minute as he looks at me and Rob and Dad and thinks about arguing one more time, but then they droop again and he walks away.

"That's how we do it," Rob says, too loudly. "Jackie, you did great with that. You didn't give him an inch, even though he was trying to play on your emotions. You were stone-cold. I love it." He holds up his hand for me to high-five him and I do, because I have no choice. I feel sick. I think about how the man will have to call his family and tell them he lost the tile cutter as I watch Rob's huge, gleaming teeth fold into a grin. "Remember, we're not here to listen to sob stories and say, 'Oh, poor you,' okay? We can't be running this business like little girls."

"Got it," Dad says.

"That goes for all of you. Even the little girls. Jackie, don't run the business like a little girl, okay?" He laughs at his own joke and I fake laugh. Then he gets closer to me and breathes his beer breath on me and says, "For one thing, you're hardly a little girl anymore." Then he squeezes my butt, hard, and winks at me. My lungs hurt like they do when I wake up from a bad dream. I look to see if Dad or Aubrey saw what Rob did, but they didn't.

"Okay," I say, backing away from him. I don't know what else to say. I want to jump into the ocean and stay there for hours.

"You could run this place someday, Jackie. You know that. You've got that killer instinct," Rob says. Dad smiles like he's proud of me. I fake smile, but I feel like throwing up.

CHAPTER 22

WHEN WE GET HOME, DAD GOES IN HIS ROOM TO FaceTime with a woman named Kristin from a cruise ship. I take off my clothes and get in the shower and scrub my butt as hard as I can to try to make the feeling of Rob's hand on it go away. I scrub my scalp to try to get the thought of the tile cutter guy's sad eyes out of my head. I try cold water and steaming hot water, but nothing works. I still feel gross. I kneel on the living room floor and put my head between the couch cushions and scream. Then I run outside and get on my bike. The air is still pink from the sunset, but it's turning gray fast. I pedal to Kayla's house, lock my bike to her fence, and climb up her fire escape. Bobby and Mason are curled up in her bed and she's reading them a story. Bobby is sucking his thumb. I tap on the window. I'm worried she'll be annoyed, but she sets down the book, moves Mason's head off her leg, and crawls across the bed to open the window for me. I climb in.

"Hey," she says, and gives me a hug. "You okay?" I nod into her shoulder. I finally feel like I can breathe. "You want to hear the rest of this story?" she says. I nod again. I slip under Kayla's ballerina comforter that she's had since we were three, and snuggle against her.

"You can use this pillow, Jackie," Mason says sleepily.

"Thanks," I say. Kayla keeps reading about the Hungry Caterpillar who eats plums and chocolate cake and leaves and then grows up and turns into a butterfly. It's a book Giselle used to read to us when we were little and thought growing up was fun and simple like that—just eating food, waiting, and eventually being beautiful. The Hungry Caterpillar doesn't have to worry about lying to people or needing a bra or getting touched by old, scary, drunk caterpillars when he grows up.

When the story is over, Kayla lifts Bobby into his bed and tucks the blankets around him. Mason climbs back into his bed, and I lie down beside Kayla. Then Giselle comes in.

"Hey, Jackie. You sleeping over tonight?"

"Yeah, if that's okay," I say. "I just needed to be here for a little while."

"Okay, baby," she says, and squeezes my arm. "Are you alright?" I nod. "Your dad knows you're here?"

"Can you text him that I'm sleeping over?"

"Sure, sweetheart," she says, and kisses my forehead.

"Can we say good night to the baby?" Bobby says.

"Yeah. Come here," Giselle says. Bobby rests his little cheek on Giselle's stomach and whispers, "Good night, baby sister."

"Good night, baby sister! Good night!" Kayla and Mason echo.

"They say good night, too," Bobby says, like he's on the phone with the baby. Giselle lifts Bobby back into his bed.

Then she sings the lullaby about the cherry with no stone and the chicken with no bone. Kayla wraps her warm arms around me, and I think about how lucky the baby is to have a mom like Giselle and a sister like Kayla and how I would give up all the good parts of growing up to feel this little and safe for the rest of my life.

When Giselle leaves and the boys are asleep, I say to Kayla, "You missed a weird afternoon at the store today." She lets go of me and rolls onto her back.

"I'm going to miss so many days at the store now that I'm student council president," she says. She talks about how she's getting recycling bins for the lunchroom and she gets to tell the whole school about it over the intercom.

"That'll look good on your St. Bridget's application," I say.

"I guess," she says. "It's good for college applications, too. The girl who is council president for the seniors got a full ride to University of Florida."

"Oh," I say. The thought of Kayla leaving me to go to college hurts to think about.

"Going to college is the way to get seriously rich—classy rich, not just, like, pawnshop rich."

"What do you mean, 'pawnshop rich'?"

"Like your dad or Rob," she says. The warm, cozy feeling floods out of me, and I shiver.

"Don't say that," I say.

"What?"

"My dad isn't anything like Rob," I whisper-yell.

"Geez, sorry," Kayla says.

"Rob touched my butt at the store today," I say. I start to cry. My shoulders shake the whole mattress. Kayla grabs on to me and holds me against her chest.

"I'm sorry," she says. "I'm sorry I said that, and I'm sorry I wasn't there to help. Fuck Rob."

"Yeah. Fuck Rob," I say. I've never said that word out loud before. "Fuck Rob," I say again. I sit up and punch my pillow like it's Rob's face. "FuckRobfuckRobfuckRobfuckRob!" I whisper-scream. Kayla punches her pillow, too. I ball up my hands so tightly that no blood can get into them. I punch the wall, and it doesn't even hurt.

"Shh, you'll wake everyone up if you do that. Hang on," Kayla says. She slips out the bedroom door. When she comes back, she hands me an orange and she spreads a plastic grocery bag out between us. "Here. Squeeze this. Just don't get the juice on my sheets," she says. I mash my fingers into the orange like it's Rob's organs and bank account and face all packed into one slippery ball. I imagine him screaming. My fingernails pierce the orange's skin. Gleaming pulp rockets through my fingers. Juice gets into the blister on my palm that I got from mopping the floor to get ready for Rob's big, muddy feet. The blister stings and I mash the orange harder.

"Do you want some?" I say to Kayla. She nods. I rip the orange in two and pass half to her. It looks like muscles attached to skin. Kayla closes her eyes and squeezes her orange like she's choking an animal. When there's a pool of sticky juice on the plastic bag and our orange halves look like tissue paper, we breathe out together.

"We should clean this up," Kayla says.

"Yeah," I say. We each pinch two corners of the bag and we carefully walk to the kitchen to throw it away. Then we wash and dry the stickiness off our hands and it's like nothing ever happened.

"This is the difference between people like us and people like Rob," I say.

"What is?" Kayla says.

"When we get mad, we have to do it in the dark and then clean it all up so it doesn't bother anybody. We have to take it out on oranges. We can't just go around making other people miserable when we're miserable. I get mad at my dad and at you, but that's it. Sometimes I wish we could just slap random people around and yell at them and ruin their days. That's what rich people get to do." Kayla drapes her arm around my shoulders.

"You don't really wish that, though, do you? When we're rich, we're not going to make people miserable. That's part of being classy rich. Turn the other cheek, like Jesus." I suck on the blister on my palm. It still stings.

"I guess," I say. I think Kayla is a better person than I am.

CHAPTER 23

I THINK MAYBE DAD KNOWS THAT ROB DID SOMEthing creepy to me. I wish he would just ask me about it, but he doesn't. He just starts being extra nice to me. When I ask him if I can go out to lunch with Beth and Beth's dad and Beth's dad's girlfriend, Maya, on a Saturday when Rob will be at the store, of course I expect Dad to say no. But he says yes. He says I can have two and a half hours off.

Beth can't stop talking about the lunch. We're going to a Brazilian steakhouse. She says the food will be amazing and her dad and Maya will be amazingly annoying. It doesn't matter to me if they're annoying. I have my own family, and I have Kayla's family. I can stand Beth's family being annoying if it means I get access to a Brazilian steakhouse. Beth says her dad can pick me up at my house, or wherever I want. Beth's dad has a Jaguar, which would be fun to ride in, but I don't want

Beth to see Paradise. I tell her that I'll bike and meet them at the Brazilian steakhouse. She doesn't argue. She thinks it's really cool that I bike everywhere. I think she thinks that I bike places because I care about the environment. It doesn't register to her that I need to bike because I don't have a nanny to drive me around.

The lunch is at 1:00. I plan to work until 12:20, then bike to the Brazilian steakhouse, which is a thirty-five-minute bike ride away from Paradise Pawn. When I get there, I'll change out of my uniform and into the sundress I packed this morning. I don't want Kayla to see me in my sundress. I feel weird about telling her that I'm going to a fancy lunch in the middle of a workday. I thought about asking Beth if I could invite Kayla to lunch, but then thinking about trying to introduce Beth and Kayla gave me a stomachache. I like getting to be one Jackie with Kayla and one Jackie with Beth. I don't know which Jackie I would be if I was at a Brazilian steakhouse with both of them, and Beth's dad, and his girlfriend.

IN THE MORNING as we're unloading the jewelry from the safe, Dad gets a call from Rob.

"Sounds like he's running a little late," Dad says.

"Why, 'cause he's drunk?" I ask.

"That's none of our business," Dad says. "He's going through a lot right now."

"Fuck Rob," I whisper. Kayla giggles. Dad slams a box of jewelry down on the counter.

"Jackie, what did you just say?" he says.

"Nothing," I whisper. I scuff my shoes against the jewelry cases.

"We have to be respectful of Rob," Dad says.

"But he's not respectful of me!" I say. Dad's face wilts a little.

"I know," Dad says. "You have to set a good example for him, though. Okay?"

"Whatever," I say. I walk away to turn on the TVs, and Dad cracks all of his fingers.

The morning drags. Everyone's eyes keep drifting away from customers' eyes toward the parking lot, waiting for Rob. My eyes keep drifting to watches to see if it's time for me to leave for lunch.

When it's slow, me and Kayla go in the back and work on jewelry inventory. We slide diamond rings out of their envelopes and stack them on our fingers. Usually, Kayla would say we need to get to work, but she doesn't. She's in a good mood. It almost feels like a waste for me to leave and go to lunch and miss out on a day with Kayla when she's in a good mood.

I twirl a size twelve diamond ring on my thumb. It's probably the only size twelve engagement ring in Cherry Beach, so it's easy to keep track of. It first came into the store about three years ago. This guy with the thickest glasses I've ever seen brought his girlfriend to Cherry Beach to propose to her, but she said no and then he came into the store crying, trying to sell the ring to pay for a separate hotel room and a plane ticket home. Then a few other people bought it, pawned it, and defaulted on it. One was a Russian lady who bought it for herself to make her family think she had a boyfriend. Now it's on layaway for a guy who works as a clown on cruise ships. He says he wants to propose to his girlfriend before her grandma dies, so he's been pawning his Xbox and his iPad and even his air compressor that he uses to blow up balloons when he's a clown so he can make layaway payments on the ring.

"I'm glad girls don't have to buy engagement rings for guys," I say.

"Why?" Kayla says.

"I don't think I could love a boy enough to spend that kind of money on him—pawn my whole life away to give him a ring. Obviously, I'd do it for you, but not for some guy who would probably just leave me. That's why best friends are better than boyfriends," I say.

"Why?" Kayla says.

"Because people can fall in love with anybody, just because they have a nice face or money or something, but people can only really have one best friend. So you can't get your heart broken by your best friend if they're really your best friend," I say. I'm feeling bad about not telling Kayla about the lunch and I want to make up for it by telling her that she really is my best friend, because she is. Beth could never take her place.

"I don't really think that's how it works," Kayla says. I feel sadness seep into my skin. Kayla reaches for my hand. "I don't mean that I'm not your best friend. I just mean hearts are stretchy. That's what my mom keeps saying about the baby. It's not like her heart is getting chopped up into slices and we'll all get a smaller slice so there will be enough love for the baby. She says a mom's heart is like a sweater that can stretch bigger and bigger forever. I think maybe that's why people cheat on people, because their hearts are stretchy. Sometimes too stretchy."

"My mom's heart wasn't very stretchy," I say. Kayla squeezes my hand.

"Hey," she says, running her fingers along my knuckles. "I didn't mean it like that."

"I was kind of joking. It's okay," I say. "Maybe that's why my heart isn't very stretchy. Like, it runs in the family. I think I only have room in my heart for you and your family and my dad and maybe one or two other people."

"I bet it's stretchier than you think," Kayla says. But I don't want my heart to be stretchy. I don't want hers to be stretchy either. She can tell I'm sad. "Here's what we'll do with our stretchy hearts," she says. "We'll get a hundred guys to propose to us, so our hands can look like this," she says, wiggling her fingers with rings stacked all the way up to her fingernails. I laugh. Then I get down on one knee and hold out a handful of rings to her.

"Kayla, darling, I'm Fred and I'm a surgeon and a banker and a hedge fund manager all at the same time. Will you marry me?" I say in a deep, silly voice.

"Maybe," Kayla says in a high voice, jamming the rings onto her fingers.

"Kayla, I'm Bob. I invented Pop-Tarts and I own a thousand hotels. Will you marry me?"

"I might," she says, giggling. "If I get unlimited Pop-Tarts for the rest of my life."

"Of course, of course, my dear," I say. Kayla takes my hands and we do a silly waltz around the storeroom until I fling my arm out to do a spin and I knock over a stack of DVDs. While we clean them up, we both laugh like it's the funniest thing ever. I love Kayla's laugh.

If I had a phone, I might call Beth and tell her that I'm sick or something, so I could stay at Paradise and hang out with Kayla. I think about just not showing up to the lunch, but then I think of Beth's eyes, hopeful like a Beanie Baby's. I think about how excited she was when I said I could come to this lunch. I can't leave her alone with her dad and Maya. I tell Kayla that I'm going to a doctor's appointment. I make sure to say it while Dad isn't around so I don't get caught in a lie.

"Is something wrong? Are you sick?" Kayla says. She seems genuinely concerned, which makes me hug her.

"No, just a checkup," I say. It's already 12:28. I'll need to bike fast if I don't want to be late. I unlock my bike and pedal as fast as I can. I sing fast songs to myself to keep up my rhythm. I careen into the parking lot of the Brazilian steakhouse at 12:58.

I lean my bike against a trash can without locking it. I don't have time, and I don't think anyone would steal a pawnshop bike at a restaurant this fancy. Globs of sweat are running down my neck. I sprint through the door of the Brazilian steakhouse. There's a guy in a white suit jacket standing at a little podium. He looks at me like I'm not supposed to be there. If I ask him if I can use the bathroom to change into my dress, I'm sure he'll say no.

I see an open door leading to the kitchen. I walk toward it, trying to look like I know what I'm doing. The man at the podium doesn't stop me. I look for a corner where I could change into my sundress, but there are people in aprons running around everywhere, carrying big tubs of dishes. I yank my dress over my uniform shirt. I pull the collar of my uniform shirt up out of the front of the dress. It's a little bunched up, but I think it probably looks okay. There isn't a mirror for me to check. I wiggle out of my pants and fold them up as small as I can. The nice thing about Beth is that she's not the kind of person to ask you why you're holding a pair of pants at a lunch.

I walk out of the kitchen at 1:02. I stand by the man at the podium. I wait for ten minutes. I can tell he's suspicious of me. I'm excited for when Beth's dad walks in and the podium guy realizes I actually do belong in his steakhouse. At 1:15 I start to get worried. I smile at the guy at the podium and try to look rich and relaxed. At 1:16, I see Beth getting out of a Jaguar in the parking lot. She's wearing cargo shorts and a weird shirt that I think she may have knit herself.

"Best friend!" she says when she walks in the door.

"Hi!" I say, hugging her.

"I like your outfit. The undershirt thing is cool," Beth says.

"Thanks," I say, feeling grateful for her. A man I assume is Beth's dad and a woman I assume is Maya walk in the door behind Beth.

"I'm Jackie," I say, holding out my hand.

"A handshake. I love it," Beth's dad says. "Bethy, you gotta learn to shake hands like this kid." Beth ignores him and keeps talking to me. Maya doesn't say anything. I don't shake her hand.

As we walk to the table, I look closely at Beth's dad's hair. Beth says he used to be almost bald, but he got a hair transplant. At first, I thought that meant they took a dead person's hair and put it on him, like a heart transplant, but they just took hair from a part of his head that still had hair and put it on the bald part. His new hair looks pretty convincing. I wonder if Maya knows about his hair transplant. I think about the family on the beach Kayla and I photographed—how the woman said she wanted her husband to stay bald so he wouldn't leave her. Maybe if Beth's dad was still bald, he wouldn't have left Beth's mom.

Maya is beautiful. Her skin is golden and glowy. She's wearing a silk scarf as a headband. She has huge boobs that are probably fake, but they look natural. She looks bored in a way that makes her prettier than she would look if she smiled.

The way a Brazilian steakhouse works, I learn, is that the waiters come around with gigantic skewers of meat and they carve little bits off for you. The meat is really good. Beth's dad eats a ton of it, Beth and I eat a medium amount, and Maya eats almost nothing. She only eats the roasted zucchini, which looks floppy and gross. She says she doesn't like meat that looks too much like meat.

"Babe, it's already dead. What's the difference?" Beth's dad says.

"This is just a boundary I'm setting," Maya says. Her voice is very low. Then Maya kisses Beth's dad on the cheek, right in front of us. There's a little crusty piece of meat on Beth's dad's chin and it almost gets in Maya's mouth, but it doesn't.

The waiters keep bringing more and more meat, and I keep eating it, because it's free and I don't know when I'll be at a lunch this fancy again. I also don't know what to say to Beth's dad and Maya, and it feels less awkward to not talk if I'm chewing on chewy meat. Beth keeps glaring at me whenever her dad says something, as if she wants me to glare at him too. He's paying for me to eat more steak than I've ever eaten in my life, so I don't feel like it would be fair to glare at him. Beth's dad starts talking about cold plunges, how he goes in one every morning.

"I'm all about discipline," he says.

"But there's no point to it. It's just making yourself miserable to prove to yourself that you can stand being miserable," Beth says. There is Brazilian steak stuck in her braces.

"It's practicing for when discipline really counts," Beth's dad says.

"But when do you actually need to use discipline in your life? You sit in a rolly chair all day," Beth says.

"I sit in an office chair making tons of money. And I know you think you're some Marxist and you want to make the world better, but someday you're going to understand that money is the real measure of how much you've made the world better," Beth's dad says. Beth rolls her eyes. Maya does too, but in a way that Beth's dad doesn't notice. It's quiet for a while, except for the sound of everyone but Maya chewing steak.

I think about how me and Kayla are rich right now. We have thousands of dollars sitting in a bathroom just a thirty-five-minute bike ride away from this steakhouse. I don't think we're rich because we made the world a better place. We're rich because we stole. I doubt that Beth's dad's money came from making the world a better place. I'm starting to be so full of steak that I feel a little sick.

"Anybody have the meat sweats?" Beth's dad says. I can tell he wants someone to ask him what the meat sweats are so he can talk about them, but nobody asks. I think it must mean when you start sweating because you ate a bunch of meat. Beth's dad is definitely sweating.

For dessert, I order chocolate lava cake. Beth tells me, in front of the waitress, that chocolate lava cake is not authentically Brazilian and I should get something called flan, which looks jiggly and gross in the picture on the menu. I get flan to be polite, even though I was excited about chocolate lava cake. When the flan arrives, it is even grosser than I thought it would be. I'm feeling sick from looking at it jiggle, and from eating endless steak. I want the lunch to be over. When the bill comes, I look over Beth's dad's shoulder. It's $270 with tax and tip. It's the most expensive meal I've ever eaten.

After lunch, we walk outside. I look at the trash can where my bike should be, and it's gone. I feel myself getting what must be a meat sweat. I can feel my meat-filled blood pumping through me. I feel so stupid for not locking it.

"My bike got stolen!" I scream.

"Oh no! Was it special?" Beth says.

"What do you mean?" I say.

"Well, like, did it have sentimental value or was it just, like, a bike and you could get a new one and you wouldn't notice?"

"It had regular value! It was expensive. It was a bike!"

"Right, of course," Beth says. "Well, do you want a ride home?" I've been gone almost two hours. If I walk back to Paradise, I won't make it there before the end of my break. Dad will be mad about my bike, but he'll be even more mad if I'm late. He'll think I think I'm better than everyone just because I got invited to a fancy lunch. He'll never give me a break like this ever again.

"Can you give me a ride to Burger King?" I say to Beth's dad. There's a Burger King down the street from Paradise. If I get out of the car there and walk to Paradise, I won't have to deal with them seeing it.

"You're still hungry? You want to eat a burger after all that?" Beth says.

"Yeah," I say. "I'm on my period, so I need a lot of red meat." I've heard from Kayla that when you're on your period, sometimes you want to eat a lot of red meat.

"Oh my gosh, me too!" Beth says. "We're synched up! That's why I wanted to go to the steakhouse today. I always crave red meat this time of the month." She gives me a hug.

"Cool, yeah," I say, pushing her off me. Beth and I get in the back of the Jaguar. I give Beth's dad directions to Burger King. He drives way over the speed limit, which is bad because it makes me carsick, but good because I'm running late, and the Burger King drop-off plan will eat up precious time. When Beth's dad pulls up in front of Burger King, my seat belt is already undone. "Thanks so much for lunch! Bye!" I yell.

"Wait, sweetheart!" Maya says as I'm about to shut the car door. It's the first time she's talked to me all afternoon.

"Bye! Thanks!" I say, pretending not to hear her. When the Jaguar pulls out of the Burger King parking lot, I sprint toward Paradise. I'm about to get Carter to buzz me in when I hear Maya's voice again. The Jaguar is in the Paradise Pawn parking lot. They followed me. Maya gets out of the Jaguar, then jogs toward me, her huge boobs bouncing up and down.

"Hon, this neighborhood is really sketchy. I just don't feel comfortable dropping you off around here alone. I'm worried you're going to get human trafficked or something," she says.

"Human what?" I say.

"Never mind, just, can we call your mom or dad and have them come pick you up?"

"I'm fourteen," I say.

"Right. You're too young to be wandering around this part of town by yourself," she says. I need to think of a way to get her to go away. I cannot have her and Beth and Beth's dad coming into Paradise.

"I just need to buy a laptop in here, okay? Don't worry about me. I'm fine. My dad will come pick me up," I say.

"Well, let me come inside and wait with you until your dad gets here, okay? This is a *pawnshop*. It's not a regular place to buy a computer. They can be kind of seedy. Have you been in a pawnshop before?"

"Yeah," I say. "I have." I see Beth and Beth's dad getting out of the car and walking toward me. This is bad. I'm desperate. I think about falling down and pretending like I'm having a heart attack just to make it all stop, but I don't act fast enough.

Carter sees me through the window. I hear the door buzz. I don't go inside. I pray to God that Carter won't come outside, but he does.

"Hey, Jackie. Welcome back," he says. Maya jumps, like she thinks Carter is going to rob her. I decide that the best thing I can do now is to keep everyone calm. Beth and Beth's dad are standing beside me.

"Do you know this man?" Maya says, like she's a police officer.

"Yeah, don't worry about it," I say. I start walking inside. I'm praying that Maya and Beth and Beth's dad will go away, but they follow me.

It's like the moment after you've knocked over a glass of water and you know it's about to spill, but there's nothing you can do to stop it.

"Jackie!" Dad says when I walk in. He's the only one behind the counter. Kayla and Aubrey and Rob must be working on inventory in the back.

"Do you know him too?" Maya says.

"Yeah, that's my dad," I say.

"Hi, Jackie's dad!" Beth says. I realize that Dad and her met at Snyder Smiles.

"Beth! Good to see you again!" Dad says. Maya seems disturbed that Dad knows Beth. Beth's dad isn't paying attention.

"Do you work here?" Beth says to Dad.

"I sure do. Jackie is my right-hand woman. I'm glad you could finally see the place," Dad says. Beth looks at me, confused.

"I didn't know she worked here, actually," Beth says. I feel my face turning red with shame. Dad looks at the ground. I don't want him to know that I'm ashamed to work at Paradise. I don't want him to think I'm ashamed of him. I want to tell him I'm sorry. I decide that I will after work. I'll explain everything to him about how hard St. Bridget's has been, and how I had to get Beth to be my friend however I could, and that meant not telling her about Paradise Pawn.

Beth's dad is walking around touching things willy-nilly. Someone will have to polish all the things that he's touched. I hear him say to Maya, "Babe, do you need a used fish tank? Fishy smell included." Then he laughs.

Dad hears the whole thing. I can tell he's mad. He puffs up his chest to make himself look stronger. Beth hears the whole thing too, but she doesn't seem bothered by it—by her dad laughing at my dad. I need them all to leave.

"I just find it so sad," Maya whispers to Beth's dad. "All these desperate people. Like, can you imagine? Pawning a wedding ring?" Maya might be a desperate person too if she weren't so pretty and dating someone so rich.

"Well, if you think it's sad, then maybe you should leave," I say to Maya as gently as I can.

"Can I go to the bathroom?" Beth says.

"Yeah, quickly," Beth's dad says. While Beth is in the bathroom, I stand there awkwardly with Dad, Beth's dad, and Maya. Something feels off and I realize what it is. I'm used to women being pulled to Dad like magnets, but Maya is different from the women who like Dad, or at least she thinks she is.

I breathe in through my nose and out through my mouth. Pretty soon this will all be over, I tell myself. Beth will ask me a few questions about it at school, but then she'll forget about it.

A John Mayer song plays on the radio. Maya and Beth's dad look at their phones. Dad polishes the jewelry cases even though I polished them earlier in the morning. I walk around to the other side of the counter to help him. Soon this will all be over, I tell myself again.

Rob carries a big Rubbermaid tub of scrap metal out of the storeroom. He's huffing and puffing. He seems a little drunk. He stops when he sees Beth's dad.

"How can I help you, sir?" he says.

"Just waiting for my daughter to use your bathroom," Beth's dad says, not looking up from his phone.

"Oh good. I thought you were with the feds for a second," Rob says, and chuckles to himself. Beth's dad looks at Maya nervously. It occurs to me that Beth's dad is probably richer than Rob, which is crazy to think about. I say a prayer that Beth will hurry up in the bathroom and they'll all leave before Kayla comes out of the storeroom.

I hear the toilet flush. Then the bathroom door swings open. Beth is holding the box of pads. One of them is open.

"I think I won a prize! I found one hundred dollars in this pad," Beth announces.

"Put that back," I hiss. I run toward Beth and try to grab the box from her.

"But it's mine," she says. She yanks the box away from me. It slips out of my grip and lands on the tile floor with a thud. Pads tumble from the box. Bills skid across the floor. I throw myself on the ground and start crawling around crazily, like an ant whose house is being destroyed, shoving the pads back into the box.

"Stop!" Rob yells. I feel like I'm going to throw up. I swallow. Everyone is staring at me. Out of the corner of my eye I watch Beth's dad usher Beth and Maya out to the Jaguar. I tell myself I can talk my way out of this. I try to smile. Rob crouches down beside me.

"What the hell?" he breathes. His breath leaves a film of beery dampness on me.

He hauls me up off the floor and screams, "What the hell is this?"

"I don't know. Just let me clean it up," I whisper. He's clamping his huge fingers into my skin and hurting me.

"You don't know? Are you lying to me?"

"No sir," I say, and I smile the most real-looking fake smile I can smile.

"Let go of her," Dad says quietly to Rob.

"So you're behind this?" Rob says, grabbing a wad of bills and shaking it in Dad's face. "Is this why the numbers have been so fucked at this store?" Dad shakes his head. Rob lets go of me and pushes his face close to Dad's. "I should have known I couldn't trust you," he says.

"I don't know anything about this," Dad says.

"Tell that to my lawyers," Rob says. "You're going to pay for this big time."

"Sir, I am telling the truth. I have no idea why this money is in here," Dad says. He is shaking.

"Also, hiding money in sanitary napkins? Gross. Have fun explaining that to a jury," Rob says, with a creepy snicker. The rest of us are silent. Dad stares at me, asking for help with his eyes. I look at the floor.

"Look, it was probably a customer," I say.

"Stay out of this!" Rob screams, glaring at me. Kayla and Aubrey come running out of the storeroom.

"What's going on?" Aubrey says.

"Someone is going to prison. That's what's going on. Y'all have about thirty seconds to explain to me why thousands of dollars are sitting here in a box of sanitary napkins or I'm pressing somebody's panic button and calling the police!" Rob yells. Kayla looks at me. I swipe my hand in front of my neck to say no. Rob is still yelling.

"We have to!" Kayla mouths. I shake my head.

"Don't you dare," I mouth. And then she does it.

"It was us," she says. "It was me and Jackie. It was so I could go to St. Bridget's." The whole store is silent. Everyone stares at us. "We're sorry," Kayla says.

"No, we're not," I murmur, but no one hears me. I reach for Kayla's hand and she pulls it away. Tears stream down my cheeks like lava. Faces swim past my eyes. Rob backs me and Kayla up against a jewelry case and screams. Dad and Aubrey yell at us too. Customers stare. Rob waves us all out of the store and into the parking lot like we're cattle. He yells at us to get off his property. We stumble to our cars.

"Can I go to Kayla's house?" I whisper to Dad.

"Absolutely not," Aubrey says. I try to meet Kayla's eyes, but she won't look at me. In the car, Dad won't look at me either.

His chin is quivering. We lurch through a red light. He blinks and a small tear slips out of his eye. Then a huge sob falls out of his throat. It's a sound I've never heard him make in my life.

"It's okay," I say. I rub his back like he's the daughter and I'm the dad. I don't think I'm doing it right.

“It’s not okay,” he says. “Really not okay. I’m going to lose my job. Aubrey’s going to lose his job, too. Rob could press charges. What the hell were you thinking?” he says.

“It was so Kayla could go to St. Bridget’s,” I say.

“But it was illegal. It was so, so wrong. Do you not understand that?” Dad says.

“It wasn’t nearly as wrong as a lot of other things people do. It’s so wrong that Rob is evil, but he’s the one who gets to be rich. It’s so wrong that me and Kayla had to go to different schools because you have more money than Aubrey!” I yell.

“Be quiet,” Dad snaps at me, so I am quiet, and he is quiet too. We are quiet all night. He makes fish sticks and frozen peas for dinner, and we eat them in silence.

Somehow he finds out that I have more money stashed in my room—probably because Kayla told her parents and they told Dad. I hand it over to him to give to Rob. When Dad goes in his room, I call Kayla’s house but no one picks up. Later, the phone rings, and I run to get it, but Dad gets there first.

“Hello, sir,” he says. It’s Rob. Dad says, “Yes, I understand,” and then, “I can’t tell you how sorry I am,” and then, “Thank you for all the good years.” I hear him hang up and then I hear him crying. I shuffle into the living room. I sit on the edge of the couch as far away from him as I can. I expect him to tell me to go away, but he lifts up his arms to hug me. I scoot toward him and melt into his shirt. He’s crying more than I’ve ever seen him cry before. We must look like the statue in Kayla’s church of Mary crying and holding dead Jesus, except that we’re on a couch instead of a rock, and we’re both crying, and we’re both alive.

“Did you get fired?” I ask. He nods. “Aubrey, too?”

“Yeah,” Dad says.

“I’m sorry,” I whisper.

"I'm sorry, too," Dad breathes. "Rob's not pressing charges against you and Kayla, or against me and Aubrey, which is good, I guess. He definitely could have gone after all of us. What you did was wrong, but I should have been paying closer attention—to the numbers, to you, to Kayla. I was so proud of how good you were doing that sometimes I forgot how young you are. I just have no idea how to raise you anymore, and clearly I'm doing it wrong," he says, blowing his nose on a paper towel.

"You're not doing it wrong," I say.

"But how have I messed you up this bad?" he says. That makes me cry harder. I don't want Dad to think I'm messed up. I don't know what to say, so I smooth his hair the way he smooths mine. He has some gray hairs that I've never seen before.

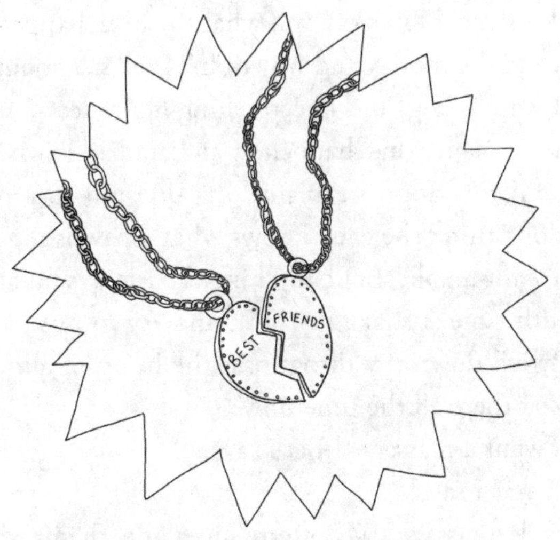

CHAPTER 24

THE NEXT DAY AT SCHOOL, I FEEL LIKE I'M CONtrolling a big, floppy Jackie marionette who smiles and walks around while the real Jackie is shriveled up inside.

In global studies, I start crying without even realizing it. A girl beside me asks me if I'm okay, and I give myself a paper cut so I can show her and say I'm crying about that. Some blood gets on my uniform shirt, but it doesn't matter. I'll only be wearing this uniform for a few more months.

Dad says I'll have to go to public school next semester since he doesn't have a job anymore. I was a little sad when he told me, but it means me and Kayla will get to be together at school again. Obviously, Kayla won't be going to St. Bridget's. I call Kayla's house every night and leave long, teary messages. I know she'll call me back eventually.

I still sit with Beth at lunch. I have nowhere else to sit. She keeps asking me if I'm okay and what the heck happened with the pads and the money and why didn't I tell her about my job and do I want a hug, and I keep telling her to leave me alone. Trying to explain what happened at Paradise Pawn to Beth would be like trying to explain long division to a newborn baby. I don't think she even knows what a pawnshop is.

"You want to talk about anything?" Beth says for about the thousandth time. I shake my head and try to push a glob of my sandwich down my throat past the lump of almost-tears that hovers there all the time now.

"You want a massage?" Beth says.

"A what?" I say.

"A back massage. My mom gives me them when I'm stressed. It helps relieve tension. I don't know what's going on, but I do know you're stressed." Beth's mom also thinks that certain kinds of crystals can cure cancer or make you stop being in love with someone.

"I don't think so," I say.

"Want to try it for a minute and if you don't like it, I'll stop?" Beth says. She's so good at thinking of weird ways to be nice to me.

"Okay," I say.

"Okay," she says. She stands behind me and puts her hands on my shoulders. I can feel the warmth of them through my uniform shirt. They make my whole body feel warm. She squeezes and pushes my shoulders like she's trying to wring soapy water out of them.

"Woah," I say.

"Tell me if it hurts," she says.

"It doesn't hurt," I say.

"Good," she says. I let tears out of my eyes. My back is to Beth, but I know she can tell I'm crying.

"Sorry," I say.

"For what? You don't have to be sorry to me."

"Okay," I say. I wipe my dripping nose with a napkin. Beth runs her fingers through my hair. I feel tingly and safe. "Have you ever done something that you thought was the right thing to do but it turned out to be really wrong?" I say softly.

"Yeah, of course. I think everybody has," she says. Her hands rest on my shoulders. "Almost nobody wakes up in the morning and is like, 'I'm going to do something wrong today.' People just make mistakes. Like tons and tons of mistakes."

"Yeah," I say. Beth runs her fingers down my back in little squiggles.

"You don't have to tell me what was going on at that store Saturday, but if you want to get it off your chest, I promise I won't judge," Beth says. A sob quivers inside me. I think about trying to start from the very beginning and explaining everything to Beth, but instead I just say, "I did something for my friend because I really love her, but it completely backfired." The napkin I used to wipe my nose is soaked. I try to wipe my tears with it and I end up smearing snot on my cheeks. Beth sits beside me and squints at my eyes like she's looking in a telescope.

"Do you know what you have to remember?" she says.

"What?" I say, sniffing.

"Just because you did something bad, it doesn't make you a bad person."

"How do you know?" I say, blinking hot little rivers out of my eyes. Beth reaches for my arm and rubs it gently.

"Because I know," she says. "Like my dad. He didn't mean to mess up my life. That's what my therapist always says, and for a while I didn't believe her, but I think it's true. My dad did what he did because he really loves Maya, and when you love somebody, you go a little crazy."

"Yeah," I say. It's true. What me and Kayla did was crazy. I know it's wrong to steal. I know some people have money and other people don't. I know some people get to have their dreams work out and other people don't, and that's just the way it is. But I wanted to be one of the people whose dreams work out. I wanted Kayla to be one too, and I love her so much that I went crazy and thought we could be those people.

I look at Beth—goofy Beth, who is so nice to me—nicer than I deserve. I love her, too. I would do crazy things for her, too. Not steal money, because she doesn't need money. She has all the money she could ever want. But I would do other crazy things for her if she needed me to. I don't know if Kayla loves me anymore, or if she would do crazy things for me ever again. Maybe not. Maybe that kind of love wears off when you grow up, for most people. If it doesn't wear off a little bit, you end up in jail. Jail is probably full of people who did crazy things for people they loved.

Beth leans toward me to give me a hug, and I melt into her. I haven't hugged Kayla in five days, which might be the longest I've ever gone without hugging her in my life. I imagine what it would be like to never hug Kayla again—for Beth to become the person I hug most in the world. It makes me feel terrible to think about. If you've done a crazy thing for someone, it seems like you should have to love them and they should have to love you forever, but I'm not crazy enough to think that's how it works.

My face is still pressed into Beth's collar. Tears are leaking out of my eyes and soaking her shirt.

"I think I'm going to a different school next semester," I say.

"Why? 'Cause everyone at this school sucks except for us?" Beth says with a little laugh.

"No, because my dad doesn't have money for tuition anymore," I say.

"Oh," Beth says. I watch her face droop. I wonder if she's thinking about her dad. Her dad can pay her tuition, but there are so many other things my dad does for me that Beth's dad can't do for her. "Well, that's going to be a huge blow to the ratio of cool people to non-cool people at this school. You're the coolest person here, just FYI," Beth says.

"No, I'm not," I say. I feel myself smiling a little. It's the first time I've smiled in days.

"I'm serious," Beth says. "And don't think that just because you're going to a different school we're going to stop hanging out."

"Really?" I say, lifting my head up off her shoulder and looking into her eyes.

"Duh," she says. She nods her head toward the rest of the cafeteria. "You think I want to hang out with all these clones? No, thank you." I laugh a little and squeeze her. She squeezes me back, and for a moment I feel like everything might be okay someday. Maybe not tomorrow. Maybe not in a month, or even a year, but someday.

WHEN I GET HOME FROM SCHOOL, Dad and two other guys are moving our couch and our dining room table and chairs and Dad's bed frame into the back of a truck.

"Dad, what's happening?" I say.

"I don't have a job, remember?" he says. "We'll get new, nicer furniture when I get a new job."

"Oh," I say. I go into my room and press my face into my air conditioner until it leaves red stripes on me. It was nice of Dad not to get rid of anything in my room.

I hear the men's truck pulling out of the driveway and I come out of my room. Dad's mattress is on the floor of his room. He's set up a card table and two wobbly plastic chairs in the dining room. The living room is empty.

"Look," he says, fanning out a stack of bills. "Make it rain! Who needs a job?" He tosses the bills around the empty living room. Then he looks embarrassed and picks them up. "I'm kidding. I'm looking for another job. It shouldn't take too long to get one." I sit down on the floor where the couch used to be. Dad sits beside me.

"You know," he says. "Most dads would have been chewing you out all week for what you did, but I feel like all this is punishment enough."

"Yeah," I say quietly.

That's the weird thing about growing up. Punishment is fake when you're little. It doesn't actually matter if you stay up past your bedtime or you eat sand because you want to know what it tastes like, but what Kayla and I did mattered, so there are all kinds of punishments that our parents can't even control.

"The other reason why I don't feel like I can punish you is because I get why you did it," he says. "It's like that whole store just prints piles of money for one guy. And it's all so in your face—the unfairness of it, when you have to stand there looking at all the diamonds and gold every day."

"Yeah," I say into his shoulder.

"You know, I stole little bits over the years, too, especially when you were a baby," he says.

"Really?" I say.

"Yeah, I mean not on the same scale as what you did, but I lifted a couple hundred-dollar bills every once in a while, when I had to buy diapers and stuff for you, or I couldn't pay rent." He's trying to make me feel better, but it's making me feel sick. I want Dad to be better than people who do crazy things for love—people like me and Beth's dad.

"If you think about it, anybody who's rich got there by stealing in some type of way—legal or not," he says.

I feel the way I felt when Dad told me he bought my Christmas presents at Paradise Pawn—that they didn't come from Santa. He wanted to tell me himself that Santa wasn't real so I didn't find out from kids at school, but that's not how it's supposed to work. Grown-ups are supposed to keep pretending the world is good and fair, and that they are perfect, even after kids figure out that they're lying.

"This isn't making me feel better," I say. Dad looks at the ground. His shoulders hunch. "Okay. I guess it's not making me feel better either." He rips some fuzz off the carpet. Then he smooths my hair.

"Sorry," he says.

"It's okay," I say. I trudge back to my room. It's raining. The store would be quiet right now. Me and Kayla would be talking and laughing, or talking and fighting. It wouldn't really matter. We would be together.

Finally, on Friday, she calls me back.

"I'm not mad at you. Are you mad at me?" I say.

"Yeah, a little, but it doesn't matter that much now. I have something big to tell you."

"Like a plan?"

"I don't know. Kind of a plan, I guess. Not really a plan involving you. I want to tell you about it on Lucky Island. Can you meet me at the Radisson gate at nine in the morning tomorrow?"

"Tomorrow's Saturday. We have to be—" I'm about to say that we have to be at Paradise, but we don't. We're not even allowed to be at Paradise anymore. "Never mind," I say.

"I know. It's weird, right?" Kayla says, reading my mind.

"Yeah," I say quietly.

"Okay, see you tomorrow at nine," she says. "Bye."

"Bye," I whisper.

*

WHEN WE GET TO THE GATE, I bang on it and say I forgot my room key, and a lady with a big straw hat who's had lots of plastic surgery lets us through. We swim out to Lucky Island slowly, like the water is glue. Then we lie on the concrete and look out at the cruise ships in silence. I watch Kayla's chest rise and fall like she's an ocean and her breaths are waves.

She wraps her arms around me, and I watch droplets of water run off them and onto my arms. She takes my *Best* necklace and her *Friends* one and joins them together. Usually, I'm the one who fits our necklaces together, and it makes me happy that she's doing it.

"What were you going to tell me?" I say. I watch her take an extra-deep breath.

"I'm moving," she says.

"To a different apartment?" I say.

"No, to Pennsylvania."

"Very funny," I say.

"No, I'm not joking. We're going to live with my grandma—not the one who lives here, the one who lives in Pennsylvania. My dad got a job at a chicken farm. Not, like, killing chickens, managing money for the chicken farm." I spring up onto my feet, almost knocking Kayla into the water.

"You swear you're telling the truth?" I say.

"Yeah, I swear," she says, and smiles a little bit, looking up at me. She's still lying down.

"How are you smiling?"

"I don't know. What else am I going to do? One of my cousins is on student council at the school where I'm going to go, and she thinks I could get elected." I tell myself this must be a nightmare. I want to scream to make myself wake up, but I can't.

"I cried about it a bunch already, but now I'm feeling okay. And I'll come back to visit once my parents have some money in the bank, after the baby is born," she says. Her voice is all business, like she practiced this speech. I feel like swallowing rocks and jumping into the ocean and sinking. I don't want her to be so calm. I want her to hurt the way I'm hurting. I grab on to my *Best Friends* necklace.

"I don't want to wear this anymore," I say. As soon as the words are out of my mouth, I regret them.

"Okay," Kayla says. She stands up. I feel her fingers graze my neck and then I feel an empty space on my chest. Then she opens the clasp on her necklace and takes it off and presses both of our broken hearts together between her palms. "You're kind of right. The point of these necklaces is that you're close to the person wearing the other half and you can fit them together whenever you want. Wearing a broken heart all the time when the person with the other half lives halfway across the country is kind of sad. Plus, they're little girl necklaces," she says. I feel like a hole is being burned into my heart. I want to tell her that I didn't mean it, that we should put them back on and never take them off, but I am too stunned to say anything. Kayla wraps her arms around me.

"What if we leave them here, so they'll always bring us good luck?" Kayla says.

"Are you kidding? They're eighteen-karat gold. We can't just leave them in the ocean," I say.

"No, they're not. They're plated. They're made of nickel."

"No, Kayla, they're gold," I say.

"You think they would have given us real gold to wear when we were three years old? Remember how often the chains used to break?" She scratches our hearts on a nail poking up out of Lucky Island, then blows on them.

"See? You don't even need a loupe for that. They're plated. There's not even a fake eighteen-karat stamp on them."

"Why did I think they were real? Who told me that?"

"Not me," Kayla says.

"Oh," I say. I watch little waves throw themselves against Lucky Island and then collapse. "Can I hold my necklace?" I say in a small voice.

"Sure," Kayla says. The broken heart lands in my palm with a tiny chime. "I don't want to make you get rid of yours if you don't want to. I just thought it would be kind of special to leave them here," she says.

"No, it's fine," I say. "It's a good idea. Let's throw them in." I roll the broken heart up and down my thumb. Then I squeeze it as tightly as I can.

"Okay," Kayla says. She clasps the chains together and we each hold our half of the heart—*Best* and *Friends*. Then we launch them toward the water. The chains spin and tangle. Then the hearts hit the water without a splash. They sink like two flickering candles and then they are gone.

"How did I go all those years thinking those necklaces were real gold? How am I supposed to believe anything ever again?" I say. Kayla laughs a sad laugh. "Like, back in the day we were supposed to believe in the Easter bunny and the tooth fairy and that kind of thing. Obviously none of that was real, which is fine. But now it's like, is anything they tell us real? Like, if you're a good person and you work hard, you're supposed to have a nice life. But Rob has a nice life, and we have crappy lives. How is that fair? How is anything fair?" I say.

"We just have to try to make it fair," Kayla says.

"But we did try, and look what happened!" I say.

"We have to try again and again and again and again. Nobody is going to believe that our lives should be better if we don't believe it ourselves," she says. I nod. I don't know what I'm going to do without Kayla to explain things like this to me.

She presses her cheek into the back of my head. "I'll miss you, Jackie," she says. It's the same thing she says at the end of shifts when we know we'll see each other the next morning. Now I have no idea when I'll see her again.

"I'll miss you, too," I say.

"And even though we don't have the necklaces anymore, we won't stop being best friends," she says.

I hug her as tightly as I can, trying to make myself believe her.

KAYLA WALKS AWAY in the direction of her house, which soon won't be her house anymore. She turns around to wave just once, and I watch her until she becomes a tiny speck. I walk to the end of Five Mile Beach alone. I walk through the Save A Lot parking lot. I'm sweaty and my legs are tired. Across the street, I see a bus stop. I've never taken the bus by myself before.

The bus stop is made of glass. It's tucked inside a tangle of leaves and dry branches and little white flowers. I sit down on the hot metal bench inside and it stings the backs of my legs. I watch a spider run up the outside of the glass. It doesn't know I am here.

On the horizon, I see a crane slowly lifting a concrete pipe. The person driving the crane doesn't know I am here. Beneath the crane there's a sign for a truck stop. The neon *u* in *Truck* is burned out. Someday soon, an electrician will climb up on a ladder and fix the wires inside the sign so the *u* glows again. Once the *u* is fixed, a truck driver will see it from the highway. She'll decide to pull off and sleep. She will not know the person who fixed the *u* on the sign for her. The people who eat the oranges she drove in her truck will not know her. None of them know I am here, sitting on a hot bus stop bench, thinking of them.

There are people I don't know whose lives are different because of me—people typing on laptops that I sold, driving cars that I detailed, spending money that I loaned. There are people I don't know who sewed on the straps of my swimsuit, who drove the barge that brought the swimsuit from the factory to Florida.

A few days ago, Dad got a big stack of business books from the library. He sits on the floor where the couch used to be and reads them and takes notes on his phone. They're called things like *How to Be Highly Successful and Rich in a Year*. I don't think the books are going to work, but I don't have the heart to tell Dad that. It's not his fault. It's the books' fault.

I think they're wrong about how things work. One of them makes this huge deal about how you become the average of the five people you surround yourself with. I used to think that if I surrounded myself with one person—Kayla—I would become her and she would become me. But we were always ourselves. And we were always surrounded by every other person in the world.

On the wall of the bus stop is a map of all the bus routes in Cherry Beach. It looks like a diagram of veins in a heart. Blue and red and pink squiggly lines come and go from a dot that says *You are here*. The "you" is me. I could go anywhere. The red line would take me to Paradise Pawn. The pink line would take me home.

I breathe on the glass to fog it up. I draw a heart with veins in the fog. Then a bus pulls up in front of me. It's the one for the pink line. The bus sighs and hunches down toward the curb. The door opens and I pay the driver. Then I am squished against other people's bodies—a shoulder in a nurse's uniform, an arm with a tattoo of a turtle, a red-and-white-striped dress, the sandal of a baby sleeping in his dad's arms. I feel wrapped in all the different warmth of their bodies as we drive up the coast together.

Acknowledgments

THIS BOOK WOULD NOT BE A BOOK WITHOUT THE love and support of many, many people.

To my parents, you both inspire me more than you know. I love you.

Mommy, thank you for teaching me that everyone's story is important, no matter what their job is. Thank you for teaching me the value of hard work, and of care for the people closest to you. Thank you for every phone call answered, every meal cooked, every hug at the airport.

Daddy, thank you for teaching me to go after dreams no matter how weird or improbable they are. I would not have believed in myself as a writer without your belief in me. Thank you also for teaching me about pawn shops and the human side of business.

Will, thank you for being the first person I call to talk about writing. Thank you for reading my stories and watching my plays since the very beginning. Thank you for making art that I love. Being your sister is one of the greatest honors and joys of my life. I love you.

Grandma Ethel, thank you for showing me how to be a writer and a businesswoman. Grandma Margaret, thank you for teaching me about the power of books. Grandma Anne, thank you for showing me how to be an artist. Grandpa Ed, thank you for teaching me how to think about money and business with care. Grandpa Hugo, thank you for teaching me that life can be tragic and funny at the same time.

Thank you to all my wonderful, supportive aunts and uncles. Thank you to my cousins, Louisa, Charlotte, Richie, Mikey, Spencer, Nicholas, Thomas, Emma, Jacob, AJ, Gabriel, Eric, and Katie, for laughing with me and telling stories with me.

Peter, thank you for the calming hugs and thought-provoking conversations. Every day I'm inspired by how much care you put into understanding the world.

To my friends, this book is about my love for you. There are too many of you to list by name, but please know, if you are my friend, even if we haven't been in touch for a while, you mean the world to me. Anna, you are a north star to me. I can't wait for your daughter to read this book, if she wants to. Kling, Katie, Gideon, Matt, Ananya, Sophie, the whole City High girls cross country team and the whole Williams women's cross country team, thank you for being there for me since I was a teenager and helping me become who I am.

Charlee, Eva, Hannah, and Manola, thank you for being lighthouses in the storm that is being a writer. Everyone in the Center for Cartoon Studies class of 2026, thank you for helping me feel more like myself than I knew was possible.

Thank you to everyone on Team CashWiz for working with me and teaching me about pawn shops and people.

To all the phenomenal teachers I have had throughout my life, thank you. Thank you to Barbara Schelar and Carly Andrews at Willowwind. Thank you to Beth Fettweis at City High. Thank you to Katarzyna Pieprzak, Karen Shepard, and Jim Shepard at Williams College. Thank you to Nelini Jones, Susan Bernofsky, Heidi Julavits, Elissa Schappell, Julie Orringer, and Gary Shteyngart at Columbia University. Thank you to Natalie Norris, Emma Hunsinger, Tillie Walden, Dan Nott, Jason Lutes, and James Sturm at the Center for Cartoon Studies.

Thank you to Reiko Davis and Elizabeth DeMeo for believing that this story could be a book before most other people did.

Thank you to the incredible people at Zando and Tin House. You have all made a dream come true for me. Thank you to my fantastic editor, Alyssa Ogi, for caring about Jackie and Kayla and helping their story shine. Thank you to Laura Schmitt for guiding me through the process of getting this book out into the world. Thank you also to Masie Cochran, Beth Steidle, Meg Storey, Rebecca Munro, Becky Kraemer, Julia Talley, Zoey Cole, Nanci McCloskey, Jennifer Freilach, and Molly Stern.

Lastly, thank you to you, the reader, for reading about Jackie and Kayla and their world. I may not know you, but I appreciate you (yes, you!) spending time with this piece of my heart.

Reading Group Guide

1. Jackie and Kayla have been best friends since they were babies, yet their lives differ in fundamental ways: in personality, family structure, and socioeconomic status. Where do we first see these differences begin to strain the girls' understanding of each other?

2. How does working at Paradise Pawn—and living in Cherry Beach, Florida—influence Jackie and Kayla's awareness of class? Do you think the two girls know more about money than today's average fourteen-year-old?

3. What does attending high school at St. Bridget's represent for Jackie, and why does the possibility of Kayla not going feel so destabilizing to her?

4. "It's all about N.E.H.A.—Need, Emotional attachment, History of paying us back, and Ability to pay. If we know people aren't coming back, we do the plan. If we know that they are, we don't" (91). A big part of Jackie's success at Paradise Pawn

hinges on her ability to see and assess customers accurately. Do you think she sees herself and Kayla accurately?

5. Throughout *Paradise Pawn*, characters often employ fake smiles and fake laughs. What does the novel suggest about performance as a strategy in retail jobs and in daily life? How does gender impact who must perform happiness, and under what circumstances?

6. Many different customers and items come through the doors of Paradise Pawn. Did you have a favorite store interaction or one that surprised you the most?

7. Father-daughter relationships feature prominently in the novel. What did you think of "the dads," and Devon and Jackie's relationship in particular? How are traditional ideas of masculinity and parenting challenged in *Paradise Pawn*?

8. Consider Jackie's experience of puberty. Do you think she wants to grow up? In your own childhood, were you excited to become an adult? Why or why not?

9. Consider the title. In what ways are Jackie, Kayla, the dads, and other characters in the novel seeking a form of paradise?

10. If you were ever in a situation where you had to pawn an item, what would it be and would you try to get it back?

11. In addition to being a writer, Meg Richardson is a talented illustrator and cartoonist. What did you think of the illustrations throughout? Did they add another layer to the story?

DANA READ

Meg Richardson is a writer, translator, and cartoonist. Her work has appeared in *The New Yorker*, *The Rumpus*, and elsewhere. Originally from Iowa, she currently lives in Vermont. *Paradise Pawn* is her first novel.